Tortuga

TORTUGA

A Novel by

Rudolfo A. Anaya

University of New Mexico Press
Albuquerque

Library of Congress Cataloging-in-Publication Data

Anaya, Rudolfo A.
Tortuga.

I. Title.
PS3551.N27T6   1988   813'.54   87-35665
ISBN 0-8263-1074-5

Dedicated with love to my wife, Patricia.
She walks the path of the sun.
She sings the songs of the moon.

1

I awoke from a restless sleep. For a moment I couldn't remember where I was, then I heard Filomón and Clepo talking up front and I felt the wind sway the old ambulance. I tried to turn my body, but it was impossible. Upon waking it was always the same; I tried to move but the paralysis held me firmly in its grip.

I could turn my head and look out the small window. The cold winter rain was still falling. It had been only a gray drizzle when we left the hospital, but the farther south we went into the desert the sheets of icy rain became more intense. For a great part of the trip we had been surrounded by darkness. Only the flashes of lightning which tore through the sky illuminated the desolate landscape.

I had slept most of the way; the rain drumming against the ambulance and the rumble of the distant thunder lulled me to sleep. Now I blinked my eyes and remembered that we had left at daybreak, and Filomón had said that it would be mid-afternoon before we arrived at the new hospital.

Your new home, he had said.

Home. Up north, at home, it would be snowing, but here it was only the dark, dismal rain which swept across the wide desert and covered us with its darkness. I tried to turn again, but the paralysis compounded by the bone-chilling cold held me. I cursed silently.

"It's never been this dark before," I heard Clepo whisper.

"Don't worry," Filomón answered, "it'll get better before it gets worse. You have to know the desert to know rain don't last. It can be raining one minute and blowing dust devils the next. But the clouds are beginning to break, see, to the west."

I turned my head and looked out the window. In the distance I could see the bare outline of a mountain range. Around us the desert was alkaline and white. Only the most tenacious shrubs and brittle grasses seemed to grow, clinging to the harsh land like tufts of mouldy hair. Overhead, the sun struggled to break through the clouds. To the east, a diffused, distorted rainbow stretched across the vast, gray sky.

I remembered the rainbows of my childhood, beautifully sculptured arches reaching from north to south, shafts of light so pure their harmony seemed to wed the sky and earth. My mother had taught me to look at rainbows, the mantle of the Blessed Virgin Mary she called them. When a summer thunderstorm passed she would take me out and we would stand in the thin drops which followed the storm. We would turn our faces up to the sky, and the large, glistening drops of rain would pelt our faces. She would open her mouth and hold out her tongue to receive the large, golden drops. She would stir the muddy ponds and pick up the little frogs which came with the rain. "They are like you," she told me, "blessed by the rain, children of the water." When I was hurt she would take me in her arms and sing . . . .

> Sana, sana
> colita de rana
> Si no sanas hoy
> sanarás mañana . . .

And her touch could drive away the worst of pains. But then the paralysis had come, and suddenly her prayers and her touch were not enough. Her face grew pale and thin, her eyes grew dark. "It is God's will," she had said.

"It's clearing now," Filomón said, "see, the sun is beginning to break through!"

"Yes, the sun!" Clepo shouted. He was Filomón's assistant, a small impish man with hunched shoulders. I noticed he limped when they loaded me on the ambulance.

"I think I see the top of the mountain!" Filomón cried cheerfully.

I was fully awake. The last images of the dreams faded as the darkness of the rain moved over us and eastward. Only occasional peals of thunder rumbled across the sky. Beneath us the ambulance rocked like a ship. Memories of my life moved in and out of my troubled consciousness. My mother's face appeared again and again. She had cried when they loaded me on the ambulance, but she knew it was necessary. The doctors there had helped as much as they could. Now, they insisted, they had to move me to this new hospital in the south where they specialized in taking care of crippled children. If there was any hope of regaining the use of my stiff limbs, it was there. So early in the morning they wheeled me on a gurney to the outpatient area, loaded me onto Filomón's ambulance and the journey began.

"There!" Filomón shouted again, "There's the mountain!"

I tried to turn my head to see, but I couldn't. "What mountain?" I asked.

2

"Tortuga Mountain," he said and looked back, "it's right by the hospital. Don't worry, I'll stop so you can see it." He sounded happy, revived, after the long, monotonous drive across the desert. I felt a sense of urgency as he pulled the ambulance onto the shoulder of the road. We bounced along until he found the right spot, then he stopped the ambulance and turned off the motor. He climbed over the seat to where I lay strapped on the small cot.

"Ah, Filo," Clepo grumbled, "you've stopped here every time we bring a new kid. Don't you ever get tired of showing them that damned mountain?"

"It's always a new kid," Filomón smiled as he loosened the straps that held me, "and each kid deserves to see the mountain from here. I want the boy to see it."

Filomón was an old man with a deep wrinkled face and rough, calloused hands, but he moved like a younger man as he lifted me tenderly so I could look out the window and see the mountain.

"There it is," he nodded, "that's Tortuga." His eyes sparkled as he looked at the volcanic mountain that loomed over the otherwise empty desert. It rose so magically into the gray sky that it seemed to hold the heavens and the earth together. It lay just east of the river valley, and the afternoon sun shining on it after the rain covered it with a sheen of silver.

"It's a magic mountain," Filomón whispered, and I felt his heart beating against me as he held me. "See!" he whispered, "See!" I tried to see beyond the volcanic slabs and granite boulders which formed the outline of a turtle, I tried to sense the steady rhythm of his pulse which seemed to be draining into the giant mountain, but I couldn't. I was too tired, and my faith in magic had drained out the night the paralysis came and in the ensuing nights and days which I spent without movement on the hospital bed.

I shook my head.

"That's okay," he smiled, "it comes slowly sometimes. But now at least you know it's there—" He seemed very tired. It had been a long trip for him too. He had had to keep the ambulance on course through one of the worst storms I could remember. But now we were almost there.

"Where's the hospital?" I asked.

"It's on this side of the river, you can't see it from here. See the smoke rising in the valley? That's Agua Bendita. It's a small town, but people come from all over to bathe in the mineral waters from the springs which drain from the mountain—"

"It's a town full of old arthritics," Clepo giggled, "old people who think they can escape the pains of old age by dipping themselves in the mountain's water, but they can't run fast enough from death!" He slapped his thigh and laughed.

Filomón didn't answer. He sat beside the cot and looked out the window into the desert. "Even as terrible as the storm was for us, it will be good for the plants in the spring. After a good, wet winter the desert blooms like a garden," he nodded and rolled a cigarette. There was something about the way he spoke, the strength of his face, that reminded me of someone I had known—my grandfather perhaps, but I hadn't thought of him in years.

"These old villages cling to the river like the beads of a rosary," he continued, thinking aloud.

"Whoever crosses this desert has a lot of praying to do," Clepo agreed, "it's a journey of death."

"No, a journey of life. Our forefathers have wandered up and down this river valley for a long, long time. First the Indians roamed up and down this river, then others came, but they all stopped here at this same place: the springs of Tortuga, the place of the healing water—"

He talked and smoked. The dull sun shone through the window and played on the swirling smoke. I was fully awake now, but I felt feverish, and I couldn't help wondering what a strange day it had been to ride all this way with the old man and his assistant. I shivered, but not from the cold. The inside of the ambulance was now stifling. It glowed with white smoke and golden light which poured through the window. Filomón's eyes shone.

"How long have you been bringing kids to the hospital?" I asked.

"As long as I can remember," Filomón answered. "I bought this old hearse in a junk yard and I fixed it up like an ambulance. I've been transporting kids ever since."

"We get thirty dollars a kid, dead or alive," Clepo laughed. "And we get to hear a lot of interesting stories. We've taken every kind of diseased body there is to the hospital. Why, Filo and I could become doctors if we wanted to, couldn't we Filo? But we don't know anything about you. You slept most of the way." He leaned over the seat and peered at me.

"He's tired," Filomón said.

"Yeah, but he's awake now," Clepo grinned. "So how did he get crippled? I know it ain't polio, I know polio. And how come his left hand is bandaged, huh? There's quite a story there, but he hasn't said a word!"

He seemed put out that I had slept most of the way and had not told the story of my past. But since the paralysis the past didn't matter. It was as if everything had died, except the dreams and the memories which kept haunting me. And even those were useless against the terrible weight which had fallen over me and which I cursed until I could curse no more.

"Do you take the kids back?" I asked.

"No, we don't!" Clepo said, "That's against the rules!"

"I picked you up," Filomón reminded him.

"I was hitch-hiking," Clepo said smartly, "somebody would have picked me up."

"You were lost. I found you in the middle of a sandstorm, crying. Lucky for you I came along."

"I wasn't crying, I had sand in my eyes," Clepo insisted.

Filomón smiled. "It doesn't matter, you've been a good assistant." That seemed to satisfy Clepo, he grunted and sat back down. Filomón drew close and looked at me. "We can't take anybody back, that's not our job. But when you get better you can make the trip back home by yourself. Just wait till spring, and you'll be better. I know it looks bad now, but in the spring the river comes alive and the desert dresses like a young bride. The lizards come out to play in the warm sun, and even the mountain moves—" He touched my forehead with his fingers, then he leaned close to me and I felt his forehead touch mine, perhaps he was just leaning to retrieve one of the straps to tie me up again, but I felt his forehead brush mine, and I felt a relief from the paralysis which I hadn't felt since it came. Then he tied the strap and climbed back into the driver's seat.

"Filomón says you gotta keep your eyes on the mountain," Clepo said to fill in the silence.

"Well, it's helped us," Filomón answered, "it's been our faith in this wasteland . . . and it's helped a lot of kids. There's a strong power there."

He started the ambulance and let it coast down the long slope of the hill into the valley. I knew he was still looking at the mountain, still feeling the strange power that resided there for him.

"The water from the mountain springs is holy," he mused aloud, "long ago the place was used as a winter ceremonial ground by the Indians. They came to purify themselves by bathing in the warm waters . . . the waters of the turtle . . . Later, when the Spaniards came, they called the springs Los Ojos de la Tortuga, and when they discovered the waters could cure many illnesses they called the village Agua Bendita . . ."

"Who lives here?" I asked. We had entered the edge of the small town. Through the window I could see the tops of rundown gas stations, motels and cafes. There was a dilapidated movie house, a brownstone hotel, and many signs which creaked in the wind as they advertised the hot mineral baths.

"Mostly old people who come for the baths, people who work at the hospital, and a few of the old people who try to make a living from the small farms along the river—"

Filomón turned the ambulance and I caught a glimpse of a weathered sign that read *Crippled Children and Orphans Hospital*. The arrow pointed up the hill, so from the highway which ran through the small town we had to turn up the hill again towards the washed-out buildings which huddled together at the top. I struggled to turn to see more, instinctively, as I had so many times before, but it was useless, I couldn't move. I could only turn my head and watch the mountain across the valley. An air of hopelessness brooded over the dull mountain as the remaining winter clouds huddled at its peak. It seemed lost and out of place in the immense desert which surrounded it, and I wondered what secret rested in its core. Whatever it was, it was something that made Filomón's voice ring with hope and made his eyes sparkle even after the fatigue of the long journey.

"The doctors here can work miracles," Filomón was saying, "they've got ways now of straightening out bones and sewing together nerves and flesh—"

"Yeah, but they didn't fix my limp," Clepo said. "And they sure as hell don't believe in all this mumbo jumbo you've been giving the kid."

"Don't mind Clepo," Filomón laughed, "he just likes to act tough, but deep down inside he knows—"

But what is there to know, I wondered, as the huge bulk of the mountain held me hynotized. The shape of the old volcano was obvious. Its hump curved down like a bow to a reptilian head. Huge, volcanic slabs of dark lava formed the massive plates of the shell. Near the bottom, jagged hills and the shadows of deep ravines created the illusion of webbed, leathery feet. Even the glaze of rain glistening on its back reminded me of the way the back of a snake or a toad will shine with oily rainbow colors. The more I gazed at it the more alive it grew, until I thought I was actually looking at a giant turtle which had paused to rest for the night. But where was its magic? Nothing seemed to grow on its sides; it was bare and dark and gloomy.

"Listen carefully and you'll hear the underground river which flows from Tortuga," Filomón was saying. "There are huge caverns beneath the mountain, and through them run powerful rivers, rivers of turtle pee. Yes, that old mountain is alive . . . a real sea turtle which wandered north when the oceans dried and became deserts. But it's alive, just waiting for another earth change to come along and free it from its prison. And it will happen. The old people told the stories that everything comes in cycles, even time itself . . . so the oceans will return and cover everything as they once did. Then Tortuga will be free—"

"You're crazy, Filo," Clepo laughed.

"And is that its secret," I asked bitterly, "to wait until the ocean returns? I don't want to wait that long! I want to move, now!" I cursed

6

and struggled against the paralysis which held me as tight as the earth held Filomón's turtle.

"It takes time," Filomón said.

"Yeah, time," Clepo agreed.

"How much time?" I asked aloud, "How much time?" I agreed with Clepo, Filomón was crazy. The sea would never return. The earth was drying up and dying. Even the rain which pelted us during the trip fell hot and boiling on the empty desert. I had no faith left to believe his crazy story. Already the paralysis seemed to have gripped me forever.

"Here's the hospital," Filomón said. He had turned into a graveled driveway bordered by bare trees. I looked out the window and caught sight of the grey buildings. Winter-burned juniper bushes pressed against the wind-scoured hospital walls.

"It was a long trip," Clepo stretched and yawned, then he added, "I'm glad I'm not at this damned place anymore, Gives me the shivers—"

"It's always a long trip," Filomón said as he turned the ambulance and backed it up to the door, "and just the beginning for him—" I knew he meant me.

Clepo jumped out and opened the door. The cold air made me shiver. Overhead the wind drove the thin, icy clouds towards the mountain.

"Looks like snow," I heard someone say. "This the new kid?"

"It ain't Goldilocks," Clepo chattered. The voice belonged to the attendant who had brought a gurney. Together they slid out the cot and lifting me gently onto the gurney, covered me with a blanket, then pushed me through the open door and into the darkness of an enormous room.

"Filomón!" I called.

"Right here," he answered.

"Are you going back now?"

"As soon as the doctor signs the papers—"

"As soon as they sign the papers we're no longer responsible for you," Clepo added.

"Where are we?" I asked. The size of the room, its gloom and staleness were disturbing. I turned my head and peered into the darkness. I saw people lining the walls of the room, mostly women. They were dressed in dark clothes. Some held small children in their arms. All seemed to be crippled. Some wore braces, some crutches, others sat quietly in wheelchairs. Above them, on the high walls, hung huge portraits of solemn-looking men.

"This is the receiving room," Filomón explained. "Everybody that comes to the hospital gets admitted here. All the doctors' offices are up here, behind them is the surgery ward. Don't worry, as soon as the doctor checks you in you'll get sent to a ward in the back."

"How many wards are there?" I asked.

"Too many," Clepo answered. "I'm going to buy a Coke," he said and wandered off.

"It must be visiting day," Filomón continued, "the parents who live close by can come and visit their children." Then he added as if in warning, "Your folks are way up north, and it's hard to make that long trip across the desert... don't expect too many visits."

"I know," I nodded. How well I knew the poverty and misery which surrounded us and suffocated us and held us enslaved as the paralysis held me now. There would be no money, no way for my mother to come, and perhaps it would be better if she didn't come. What could she do for me now, sit and look at me as the women who lined the walls sat and looked at their crippled children? No, that I didn't want. Better to write her and tell her not to worry, or to send a message with Filomón and tell them that I understood how hard times were and that whatever happened to me here at the hospital it was better if I worked it out alone. Pity could not help me, and I had long ago lost the faith in my mother's gods.

"Tell them not to come, if you see them," I said to Filomón.

"I will," he nodded. At the same time a young girl appeared by the side of the gurney and Filomón's eyes lit up. "Ah, Ismelda," he smiled. "What are you doing here?"

The girl smiled. "I'm helping the nurses bring the kids from the wards for their visits... it's been a busy day, in spite of the cold. Is this the new boy?" she asked and looked at me. She had a warm smile. Her dark eyes and long hair set off the most beautiful oval face I had ever seen. She was about my age, maybe a little older, but dressed in the white uniform of a nurse's aide.

"Yeah, we just brought him in," Filomón nodded.

"Paralysis," she murmured as she touched my forehead and brushed back my hair. Her touch sent a tingle running down my back and arms. Her eyes bore into mine with the same intensity I had felt in Filomón's eyes. She rubbed my forehead gently and looked at Filomón.

"He busted his back," Filomón said, and added, "he's from up north."

"I can tell that from his dark, curly hair," she smiled. "And he's thirsty." She disappeared. How she knew I was thirsty I didn't know, but I was. My throat felt parched and I felt a fever building up deep in my guts.

"What does she do here?" I asked Filomón.

"She lives with Josefa in the valley, just on the outskirts of the town. They both work here. They do beds, sweep floors, help in anyway they can—"

She returned and held a straw to my lips. I sucked greedily and felt the cold water wash down my throat. It was the first drink I had had all day and it instantly refreshed me.

"Good," I said when I had finished, "tastes strong."

"The water of the mountain is strong," she nodded, "that's because it's full of good medicine."

I didn't know if it was the water which had refreshed me or her touch, but I felt better. When I looked from her to Filomón I had the strange feeling that they knew each other very well. They had greeted each other like old friends and the sense of ease that passed between them helped to dispel the dread which had filled me the moment I entered the room.

"I have to go," she said and touched my hand. "Visiting hours are almost over and we have to return the kids to their rooms. But I'll come and see you." She squeezed my hand and I felt the pressure. Instinctively I squeezed back and felt my fingers respond, lock in hers for a moment, felt a surge of energy pass through our hands, then she was gone. Someone stuck a thermometer in my mouth before I could call her name.

"You'll dream about that girl," Filomón smiled, "she's very strong . . . knows the mountain."

Clepo reappeared. He had poured salted peanuts into his coke bottle and when he held it up to drink his red tongue reached into the bottle in search of the illusive, floating peanuts.

"Want some?" he asked me. I shook my head.

The nurse pulled out the thermometer, glanced at it and motioned for an orderly. "Get this kid over to Steel's receiving room," she snapped. "That's it, Filomón," she said as she signed the paper on his clipboard, then she walked away.

"Hey, you're getting Steel for a doctor," Filomón whispered, "he's the best."

"The kids like him," Clepo nodded, "he used to be my doctor."

The orderly began to push the gurney. Filomón stopped him for a moment, leaned over and whispered, "Remember, keep your eye on the mountain, that's the secret. Watch this girl Ismelda, she and Josefa know a lot of strong medicine . . ." Then the orderly began to push the gurney again and I saw Filomón and Clepo wave goodbye.

"Wait till spring!" Filomón called, and Clepo repeated, "Yeah, wait till spring!"

Somewhere in the enormous room a harsh voice called, "Visiting hours are over!" The people rose and began to leave, some of the children cried. I turned my head to call to Filomón, because the dread of the hospital had returned and I didn't want to be alone, but I couldn't see him.

9

"See you in the spring!" I thought I heard him shout above the noise of departure, "Just wait till spring!" then the orderly pushed me out of the room and into a long quiet hall. He pushed the gurney into a brightly lighted room and left. The glare from the overhead lamp hurt my eyes, so I closed them and waited. In my mind I could see Filomón and Clepo waving goodbye. I tried to recall the desert we had crossed, but it was so wide and lifeless that I couldn't remember its features. The sun seemed to burn it lifeless. Whirlwinds rose like snakes into the sky. Then the rain came and pounded us and made me sleep.

Now here I was, somewhere in the middle of that desert, but I really didn't know where. My last contact with home had been Filomón and Clepo, now they were gone. But the girl, Ismelda was here. I could still feel her touch, and I could remember her face clearly.

A nurse interrupted my thoughts. She took my temperature again, felt the pulse at my wrist and asked me if I had had a bm. I laughed. It was such a crazy question. She smiled and went on to ask me other questions. She recorded the answers on a chart. When she was done she said the doctor would be in shortly and left. I closed my eyes again and lay listening to the sounds of the hospital.

I could hear the sound of kids yelling; sometimes they seemed to pass by outside. I listened very closely and thought I heard the sound of water gurgling far beneath the earth. I floated in and out of light sleep and dreamed of my mother, and she said that all was the will of God and could not be questioned . . . and then my father appeared, and he said that each man was forced to live by his destiny and there was no escaping it . . . and I was about to curse both views which sought in vain to explain my paralysis when someone touched my shoulder.

"Sleeping?" the doctor said. He held my wrist and felt my pulse. His eyes were slate blue, piercing. He smiled. "It was a long trip, wasn't it?" I nodded. He placed his stethoscope to my chest and listened. "Any pain?"

"I think the bedsores on my ass and feet are burning again," I said. The first week I was in the hospital they had kept me in traction and on my back so the bed had burned sores which bled into my buttocks and my heels. Now Steel looked at them and shook his head.

"Bad burns," he said. "The trip didn't help any. I'll have the nurse clean them and put something on to relieve the burning and itch. He gave me a long examination, jabbing a pin up and down my arms, trying to find a live spot, asking me to try to move different muscles in my legs which seemed completely dead. When he finished he said, "We're going to do some x-rays and have a look at the back—" and he gave instructions to the nurse and she and the orderly wheeled me into the x-ray room. They slid me onto the hard, shiny surface of the table, the technician straightened me out and from somewhere behind a screen told me to hold my breath. I looked up and saw the metallic shutter wink, felt something like a warm liquid pass through my bones, then the whirring sound died. The technician repeated the procedure, propping me on my side to get side views, and took over a dozen pictures. It was uncomfortable and painful The more he worked over me, the more I felt the fever returning inside my stomach. Finally I closed my eyes and tried not to think about the clicking and the buzzing of the machine and the "Hold your breath," "Just one more" of the pale, thin technician. I thought of Filomón riding across the empty desert in his remodeled hearse, and I laughed bitterly to myself. Maybe I had really died and the whole idea of the hospital was just a dream to keep from facing that reality . . . and I suddenly thought about how much Filomón reminded me of my grandfather. He used to come riding across the wide plain in a mule-pulled wagon, the most beautiful cream-colored mules in the entire country . . . lashing the air with his whip . . . coming to visit us . . . .

"Just one more fuckin' time!" the technician swore beneath his breath. Sweat poured from his forehead. "That Steel is a sonofabitch. If it's not just right he'll send it back—"

But Steel didn't reject any of the x-rays. When they were dry and hanging on the illuminated glass he looked at each one carefully, made some notes, then he turned around.

"Okay," he said, "looks good. How long were you in traction?" he asked.

I didn't remember. I only remembered the long, agonizing nights, the suffocation, the heat, the sweat which wet the sheets, and how I tried not to sleep because I thought if I did I would die.

"It doesn't matter," he said, "they did a good job. You don't need surgery. I think the best thing for you would be a nice sturdy body cast, from the belly button to the top of your head. That way we can start you on physical therapy as soon as possible. You need that if we're going to try to save the legs. Do you understand?"

I nodded.

"Good. If there's anything left in those legs I'm going to find it, and we'll go as far as we can. But you've got to help. I don't want you to give up." His voice was firm, but it was sincere. He wanted to help. "You have to keep working at it all the time," he said. He placed two fingers in my hand and said "Squeeze," and I squeezed. "That hand is strong, so's the arm—"

It was strange, but I couldn't remember squeezing anything with my hand up to the time Ismelda held my hand. Now my body seemed to want to come alive. It was a new sensation, especially sharp because of the dread I had lived with since the night of the paralysis.

"I do want to walk," I said eagerly. I did want to walk and run free again!

"Good," he nodded, "then you and I are in business. Let's get with it. First the barber. He's going to cut your hair, shave it. It'll be more comfortable and easier to work with when the cast goes around your head," he explained as a short, pudgy man entered the room. "Okay, Cano, make him bald."

"Yes sir," Cano said and snapped open a cloth which he threw around me. "How you doin', kid," he smiled and began cutting. He talked continuously while he cut, and when he smiled his thin, penciled mustache turned up at the edges. "You got good hair, dark and wavy, the kind girls like," he winked and rolled his eyes, ooh-la-la. "My poor mother, she used to say hair like this should be burned so the witches don't get hold of it . . . they like to build nests in it. Just like a woman, huh, build a nest in your hair!" He roared with laughter and swept aside the hair he had cut. "My mother believed in witches . . . see?" he held up his hand. He had only four fingers. "She says I got this cause a curse was put on her when I was in her belly. Who knows. Dr. Steel, he wanted to make me a new finger, and I bet he could, these doctors can do anything nowadays, they're getting too much power, like God, but I said, 'No thanks, Doc, if I can clip hair with four fingers then I'm happy. Don't go tampering with God's ways', I said to him . . ."

He finished cutting, lathered the top of my head with thick, warm soap, slapped his razor on a leather strap and began shaving.

"So how old are you, kid?" he asked.

"Sixteen," I answered.

"You're lucky, you still got lots of time in life. You'll like it here. They got everything for you, a swimming pool, school, church, good food, TV, games, everything. For some of the kids it's better than home . . . some don't wanna leave after awhile . . ."

I felt cold as the razor shaved swathes across the top of my head.

"So what happened to you?" he asked as he wiped his razor on a cloth on my chest.

"Accident—"

"Ah, life is full of accidents. Too many kids get hurt nowadays. Polio, epilepsy, everything . . . sometimes I get sad when I see it all. Wonder why God would do a thing like that. One day I asked Filo. You came with Filo, right? Well, he's a smart man. Must be over a hundred years old and still carting the kids around. Anyway, you know what he said? He said it's just a waystation on the journey of life. I don' know what he meant. Do you?"

I shook my head. He wiped my bald head with a wet cloth then dried it. "No, I don' know what he meant. 'This is like a station', he said, so that means there are more. And here they sew you kids back together. They can take a piece of bone from the tail and put it in your arm. They can take bones broken in ten places and put them together with steel pins. They can make crooked feet straight. Kids you think are dead, they bring to life . . . damn, one of these days they are going to put a motor in you and make you walk whether you want to or not!" He laughed uneasily. His mood had grown serious. "So that's it, kid," he smiled and held up a hand mirror. I looked at my shiny bald head. My arched nose and dark eyes seemed more pronounced without the hair.

"Don' worry," he said, "it will grow back. Better than my finger, which never grew. You know, they say hair grows even on people who are dead—" He gathered up his tools and went out waving and saying, "Don' worry, kid, it will grow back . . ."

I closed my eyes and thought, but if it grows equally on the dead and the living, how can one tell if he is alive or dead? And this Dr. Steel, I thought, the miracle worker according to Cano, what in the hell is he going to do with me? How in the hell is this cast going to help me walk? What do I have to find inside this broken body to make it move again? I strained and pushed my legs, but felt nothing. Damn, I cursed, damn!

Then I lay quietly and listened to the hospital sounds. I thought I heard a group of girls calling to each other. Clepo had said something about a girls' ward. Somewhere someone strummed on a guitar and sang softly . . .

> *It's been a blue, blue day*
> *I feel like running away*
> *I feel like running away from it all . . .*

Dr. Steel reappeared with two other doctors. "These are the plasterers," he said as he inspected my head. "Cano did a good job, not a scratch." He ran his hand over my bald head.

"Looks as bald as the mountain," one of them joked.

"Well, let's give him a shell, then. You ready?" Dr. Steel asked. I nodded and they went to work. They worked quietly and efficiently. One of them mixed the gypsum with water and a smell of fresh, wet earth filled the room. Dr. Steel and the other man covered me with cotton bandages and a thick gauze. They wet the bandages in the mixture and covered me with them, winding the bandages around and around. The cast grew quickly, covering me from my hips to the top of my head with a hole left for my face and ears. I closed my eyes as the shell grew. With Dr. Steel directing the operation I felt in safe hands. He was a cold, methodical person, but he knew what he was doing. So I lost interest in the process and retreated into my thoughts, and there I saw the image of the mountain, imprisoned like me, until, as Filomón said, an earth change would come and free it. Did he mean that I would have to learn to be patient like the mountain, to sleep in my shell until the blood clotted and I was barely alive . . . just waiting for the spring . . .

13

"But why the spring?" I wondered aloud.

"Yeah, almost through," the doctor answered.

The shell tightened around me, from my navel to the top of my head, with holes for my arms so I could drag myself around like Tortuga, when the sea swept over the desert again . . . white and pure as the plaster my mother's saints were made of . . . . Outside the winter wind moaned and I wondered what time it was. Someone sang

Who'ca took'ca my soda cracker
Does your mama chew tobaccer . . .

"Damn kids," the doctor laughed. He leaned back and lit a cigarette. They were done. Only Steel continued pulling and tugging at the cast, trying to get it perfect.

"Good enough to dry," one of them said. They looked at Steel. Finally he nodded. "Yes, good enough to dry. It's going to set straight as a ramrod."

So I was safe, safe in my new shell, safe as the mountain, shouldering a new burden which was already tightening on me.

"You'll feel it tighten a bit," Steel said, "but that's normal. We'll give it a little while to dry and then we'll x-ray to make sure it's set straight. Then you're on your way," he patted my arm and they went out of the room, closing the door behind them.

Safe as hell, I thought. Safe in my new shell. Safe as the mountain. With the door shut the room grew hot and stifling. I drifted in and out of troubled sleep. Once I thought I heard someone open the door.

"Hey, there's somebody in here."

"One of Steel's new ones . . . drying out, looks like."

"Let's use another room."

"Whatever you say nurse . . ."

They went out and so did the lights. The dark grew more oppressive. The cast tightened like a vise around my chest, its sharp edges dug into my stomach. I called out a couple of times, but no one heard me. With the door shut I couldn't hear any of the sounds in the hall, but if I lay very quietly I could hear the sound of water running somewhere. I listened to the rushing sound for a long time, then no longer able to hold my own water I wet the gurney mattress and the sheet that covered me. I cursed, tried to turn my head and discovered that I no longer had even that freedom. I cursed again and tried to sleep, but I couldn't with the cast tightening in on me and the heat of the room suffocating me. The nurse had cleaned my bedsores and powdered them with something, but they were hurting again, burning and sending stabs of pain up my back. I was about to call again when I heard the door open, saw the shaft of light on the ceiling, then heard it close.

"Doctor!" I called out. "Nurse!" But there wasn't anybody there. Someone had just looked in and I had missed my chance. Then I felt a presence in the room. Someone had come in and was standing by the door! I held my breath and listened and I heard someone moving very softly towards me.

"Who's there?" I asked. There was no answer, but someone was in the room. "Who's there?" I called again.

"I been watching you since you got here," a voice answered.

"Who are you?"

"Never mind who I am! But I know who you are," the voice answered. There was a threat in the sharp answer.

"Call the doctor," I said.

"No!"

"Then I'll call him myself—" I started to shout but a thin, withered hand clamped my mouth shut. I gagged at the rancid fishy smell on the hand. I spit and tried to shout but the dirty, scaly hand held tight.

"The doctors are all on a coffee break," he taunted, "and by the time they get back it will be too late, turtle!" He laughed and drew closer and I could smell his bad breath and see his yellow eyes shining in the dark. "Don't shout!" he hissed, "Don't shout and I'll let you loose—" Slowly he removed his dry, twisted hand from my mouth.

I gasped for air. "Who are you? What do you want?"

"I heard you were here . . . you came today with Filomón. Did he tell you his crazy stories about the mountain?"

"I don't know what you're talking about," I answered. He sounded crazy.

"Oh yes you do, Tortuga!" he snapped. "Don't get smart with me! I saw Filomón bring you in! I know Cano cut your hair! Now they put you in this turtle shell, trying to make you like a turtle! So Filomón says everytime the mountain moves somebody in here moves! That's his story. And he thinks you can beat the paralysis that keeps you on your back like an overturned turtle. Well, I think that's a bunch of bullshit! You hear me, Tortuga? Bullshit! Go ahead! Try moving! Try it!" His voice rose, shrill and insane.

"You're crazy," I said.

"Crazy, huh," he sneered. "See this hand?" He held up his withered hand for me to see. "It's been drying up like this for a year, and nobody can do anything about it! I used to believe in Filomón's crazy stories, but that didn't do any good either!"

He was shouting and panting. His spittle fell on my face, and his eyes opened wide and glowed in the dim light.

"So you're supposed to be the new Tortuga, huh! They gave you a large shell, just like the mountain, huh! Well I'm going to find out if Filomón's story is true or not! Let's see if you can move!"

15

He struck a match. The light flared in the dark and filled the air with the sharp smell of sulphur. In the light I could see his face, twisted and angry, and his withered hand which was brown and wrinkled.

"I'm going to find out if you're Tortuga!" he shouted and brought the match close to my eyes.

"Tortuga!" I shouted, "You're crazy!" I tried to turn my face from the hot flame but I couldn't.

"Move!" he shouted. "Move, mountain! Come and cure my hand! Move, Tortuga!"

"No!" I cried. "I can't!" I closed my eyes and smelled my singed eyelashes.

"Move, Tortuga!" he shouted insanely, "Move! Show us the secret!"

Just as the hot flame seared my eyes I heard the door open and somebody shouted, "Danny! What the hell are you doing in here!"

Lights flooded the room. The hot flame quickly disappeared.

"Nah-nothing," the boy named Danny whimpered and drew away. I opened my eyes and saw him move around the gurney. "I was just visiting, Mike, I, I was just visiting with Tortuga—"

"The hell you were!" Mike shouted at him. "You're up to no good again! Get the fuck outta here or I'll break your goddamned arm!"

I heard Danny run out of the room, then the squeak of a wheelchair as Mike approached me.

"You okay?" he asked.

"You came just in time," I answered. "I don't know why he did it, but he was holding a match up to my face—"

"He's crazy," Mike swore, "he does crazy things. Once I lay the law on him he behaves pretty well— Hey, you're the new kid the ward is talking about. Just got in with Filo, huh? I'm Mike. I heard Danny call you Tortuga, like the mountain, fits now that you got that body cast . . . you kinda look like a turtle, you know." He tapped the cast. "They did a beautiful job on it, bet Steel did it."

"Someone taking my name in vain," Dr. Steel said as he entered the room.

"Hey, doc, how you doing? I was just talking to Tortuga here, praising your work . . ."

"Tortuga," Dr. Steel murmured as he tapped the cast and felt its dryness, "so Mike's given you a nickname already—"

"Fits, don't it?" Mike smiled. "Besides, Danny beat me to the punch. Danny gave him the name."

Dr. Steel smiled. "Yeah, Tortuga fits just right. How does the cast feel?"

"A little tight."

"You'll get used to it," he nodded.

16

"Cuts around the stomach, shoulders—"

"That's no problem. We trim that and tape it. Feel up to an x-ray?"

"Sure."

"Okay, let's see how it set—" He pushed the gurney out of the room while Mike asked him if I could stay with them when I got back to the ward.

"He's from my part of the country," Mike said.

"We'll see," Dr. Steel nodded and pushed me into the x-ray room. The x-raying didn't take long, a couple of shots and Dr. Steel was satisfied that the cast had set right. "You're ready for some rest, and some supper." He trimmed the edges of the cast with a small electrical saw, then quickly taped them. It felt better, though the weight of the cast was still strange to me. "It's been a long day," he said as he finished the taping, "we had visiting day and surgery at the same time, that's why there's been so much confusion in the halls. It'll be more quiet in the ward. I'll prescribe something for you to sleep tonight, then I'll see you in the morning, okay?" He called for an orderly and a slick, gum-popping man jumped forward and saluted.

"At your orders, doc."

2

"My name's Waldo," he said, "but everybody calls me Speed-o. Jack of all trades, orderly, driver, I can get you anything, I mean anything you want from town. And I take care of a few of the nurse's aides around here." He leaned over me and winked as he pushed the squeaking gurney down the deserted hall. I could smell the sweet smell of pomade on his hair and the Dentyne gum he chewed. "What's your name, kid?"

I thought awhile then answered, "Tortuga."

"Tortuga! Hey, that's all right daddy-o! I like that!" Then he burst out singing.

> *Hey, watch out!*
> *Turtle man coming down the road*
> *And he's carrying a heavy load*
> *Just looking for a place to sleep tonight!*

"Like that, huh?" he snapped his fingers. "I'm a real swinger, just a real cool swinger!" He stopped suddenly and pushed the gurney into a dark corner. "Hey, Tortuga, you don't mind if we slide in here for a minute, right. There's a new nurse in this ward that is bad. I mean really bad! but she likes you know what. Everytime I pass by we slip into the linen closet for a quickie." He giggled crazily. "Whad'ya say?"

I was about to answer, but he was already gone. I just wanted to get somewhere and rest, I wanted to put everything in perspective and get a sense of where I was. But why did the girl Ismelda keep popping in and out of my thoughts. I had only been here a few hours and already met some crazy characters . . . what would the future hold for me? How soon would the doctor start the therapy? And how much movement could I recover from my legs?

I closed my eyes and listened to the sounds of the hospital. Somewhere dishes clanged and kids shouted to each other. From faraway I thought I heard the whimper of babies crying. Along the wall the steam radiators pinged and groaned as they swelled with steam. Overhead the cold wind moaned . . . and if I listened very carefully far beneath the frozen earth I could hear the sound of water, Tortuga's warm pee cutting new channels through the frozen wasteland . . .

Follow the river, Filomón had said, and yet even he seemed lost in the storms which racked us as we crossed the barren desert.

Wait till spring . . .

Pray to God, God's will be done . . .

I prayed, a million times I prayed, why the paralysis? Why me? What did I do to deserve this punishment? Why? Why? Why?

I awoke in a sweat. "Where am I?" I asked, and in the darkness I heard an answer, I heard someone moving around the gurney and for a moment I thought Danny had returned.

"Is this Tortuga?" the voice asked.

"Yes, he has come to live with us."

"Filomón brought him."

"Is he an orphan, like us?"

"Will he go to live with Salomón?" the voices whispered.

"Pray he doesn't, sister, but Salomón knows he's here."

I thought I was dreaming. Dark figures shuffled around the gurney, wheelchairs squeaked. "Who's there?" I asked.

"Are you awake, Tortuga?"

"Who is it?" I asked.

"Your brothers and sisters," came the answer.

Someone tapped on the cast, but because the gurney was high I couldn't see anyone. Then I felt a tug as an arm wrapped itself around my cast and pulled. At first I thought they were pulling me down and when the face of the girl appeared suddenly over me I realized she had pulled herself up. I gasped with fear. Her twisted face was gray and wrinkled, the face of an old woman. She drew closer and I saw the hump on her back. She was a small, deformed creature. She had clawed her way to the top of the gurney, now she smiled at me.

"Who are you?" I cried. Around me the others also squirmed their way up the side of the gurney, giggling and calling out, "Is that Tortuga?" "Does he look like Tortuga?" "Lemme see—"

"Yes, it is Tortuga," the hunched back girl smiled. Her eyes were pale green in the dark. Her breath was sweet on my face, but her face was twisted and deformed.

"Who are you?" I cried again.

"Cynthia," she whispered.

"Is he going to stay in our ward?" another one asked.

"Salomón will say," she answered, studying me closely, curiously, and drawing closer and closer as if to kiss me.

"No!" I finally screamed as loud as I could, "Get away! Get away!"

"Shhh—" she tried to quiet me by placing her thin fingers over my mouth. "It's okay . . . we know . . ."

I gagged with panic, heaved and shouted again. "Get away! Get away! Don't touch me!"

They were swarming over me now, pulling themselves over the side of the gurney, their twisted gnome faces looming over me, whispering, giggling, poking at the cast, calling it a turtle shell, celebrating my arrival, vying for my friendship, then suddenly scattering as I shouted and cursed at them. They disappeared quickly, dropping off the gurney and scrambling away. I was still shouting when I felt Speed-o's hand clamp over my mouth.

"Shh—Hold it! What the hell's the matter with you, kid? You wanna wake the dead?"

"Freaks," I gasped, "freaks—"

"Oh, that group," he said and shook his head as he lit a cigarette. "That's Cynthia's group . . . they prowl the halls at night . . . know everything that goes on in this hospital . . . but they don't come out during the day . . . bad cases . . . but if you ask me the whole place is crawling with freaks . . ."

He pulled the gurney out of the corner and pushed it down the hall. Somewhere the sun was about to set because the pale ochre light which touched the high windows which faced the patio created a haze in the dim hallway. At the end of the hall he stopped at the nurses station and rang the bell on the counter. He paced nervously back and forth, muttering "I wonder where in the hell everyone is? I'm asked to deliver a body and there's no one waiting at the gate! This is your ward . . . but I wanna get back to that quickie I didn't finish. Nooooorse! New boy!"

"They're gone," someone whispered.

"Where?" Speed-o asked.

"Supper."

"And the nurse?"

"Chasing Danny."

"What'd he do now?"

"Started throwing spagetti in the dining room. Big fight. Lots of fun."

"For cryin' out loud," Speed-o groaned. "I can't stand around and babysit this turtle man . . . he's gotta get to bed and I gotta get back to my beaver . . . Any empty rooms around here?" he asked the kid.

"Maybe up the hall, some—"

"Well let's go," Speed-o said and pushed me hurriedly down the long, empty hallway. "We'll find you a room, ole buddy, we'll find you a nice and private place—"

We went deeper into the ward until he found a room without a name tag on the door, there he turned the gurney in and swung it alongside the only bed in the otherwise empty room.

"This will do fine," he nodded. He grunted and pushed and managed to slide me off the gurney onto the bed. "Just fine, just fine," he smiled and covered me with a sheet. "The nurse will be here in no time," he smiled and smoothed back his slick hair. "I'll see you in the funny papers, Tortuga," he winked and went out singing

If all little girls
Were like bells in a tower!
And I was the preacher
I'd bang them each hour!

Then the door clicked shut and I could only hear the echo of his song in the hallway.

The room was dark and silent. Through the window I could see the top of the mountain, glowing magenta as the winter clouds lifted long enough to let the setting sun shine on its back. The gigantic mass of boulders seemed to breathe with life as the color grew a soft watermelon pink then salmon orange. The light glowed from within the mountain as Tortuga seemed to lift his head into the setting sun . . . he turned to look at me, another crippled turtle come to live at his feet. The rheumy eyes draped with wrinkled flaps of skin bore into my soul and touched me with their kindness. For a moment the mountain was alive. It called to me, and I lay quietly in my dark room, hypnotized by the sight. Now I knew what Filomón had meant. There was a secret in the mountain, and it was calling me, unfolding with movement and power as the dying rays of the sun infused the earth with light.

Then a gray wash fell over the desert and the golden light was gone. The cold wind rattled the roof of the hospital. Brittle tumbleweeds rolled across the frozen waste. The fatigue of the journey settled over me and I fell into a troubled, restless sleep. In my dream I saw myself crawling across the desert like a crippled turtle. I made my way slowly towards the mountain, and when I was there I found the secret ponds and springs at the foot of the mountain. A ring of young girls danced around the water . . . they sang and danced like the group of first communion girls who had shared my holy communion so many years ago . . . when I was only a child. Then one of them, a dark-haired girl with flashing eyes, broke loose from the dance and ran towards me, calling my name as she ran. Tortuga! Oh, we're so glad you've come. Come and swim in the holy waters of the mountain! Come and hear Salomón tell his stories! I recognized Ismelda, dressed in flowing white and singing a song of joy . . . She took my hand and together we tumbled into the warm, bubbling waters. I'll drown! I cried, I'll drown! No, she cried, you will not drown in the mountain's waters. And holding me tight she taught me how to move my turtle flippers until I too could

21

swim in the rushing water. Around me golden fish swam as effortlessly as birds float and glide in the air on a still day. See! she shouted with joy as she led me deeper and deeper into the mountain's heart, see the blood of the mountain. I looked and saw the rivers which fed the springs, one molten and red with burning lava and the other blue with cold water . . . and where the two rivers met the water hissed and became a golden liquid, apricot scented. This is where the waters meet, she whispered to me as we swam towards the shore, this is the place of power. Look! I looked and there on the bank sat a small, thin boy surrounded by cripples. He smiled and waved to us. This is Salomón, Ismelda said, and you have come to hear his story. Salomón knows the magic of the mountain . . . he is the mountain. Listen to his story. I listened as the frail, angelic boy opened his lips to speak. Then in the deep night and in the dream there was only silence as Salomón began his story . . .

Before I came here I was a hunter, but that was long ago . . . Still, it was in the pursuit of the hunt that I came face to face with my destiny, so I will tell my story and you will know.

We called ourselves a tribe and we spent our time hunting and fishing along the river. For young boys that was a great adventure, so each morning I stole away from my father's home to meet my fellow hunters by the river. My father was a farmer who planted corn on the hills along the river. He was a good man. He kept the ritual of the seasons, marked the path of the sun and the moon across the sky, and he prayed each day that the order of things not be disturbed.

He did his duty and tried to teach me the order in the weather and the seasons, but a wild urge in my blood drove me from him. I went to join the tribe along the river. At first I went willingly, the call of the hunt was exciting, the slaughter of the animals and the smell of blood drove us deeper and deeper into the dark river until I found that I was enslaved by the tribe and I forgot the fields of my father. We hunted birds with our crude weapons and battered to death stray raccoons and rabbits. Then we cooked the meat and filled the air with the smoke of roasting meat. The tribe was pleased with me and welcomed me as a hunter. They prepared for my initiation.

I, Salomón, tell you this so that you may know the meaning of life and death. How well I know it now, how clear the events are of the day I killed the giant river turtle. I tell you this because since that day I have been a storyteller, forced by the order of my destiny to reveal my story. So I speak to you to tell you how the killing became a horror.

The silence of the river was heavier than usual that day. The heat stuck to our sweating skin like sticky syrup and the insects sucked our blood. Our half-naked bodies moved like shadows in the brush. Those ahead and behind me whispered from time to time, complained that we were lost, suggested that we turn back. I said nothing, it was the day of my initiation, I could not speak. There had been a fight at camp the night before and the bad feelings still lingered. But we hunted anyway, there was nothing else to do. I was just beginning to realize that we were compelled to hunt in the dark shadows of the river. Some days the spirit for the hunt was not good, fellow hunters quarreled over small things, and still we had to start early at daybreak to begin the long day's journey which would not bring us out of the shadows until sunset.

In the branches above us the bird cries were sharp and frightful, and more than once the leader lifted his arm and the line froze, ready for action. The humid air was tense. Somewhere to my left I heard the river murmur as it swept south, and for the first time, the dissatisfaction which had been building within me surfaced, and I cursed the oppressive darkness and wished I was free of it. I thought of my father walking in the sunlight of his green fields, and I wished I were with him. But I could not; I owed the tribe a debt. Today I would become a full member. I would kill the first animal we encountered.

We moved farther than usual into unknown territory. We cursed as we hacked away at the thick underbrush; behind me I heard murmurs of dissension. Some wanted to turn back, others wanted to rest on the warm sandbars of the river, still others wanted to finish the argument which had started the night before. My father had given me an amulet to wear and he had instructed me on the hunt, and this made the leader jealous. So there had been those who argued that I could wear the amulet and those who said no. In the end the jealous leader tore it from my neck and said that I would have to face my initiation alone.

I was thinking about how poorly prepared I was and how my father had tried to help when the leader raised his arm and sounded the alarm. A friend behind me whispered that if we were in luck there would be a deer drinking at the river. No one had ever killed a deer in the memory of our tribe. We held our breath and waited, until the leader motioned and I moved forward to see. There in the middle of the narrow path lay the biggest tortoise any of us had ever seen. It was a huge monster which had crawled out of the dark river to lay its eggs in the warm sand. I felt a shiver when I saw it, and when I breathed I smelled the spoor of the sea. The taste of copper drained in my mouth and settled in my queasy stomach.

The giant turtle lifted its huge head and looked at us with dull, glintless eyes. The tribe drew back. Only I remained facing the monster from the water. Its slimy head dripped with bright green algae. It hissed a warning, asking me to move. It had come out of the water to lay its eggs, now it had to return to the river. Wet, leathery eggs fresh from the laying clung to its webbed feet, and as it moved forward it crushed them into the sand. Its grey shell was dry, dulled by the sun, encrusted with dead parasites and green growth; it needed the water.

*Kill it, the leader cried, and at the same time the hunting horn
sounded its tooooo-ouuu and echoed down the valley. Ah, its call was
so sad and mournful I can hear it today as I tell my story . . . Listen,
Tortuga, for it is now I know that at that time I could have forsaken my
initiation and denounced the darkness and the insanity that urged us to
the never-ending hunt. Now I remember that the words my father taught
me were not in my heart. The time was not right.*

*The knife, the leader called, and the knife of the tribe was passed
then slipped into my hand. The huge turtle lumbered forward. I could
not speak to it, and in fear I raised the knife and brought it down with
all my might. Oh, I prayed to no gods then, but how I have wished that I
could undo what I did . . . One blow severed the giant turtle's head. One
clean blow and the head rolled in the sand as the reptilian body reared
back, gushing green slime as it died. The tribe cheered and pressed
forward. They were as surprised as I that the kill had been so swift and
clean. We had hunted smaller tortoises before and we knew that once
they retreated into their shells it took hours to kill them. Then knives
and spears had to be poked into the holes and the turtle had to be turned
on its back so the tedious task of cutting the softer underside could begin. But now I had beheaded the giant turtle with one blow!*

*There will be enough meat for the entire tribe, one of the boys
cried, and he speared the reptilian head and held it aloft for everyone to
see. I could only look at the dead turtle that lay quivering on the sand,
its death urine and green blood staining the damp earth.*

*He has passed his test, the leader shouted, he did not need the
amulet of his father! We will clean the shell and it will be his shield!
And he shall now be called the man who slew the turtle!*

*The tribe cheered, and for a moment I bathed in my glory. The fear
left me, and so did the desire to be with my father on the harsh hills
where he cultivated his fields of corn. He had been wrong; I could trust
the tribe and its magic. Then someone cried and we turned to see the
turtle struggling toward us. It reared up, exposing the gaping hole
where the head had been, then it charged, surprisingly swift for its huge
size. Even without its head it headed for the river. The tribe fell back in
panic.*

*Kill it, the leader shouted. Kill it before it reaches the water! If it
escapes into the water it will grow two heads and return to haunt us!*

*I understood what he meant. If the creature reached the safety of
the water it would live again, and it would become one more of the
ghosts of the bush that lurked along our never-ending path. Now there
was nothing I could do but stand my ground and finish the killing. I
struck at it until the knife broke on its hard shell, and still the turtle
rumbled toward me, pushing me back. Terror and fear made me fall on
the sand and grab it with my bare hands. Grunting and gasping for
breath I dug my bare feet into the sand and tried to stop its mad rush for*

24

the water. I slipped one hand into the dark, bleeding hole where the head had been and with the other I grabbed its huge foot. I struggled to turn it on its back and rob it of its strength, but I couldn't. Its dark instinct for the water and the pull of death were stronger than my fear and desperation. I grunted and cursed it as its claws cut my arms and legs. The brush shook with our violent thrashing as we rolled down the bank towards the river. Even mortally wounded it was too strong for me. Finally, at the edge of the river, it broke free from me and plunged into the water, and trailing frothy blood and bile it disappeared into the gurgling waters.

Covered with the turtle's blood, I stood numb and trembling from the encounter, and as I watched it disappear into the dark waters of the river, I knew I had done a wrong. Instead of conquering my fear, I had created another shadow which would return to haunt us. I turned and looked at my companions; they trembled with fright. You have failed us, the leader whispered, and you have angered the river gods. He raised his talisman, a stick on which hung chicken feathers, dried juniper berries and the rattler of a snake we had killed in the spring, and he waved it in front of me to ward off the curse. Then they withdrew in silence and vanished into the dark brush, leaving me alone on that stygian bank.

Oh, I wish I could tell you how lonely I felt. I cried for the turtle to return so that I could finish the kill, or return its life, but the force of my destiny was already set and that was not to be. I understand that now. That is why I tell my story. And so I left the river, free of the tribe, but unclean and smelling of death . . . That night the bad dreams came, and then the paralysis . . . .

I awoke sobbing and gasping for breath. I reached out in the dark to touch Salomón . . . I called Ismelda's name. I knew I had been there with them, listening to his sad story, sitting by the warm water which gurgled from the spring.

My arms and legs shook uncontrollably. Searing jolts of electricity surged through my body as the water bathed my tired body. The hot energy tore through my guts, gathered in my balls and erupted out of my wet, warm tool, spewing the marrow of blood and streams of hot pee on the cold bed. Ismelda's tongue flickered in my mouth, she smiled and sang, a song like the crescendo of water which kept slapping against me . . . a song burning into every dead nerve and fiber in my arms and legs.

"I'm alive!" I shouted. "Hey! Come and see! I hurt! Oh I hurt! Come and see!"

I opened my eyes, the room was dark, my cry echoed against the walls then died down, as the fire died down. I was panting and gasping for breath. The cotton lining of my cast felt moist with sweat.

"Water!" I cried. "I'm burning up! Help me!"

I jerked spasmodically on the wet bed. Then the newly wired nerves rested and the pain subsided, but I knew something had happened in the magic of my dream to help me tear loose from the paralysis. I felt the bedsores burning on my ass and my feet and still I felt like laughing. I squirmed and felt the ripple of a quiver run down my legs and tickle my toes. I looked, but it was too dark to see, still I was sure something had moved. I cried again.

"Hey! Dr. Steel! Nurse! Anyone! Come and see! Get me out of here!"

I thought I heard footsteps and listened quietly in the dark, but no one appeared. Somewhere an owl called then flew across the river towards the mountain. The storm howled again, but now in the distance, farther south. I reached and touched the cast with my trembling right hand, felt the texture of the plaster which had become my shell, touched my face which was soaked with sweat. Good, I thought, good. I closed my eyes and slept again, smiling with joy, covered with sweat and stink, but glad to be quivering with the pain of the nerves and muscles which were coming alive. By the mountain, by the side of the spring, Ismelda waited.

3

The daughter of the sun awoke to weave her blanket with pastel threads. Her soft, coral fingers worked swiftly to weave the bits of turquoise blue and mother of pearl into the silver sky. She had but a moment in which to weave the tapestry that covered her nakedness, because behind her the sun trumpeted, awoke roaring alive with fire and exploded into the sky, filling the desert with glorious light and scattering the mist of the river and the damp humours of the night. Dawn blushed and fled as the sun straddled the mountain, and the mountain groaned under the welcomed light. The earth trembled at the sight.

Light pierced my dusty window and flooded the room. I opened my eyes and gave silent thanks for the new day. The night had been long and immense, full of dreams and pain, cold with the rattling of the wind. Now the shafts of light fell on my body and drove the chill away. I tested my legs and felt a tremble in my toes. I pulled with all my might and bent my arms slightly at the elbows. A strength had returned, so slight I could barely feel it, so weak it made me sweat and quiver just to test it, but it had returned, thanks to the grace of the mountain and the strength of the girl in my dreams . . . it had returned and I knew I could build on it. My first step towards freedom had come.

I cried out for help, but no one came. Speed-o had unloaded me in an unmarked isolation room. There was no telling when I would be found. My lips were cracked with thirst, and in my stomach a hungry worm fed and made it churn and growl. I felt my body empty itself on the bed, and the mess and the blood from the open bedsores wet the sheets and mattress. I laughed and cried at the same time, felt the old hopelessness return, then I stretched and felt the movement I was guarding so carefully and felt better. For consolation I turned to the mountain, but the sun had risen quickly and a new bank of winter clouds swept over the barren height.

"Damn you!" I cursed, and the sound echoed in the bare room. "Damn all of you! Can't you see I need help! . . . I need help . . ."

Maybe this bare room was a room in hell and I was condemned to spend eternity here, wallowing in my filth, taunted by just the slight hope of movement, shouting for help in an empty void . . . I cursed again and turned my rage and the ache on the mountain.

"Move!" I cursed like Danny, "Move, Tortuga! Get your fat ass off the ground and move! Trample everything! Show us you can move. Move . . . please move . . ."

A strange thunder rumbled across the sky, winter thunder full of an eerie green light, but Tortuga remained fastened to the earth, sleeping its winter sleep. I looked at it for a long time, then I slept again . . . saw the ring of girls dancing by the lime green of the river, felt Ismelda take my hand . . . gave myself again to the illusion which had become as real as the pain of the bed.

I slept a long time, then a voice whispered my name and I opened my eyes. I blinked, looked sideways and saw Mike sitting by the side of the bed.

"I'm sorry, Tortuga," he whispered, "dammit I'm sorry—"

"It wasn't your fault," I answered. It hurt to talk. My lips were cracked and blistered and my tongue felt like a swollen wad of dry cotton. The door was open and I could hear shouting in the hall and the sound of running feet.

"I should have known better!" he cursed. "It's just that I thought they had kept you up front in one of the isolation rooms. Sometimes they keep new arrivals up there, for observation, then this morning on my way to therapy I passed Dr. Steel and asked about you and he said you were in the ward . . . Everybody knows what happens in this ward, so I knew you were lost . . . I came as fast as I could. The nurses are coming, and Steel's on his way too—"

"Do me a favor," I answered, "my legs feel like they're broken off . . . Can you rub them a little."

He nodded and pulled the sheet back. The stench made him wince. "God," he groaned, "it's a mess! A goddamned mess. You're bleeding— Nurse!" he shouted over his shoulder and began massaging. Reviving the circulation sent stabs of sharp pain through my numb legs.

"Coming! Coming!" someone shouted. The room began to fill with kids. Ismelda appeared behind Mike's shoulder. She looked at me and at Mike rubbing furiously while he cursed the nurses and she shook her head. Her eyes told me she felt my pain. She helped Mike massage my legs, working slowly to get the blood going, saying nothing.

"Oh my God!" exclaimed the first nurse to enter the room.

"The shit's going to hit the fan now!" Mike swore.

"They never checked him in! I swear they never checked him in!" she cried. Other nurses and aides and kids followed. One of the nurses stuck a thermometer in my mouth I spit it out and asked for water.

"He needs a drink! Not a gaddamned thermometer!" Mike shouted. His curses made them panic. One of them pulled out the dirty sheet beneath me and tossed it aside. Then she began making the bed. A straw touched my lips and I sucked warm orange juice which turned to acid in my stomach. Around me the room continued to fill with kids, all asking questions. Dr. Steel pushed his way through them, a worried look wrinkling his brow. He put his thermometer on my chest, calmly gave the nurses orders, asked, "How do you feel, Tortuga?"

"He could've died!" Mike cursed. The other kids picked up the refrain. "He could've died!" "They tried to kill him!" "Damn, just wait until the committee hears about this!" "Yeah, they can't kill Tortuga and get away with it." "Oh my . . ."

"Okay . . ." I answered as the thermometer reappeared and rested on my swollen tongue. I tried to push it away, but the nurse held it. I looked at Mike and Ismelda massaging my legs and tried to get their attention. "Looka mah toez," I mumbled.

"Nurse, get the kids outa here!" Steel snapped.

"Everybody out! Everybody out!" the nurse shouted. Nobody left, the confusion was great. A couple of kids had put bedpans on their heads, another one beat a urinal, all complained that the committee would hear about this, that a report would be made and the nurses fired. I didn't know what the hell committee they were talking about, I only wanted to get their attention so they could tell me whether or not my toes were wiggling when I told them to wiggle. Ismelda wiped my legs with a cool, wet cloth, and when the nurse pulled out the thermometer and read 101 degrees I caught her attention.

"My toes . . ." She and Mike looked at the same time. I strained as hard as I could, shut my eyes, groaned, sank deep into my shell and found the one live ember, blew on it softly, squeezed it, held it in my hands for Ismelda to see, and then it exploded and went flowing down my arms and legs, spastically jumping over dead nerve endings and numb muscles, flipping open long dead circuits, moving through the dark channels inside my shell, making me cry with pain as the energy of the relit fuse churned inside my stomach and jerked up my balls as it filled my groin and thighs with a warm, electric liquid, a liquid which buzzed as it flowed through my bones and dry tendons and finally exploded at the tip of my toes.

"He moved!" Mike shouted and turned to grab Steel.

"Two cc's," Steel ordered and I felt the prick of the needle in my arm, felt the syrupy heaviness spread quickly.

29

"Oh Tortuga," Ismelda smiled, worked her way around the nurses and touched my forehead.

"Water . . ." She held the straw to my lips and this time the water was cool and refreshing.

"Look, doc! Look!" Mike shouted.

"Just a spasm . . ." Steel said. He pushed up my eyelid and shone a light into my eye. "Get the kids out," he said again.

"Everybody out!" the big nurse shouted.

"Keep the sheet cold . . . bring down the fever . . . he'll be all right . . ."

"No! No! Look! He moved! Tortuga moved!" Mike shouted and pulled at the doctor.

"Tortuga moved!" one of the kids shouted and they rushed to the window to see if the mountain was indeed moving. Dr. Steel turned, looked, cautiously, cynically.

"Move it again!" Mike shouted. The kids shouted, beat bedpans, tripped over each other to get to the window.

"Damn little bastards!" the nurse swore under her breath.

"Don't cuss us, we'll report you to the committee."

"100 degrees," another nurse called, flipped the thermometer and stuck it back in my mouth.

I groaned, found the thread again, the thin light which had been gone for so long and which was now responding to my call, a fine gossamer thread burning in my brain, pounding in my heart, acrid-wet with electricity, and I said move and it moved, jumping the long-dead relays, sizzling like the rivers of fire and water deep in the mountain, it went careening through my dark flesh and withered tendons.

"See!" Mike shouted. "See!"

"Yes," Ismelda whispered and wiped the sweat from my forehead.

Dr. Steel turned and looked at me. "I don't believe it," he said, "I want to but I don't. Can you do it again? I'll watch." "I can do it again," I answered, "I can do it all day long," and I smiled and pushed the switch again.

"Doctor, the fever's down . . . perhaps an enema . . ." a nurse suggested.

"Oh my . . ."

"Yeah! It's moving!" the kids at the window shouted. They were looking at poor old Tortuga changing colors and groaning as the new storm gathered over it, and they saw it move . . . ancient dreams, reptilian flesh, cold as ice, now moving to a new found melody.

"Sharp or dull," Steel asked as he poked along my legs with his needle.

"Some sharp . . . I think . . ."

"Yahoooo!" someone shouted by the door.

"Algo es algo, dijo el diablo!" Mike responded and grabbed my leg and shook it. "It moved!"

"Nurse, get the kids out . . ."

"All right! Everybody out!"

"Down to 99 degrees—"

"Good . . . good," Dr. Steel nodded, straightened up, stood there with his stethoscope still dangling from his ears, shook his head, said, "I don't believe it," but he did, and he looked at me and winked.

I relaxed for the first time since I started straining and when I did my guts seemed to tear loose and a hot, frothy mess spilled on the bed. Gas rumbled through my empty stomach and exploded. The nurse who had just finished cleaning the bed groaned, pulled out the dirty sheet and started again.

"Dull or sharp?"

"Sharp . . . yes, I'm sure . . ." I tried to nod, felt the restraint of the cast, felt weak from hunger and pain.

"He farted!" "Damn!"

> *Tortuga, Tortuga, two by four*
> *Couldn't get to the bathroom door*
> *So he does it on the floor.*

"On the bed!" "Yeah." The kids laughed, drummed their bedpans and urinals louder and louder.

"At least he's moving." "Yeah."

"Out!" the big nurse shouted and grabbed at a young man with a harmonica who was leading the singing. "Out! Right now."

"Mike, get them out," the doctor said. "He's okay now. He just needs to rest, something to eat . . ." He turned to the nurse and told her to clean and powder the bedsores. Mike turned to the kids, repeated what the doctor had just said and they all began to file out quietly.

"Tortuga needs to rest . . . That's all, just rest . . ."

"Poor ole Tortuga . . ."

"Yeah, poor ole Tortuga . . ."

They went out singing:

> *Poor ole Tortugaaaaa!*
> *He never got a kissssss . . .*
> *Pooooor ole Tortuga,*
> *He don' know whad he misssss . . .*

"I'm sorry," Dr. Steel said and folded his stethoscope and put it in his pocket, "this won't happen again . . . Will it, nurse?" he asked the big nurse.

"No, sir! No, sir! But it was the night nurse who was on duty, sir."

"I don't care who's on duty. You run this ward, and I'm saying this won't happen again. Clear?"

"Yes sir," the nurse nodded, turned and looked at me with a scowl on her face.

"Look!" one of the aides pointed.

"What?"

"He's peeing . . ."

"Whad they say?" someone asked from the hall.

"Nothing," Mike laughed as he went out, "they just said he's peeing, that's all, just taking a good old healthy leak."

"Peeing turtle pee, I bet."

"Yeah," they laughed.

"Oh my . . . ."

They all laughed, even the nurse who had to pull out the sheet again and start over.

"It's a good sign," Dr. Steel winked and walked out.

"98.6—"

"See you later, Tortuga!" Mike called from the hallway and the rest of the kids repeated, "Yeah, see you later, Tortuga!" "Try using a urinal!" one of them added and they all laughed.

The nurses finished cleaning me up by powdering the bedsores. Somebody brought me something to eat, which I gulped down with shut eyes because the drug in the shot was already pulling me into sleep . . . Then they turned me on my stomach so the talcummed sores could dry. Face down, buried against the bed, I fell asleep, dreaming I was a turtle slowly clawing its way across a wide desert . . . towards a cool, northern mountain lake.

4

The nurse came in and checked my blood pressure and took my temperature every hour. She was a silent woman, cold and precise, so I said nothing but I felt better. The fever was gone, I was eating everything they brought, and the pain from the bedsores was better. But most exciting to me was that I could control the muscle spasms. They weren't spasms anymore, they were actual commands I could send down to my legs and they obeyed. It was an excitement I hadn't felt since the initial paralysis. Then I had tried so hard to make my legs move, and finally I had given up and withdrawn into resignation.

Now there was movement, slight and feeble, but with it returned a sense of hope. I looked out the window at the mountain. I thought of Filomón and what he had said. I thought of my first night at the hospital and the woman in the dreams, Ismelda, the woman who had led me to the springs where we entered the mountain. And Mike? How had he found me? Why? How were they working their way into my new life? In the other hospital I couldn't remember faces. Many people had come to see me, and they had gathered around my bed, looking at me with silent, sad eyes, praying they could lift the paralysis with their pleas to God . . . and my mother, growing gray before my eyes, hers was the only face I remembered. But nothing they could do or say had cut through that numbing weight of the paralysis as had these strange powers that worked their way at the foot of the mountain . . .

"You're doing fine, just fine," Dr. Steel said when he checked me that evening, and he went out shaking his head, making his rounds.

Other boys who lived in the ward dropped by to say hello. Most were my age, polio victims, cripples of every sort, but some were just kids, ten or twelve year olds who lived in a world of their own, raised hell whenever they could but quickly settled down when Mike spoke. He seemed to be the leader in the ward. He was bunking with two other boys, Jerry and Sadsack, and he was trying to get me moved to their room where there was an extra bed. In the meantime I waited, lying alone in the bare room, listening to the rush of sounds that filled the ward in the morning and which settled down as the kids went swimming or to physical therapy or to the classes that were held for those who cared to attend.

There was also a lull during mid-afternoon. I lay quietly and listened to Franco strumming his guitar and singing western or rhythm and blues songs. Somebody told me he looked exactly like Elvis Presley but that he had lost his legs to an incurable disease, so he kept to himself in his room, roaming the halls only at night in his wheelchair, taking old songs and changing the words to tell his story.

He had already composed a song for me. I lay thinking and listening to the words which drifted through the stale, antiseptic air of the ward.

> *Tortuga was a wounded turtle*
> *Cast in a lonely shell*
> *He thought of heaven*
> *And he dreamed of home*
> *But he had come to hell . . .*

Then Danny came in. "Psst. You awake, Tortuga?"

"What do you want?" I asked. After our first encounter I didn't trust him.

"I just came to see how you are," he said and moved into my sight. He stood there for a long time, looking at me, mulling something over in his mind, and I felt sorry for him because he was a pathetic kid, dressed in an oversize hospital shirt and holding his withered hand up as if he had to keep it in sight, had to keep asking himself why the hand was drying up and dying on him. His pale yellow eyes darted back and forth, from me to his hand to the window which held the mountain framed as a still life.

"You're lucky," he said finally, "the doc knows what's the problem . . . I heard your legs moved . . . you're lucky." He looked at the mountain and cursed. "Goddammit, nothing works for me." He held his hand in front of me, close so I could see the dry wrinkles and scabs which covered it, and I smelled something rancid and dying.

"At first it was only my fingers . . . They got numb and I couldn't move them . . . then they began to dry out. I came here, and they brought all sorts of specialists to look at me, and not a one of them could tell me what was the matter . . . and the curse kept spreading, now it's my whole hand . . . like cancer, but it ain't cancer, it's just dying . . . Sonsofbitches can't do nothing for me! But you," he glared at me, "you listened to those crazy stories Filomón tells about the mountain! And you believed him! Is that why they put you in a shell? Is that why you moved your legs?"

"I don't know," I answered. "Maybe it was—"

"Bullshit!" he cut me off. "Don't go getting a holier than anything idea about those crazy stories. That nurse is going to fix you. She's going to transfer you to Salomón's ward!"

"Where is that?" I remembered the boy who told the story in my dream.

"That's where they keep the hard core polio cases," he laughed. "Listen, there's just about every kind of cripple in this place, freaks all of them. They're either bent and twisted with polio or MD or club feet, pigeon toed, curved spines, open spines, birth defects, broken backs, car wrecks, under-nourished kids who can't even stand up, even VD cases, kids that were smashed by their parents, looney cases . . . every kind of gimp you can imagine is here, somewhere. But in Salomón's ward are the vegetables. Every other kid has a chance, like you, and who knows, hell, they might even find a cure for me . . . at least I can get around. But back there, that's the end of the line, and that's where you're headed." He laughed crazily, as if he was glad that I was being transfered, as if some future punishment for me would alleviate his pain, and he walked away before I could question him further.

The rest of the afternoon was very quiet. I slept. The day was warm, the fragrance of the desert filled the room, as if the earth was thawing, and then the sun fell towards the rugged mountain range to the west and everything froze again. A haze from the fires burning in the homes along the river settled over the valley. Tortuga lay frozen and stiff, weak saffron rays glanced off his tired back, but he did not respond to my presence . . . he did not acknowledge my being.

When Mike showed up he brought Ronco and Sadsack with him. Ronco was nineteen, older than most of us. The nurse kept him isolated in a room to himself. He had a record player, the only one in the ward, and Mike said his walls were covered with pin-ups. His favorite was a large poster of Marilyn Monroe, the most beautiful woman who ever lived, he said, because she was the kind of woman who could give you loving whether you were Joe DiMaggio or whether you were a poor crippled bastard dragging around in a wheelchair.

Sadsack was a polio case. He was tall and the disease had left him uncoordinated. His arms and legs flopped around like used rubber bands. He had the sad, wrinkled face of a bloodhound, and a mop of thin hair which was always sticking up. Folds of loose skin fell over his sleepy eyes. He was a complainer.

"They're moving me to another ward," I said.

Mike looked at me and nodded. "Yeah, news travels fast on the grapevine—"

"But why?"

"Ah the Nurse can be a bitch," Ronco said hoarsely. The first tracheotomy they had done on him years ago had been done by a careless surgeon so when he spoke his voice sounded like a very rough imitation of Cagney.

"She likes her name spelled with a capital N," Sadsack said, "so it's yes Nurse or no Nurse . . . she runs a tight ward."

"I guess she didn't like being chewed out by Steel, so she's taking it out on you . . . but don't worry, we'll go to Steel and get you back here."

"Where is this other ward?" I asked.

"It's down the way," Mike motioned.

"It's Salomón's ward," Danny reminded me, "it's a garden full of vegetables, a real vegetable patch!" he laughed.

"Da, dat me-means he lib-lib in dah-dah Gar-garden!" Mudo croaked in approval, his thick, swollen tongue barely unravelling the words. I knew already he was one of Danny's stooges.

"Means Tortuga's a vegetable too!" Tuerto, Danny's other crony piped up, and he looked at me with his bulging fish eyes. The three of them laughed.

"Shut up!" Mike snapped. "We'll get him out of there. He doesn't belong there . . . Salomón knows that."

"I don't believe what Salomón says," Danny countered.

"Well you better start believing you little bastard!" Ronco said harshly. "Salomón's the only one who knows what's going on here . . . might do your hand some good if you started listening to him."

"What does he say?" I asked.

"He tells stories," Mike shrugged.

"Yeah, he's really smart," one of the smaller kids I couldn't recognize said.

"He reads books . . . that's all he does, all day long, in the night . . . I bet he's read a million books!"

"He's been here longer than anyone else."

"He's a good storyteller—"

"Ah, he's a carrot!" Danny persisted. "He's king of the vegetables, that's all. And they're all stuck in their machines just like a bunch of vegetables stuck in the ground! They can't shit, they can't eat, they can't do anything by themselves!"

"Yaugh—yeah," Mudo gurgled then wiped the saliva from his mouth.

"It's not that bad," Ronco tried to reassure me, "you just have to get used to it. But if the Nurse tries to take you to any other ward then scream bloody murder. Don't let her." He glanced nervously at Mike.

"Nah, she won't do that," Mike said, "we'll fight her. We're going to go to Steel as soon as he has time . . . he's been in surgery all day."

36

"Yeah, we can report her to the Committee," one of the kids volunteered.

"Damn right we can!"

"They put me in that ward once, to punish me, cause I'd broken into the crafts room and stolen glue for the kids who like to sniff it, an' I couldn't sleep. There must be a hundred iron lungs in there, cause the bad polio cases can't breathe at night without the lungs, and at night they make a noise like a monster breathing in the dark . . . whoooosh, wouuuuu-shh, whooooosh . . . I'd rather they punish me with castor oil than to go in there!"

"Who else goes in there?" I asked. Mike shook his head. "It's not exactly a place to visit," he said.

I wanted to ask them more about Salomón but it was late in the afternoon and the supper call sounded in the hallway, calling everybody that could get there to the dining room. Those of us that were bed-ridden remained in our rooms, feeling the day end as the sad twilight filled the rooms. It was a time to think of home, of family and of warm times eating together . . . times which seemed so distant now that the memory was inseparable from a dream. I lay quietly, listening to the food trays coming down the hall, feeling the echoes in the near-empty ward, and looking at the mountain through the window. Then, beneath all the sounds, woven into them so you had to hold your breath to separate the cries, I heard the soft whimpering of babies. It was a sound no one talked about, and it seemed to come from where I guessed lay Salomón's ward.

5

The next morning the Nurse appeared with the day orderly, a grinning giant called Samson.

"Ready?" she asked. She seemed cheerful. Samson smiled down at me, his bald head shining with light. Together they rolled my bed out of the room and pushed it down the empty hall. The bed squeaked and reverberated as we went deeper into the hospital. I tried to keep track of the direction, but we made too many turns into the dimly lighted maze.

Finally we arrived at a large wooden door. It was old and cracked, and when Samson opened it the dry hinges creaked. Then we entered a long, enormous room with a high ceiling. The air was dry and stale, and only the hazy light which shone through the high, dusty windows lighted the room. Long forgotten flower pots sat on the dusty sills, unwatered and unattended, their pale yellow tendrils and vines dropped in profusion down the gray walls. Overhead a network of electrical wires criss-crossed the ceiling, dropping a single cord down to each iron lung which rested by the side of each bed. I had never seen the iron lungs before. They were cylindrical tubes of steel with a porthole at one end for the head and plate glass windows along the sides. They looked like strange caskets in the dim light. Around them hovered the shadows of nurses, old women who moved silently from bed to bed . . . and as my eyes grew accustomed to the dark I could see the beds and the thin skeletons which rested on them. At first I thought they were all dead, the thin arms which rested over the single sheet that covered them were bones covered by a thin parchment of yellow skin. I looked closer and saw their heads, skulls, shrunken to the bone and penciled with thin, blue veins.

"They're dead!" I gasped. Samson shook his head and motioned for me to look closer.

"Completely helpless," the Nurse intoned.

I looked sideways again, watched the heads turn to follow my progress, then saw the eyes, the large sad doe eyes, the haunting eyes which burned in the hollow sockets and filled me with dread. They were alive! Each thin, shrunken body was alive! Air rattled through the tracheotomies at their throats as they gasped and sucked to keep alive.

At most of the beds i-v bottles full of a yellow liquid dropped a tube which entered the permanent needles stuck in their arms. They were being kept alive with air and sugared water! The only thing they could do was move their heads and watch my arrival with their sad eyes. I cringed and felt myself draw into my cast. Damn, I cursed through gritten teeth and closed my eyes. Damn it to hell!

"They're completely helpless," the Nurse continued, while I cursed her and the room of cripples, "completely dependent . . . like you . . . but they're cared for, fed, put in their respirators at night . . . kept alive . . . Ah, here's Salomón's room. It's the only room in the ward . . . he needs privacy, and besides, he's been here the longest. No one remembers when he came, I don't, do you Samson?"

Samson shook his head, opened the door and they pushed the bed into the small cubicle. The walls were lined with bookshelves; books and magazines were piled everywhere. Small potted plants and vines dotted the shelves and the windowsill of the window which faced the mountain. I glanced at the outline of Tortuga's hump as they pushed me close to the bed in the corner and turned me so I could see the thin, frail creature they called Salomón. He looked like the others we had passed in the ward, a thin skeleton drained of life, completely paralyzed and helpless, alive only because his eyes moved . . . and what sad eyes, deer eyes which shone with light and cut through me and filled me at once with pity and hate. He knew I was already asking myself why these poor cripples were being kept alive, helpless cripples, vegetables as Danny said.

"How are you, Sol?" the Nurse asked. "We've brought someone new to the ward, someone to share your room for awhile . . . Tortuga. That's what the kids call him." She smoothed the sheets on his bed and turned to look at me. "You can see how helpless he is, and yet he never complains, he never complains . . . I've never heard him utter a single complaint, have you Samson?" Samson shook his head. "He hasn't moved an inch since the day he came . . . never will . . . but he doesn't complain. He spends his waking time reading, devours books like a bookworm. Show Tortuga how you read, Sol."

Salomón held a plastic rod or a pencil in his mouth. With his tongue he could manipulate the rod enough to turn the pages of the book fastened by its covers to the bedstand in front of him. That's all he could do, move the rod and turn the pages of the book.

" . . . reads everything we can find for him . . . prefers philosophy and books like that . . ." She looked at me. "You're going to like it here. Salomón is a good room mate. Doesn't bother anyone, just reads all day long. Say hello to Salomón," she said crisply.

"Screw you!" I muttered through clenched teeth. She jerked as if I had slapped her, a scowl replaced the smile she had put on for Salomón.

"That kind of attitude is going to get you in trouble," she said then told Samson to straighten my bed opposite Salomón's, in the corner. "The nurses here will take care of everything you need . . . they have nothing else to do with their time. And who knows, maybe Sol will teach you how to read like he does . . ." She smiled and walked away, the limp in her left leg more pronounced now than the slight favoring I had noticed she gave it earlier. Samson trailed sheepishly behind her.

The initial pity I had felt for the vegetables was gone, now only a hopeless, smouldering rage remained, filling my stomach with such anger that it cramped and hurt. I couldn't look at Salomón because I thought I'd cry, instead I gritted my teeth and let the anger out in a flood of curses.

"You bitch! You goddamned bitch! Do you think I'm going to stay here with these vegetables and rot to death! I'm not! I won't! Get me out! Call the doctor! Call Steel! Did he double cross me too! The no good sonofabitch! Get me out of here! Get me out!"

I gasped for breath, felt panic fall on me like a heavy weight, like earth being shoveled down on a casket. I struggled to bend my elbows to try to lift myself, felt the cold sweat cover my entire body, but I couldn't budge the heavy cast, and I couldn't shake the suffocation, not even with my curses. One of the old nurses, a wrinkled, hairy crone, came in, motioned for me to relax, to lie still, and I cursed her. Another one appeared and together they pinned my arms, held me while one of them stuck a needle in my arm and I felt the drug ooze up my arm and then towards my stomach.

After that they looked at each other, nodded and left the room. But I wasn't through yet. I turned what was left of my strength and anger on Salomón.

"I don't belong here!" I shouted. "I'm not a vegetable! Look! I can move!" I bent my elbows and lifted my arms as far as I could to prove my point. "Look!" I wiggled my toes. "See! I can move! I'm not a vegetable!" And again I tried to push my elbows against the mattress, willing at this time to throw myself on the floor, to crack the cast in two if need be . . . to crawl out . . . to crawl like an animal before I remained here . . . in this circle of hell.

"I . . . I'd rather die first! Hear . . . die! No life like yours . . . Freaks . . . hear me . . . never . . ."

I shouted for the entire ward to hear me. I wanted them to know that I wasn't one of them, their suffering was not mine. I heard my rage echo across the enormous room, felt it drift down the maze of halls. Then my eyes grew heavy as the morphine took over and sucked me into a dark, swirling mist. Get me out of here, I heard my shouts in the darkness—please don't torment . . . please God . . . take me from this hell . . .

40

Around me the thin, crippled bodies of the vegetables floated in the water of my dream, and in the barren and dark desert I heard Salomón say:

Ah, Tortuga, we have been waiting for you . . . and you have come to us. Why question the ways of the creation. Know only that every man, in one way or another, must cross the desert. Life is such a thin ribbon, so fragile, so easily transformed . . . But as we teach you to sing and to walk on the path of the sun the despair of the paralysis will lift, and you will make from what you've seen a new life, a new purpose . . .

I know your journey was long, and the weight of the shell is tiresome . . . but know this, every person bears that weight in one way or another. It is the same with all of us. First we question why? Then we curse the gods that send the punishment . . . then the despair enters and there is only the chaos of nothingness left . . . a void in which we sink eternally, a plane of life so still and lonely that we think all of the creation has abandoned us . . . and still, it's but a station of life, a form we cannot see. Let me tell you that long ago I came with Filomón across the desert . . . crucified to suffer the paralysis forever, I cursed God and prayed for death. I had the will left to kill myself and end the meaningless suffering, but I did not have the strength. I tried choking on my own phlegm, and they cut a hole in my throat and made me breathe. I could not eat and they fed me through my veins. When my lungs collapsed they placed me in the iron lung and forced the air to make me live. They fixed me for all time . . . in one place . . . a worthless piece of flesh rotting in the compost of self pity.

I cursed them as you have cursed them, and I cursed their God who could practice such cruelty on pitiful men . . . I cursed the sperm of my father and the marrow of my mother for giving me life . . . Life, what a cruel joke it had become . . . better death than this suspension in a plane where there was no movement, no meaning . . . so I prayed for death . . . I gave up the last of my will, let the darkness surround, and begged for death.

But it was not to be. One day I opened my eyes, and felt that I was empty of the hate and rage which had filled me. It was a soft summer day. I remember the air was sweet with the fragrance of the fresh cut hay in the fields below. Cotton from the cottonwoods drifted lazily in the warm, still air, the meadowlarks warbled their song across the fresh mown fields, all of life seemed touched by an energy which charged everything with its electric-acid. Even Tortuga rested calmly, bathing his old and tired body in the pleasant sun. Then the miracle which changed my life forever appeared at the window. I looked closely and saw a giant butterfly enter through the open window. At first I thought it was a humming bird, it was so huge this wondrous creature. It darted in and out of the sunlight, glowing with the iridescent colors of the rainbow

41

and trailing the sweet, golden nectar and pollen of early summer. It flew gracefully around the room, darting back and forth, floating like a melody and trailing a symphony of music . . . And when it hovered over me it showered me with its golden dust.

I held my breath in wonder. That day my eyes were opened to the beauty and wonder of the creation. That day I felt the golden strands of light which unite all of the creation gather in that marvelous creature . . . and I sensed a strange salvation working its way into my soul. The numinous soul of the mountain and the sky and the water gathered in the light of the sun, reflected in the fanning of the wings, made music in its flight. But there is more . . . already my eyes were opening . . . already I had been granted more than most men are granted at such a holy moment . . . no, listen, there is more. The large butterfly fluttered over me then gracefully landed on the ball of cotton which covered the opening to my throat. I thought it would fly away when it didn't find a white rose . . . but no, it knew what it was doing. Softly it pushed away the dry cotton which filtered my bitter gasps for air, and then it settled over the opening at my throat . . . and casting its future with this crippled flower, it pollinated me . . .

Yes, Tortuga, it was a rare thing . . . a love returning when I thought all love had died. Its round, butterfly eyes caressed me with their love . . . a love it had brought from the flowers which grew along the slopes of the mountain and in the desert. It fanned its wings and spread the rich colors throughout the room, preened itself as butterflies will do, cleaning the gold pollen from its feet. Then it laid its kiss softly . . . I tasted the sweetness of its touch and felt a tickle in my throat as the tiny eggs and the pollen entered my throat. For the first time since the paralysis another form of life had come to touch me . . . as you have been touched by Filomón and Ismelda . . . and as you will be touched by the mountain and all the forms of life that live at its feet. I cried with joy as the tiny eggs burrowed into my blood and wrapped themselves in soft, chrysalis shells to sleep. I wanted to shout for the first time that I had felt the secret of all life . . . Instead I lay very quietly . . . watched the giant butterfly rise and disappear out the window . . . watched it until it became one with the desert and the mountain. I slept . . . and felt the death all flowers feel when pollinated. But inside I felt a new life growing, like the flower which wilts is born again in its own fruit, I felt the little chrysalises ripening, gnawing through their shells and rising to my throat to seek their freedom. These new winged beauties now burst from my mouth each time I speak. They fly from my soul to carry the words of love I learned that day. Each carries a new story, but all the stories are bound to the same theme . . . life is sacred, yes, even in the middle of this wasteland and in the darkness of our wards, life is sacred . . .

They are my children, Tortuga . . . they are the cries and whispers of my soul. They say the sun sanctifies all life, and it is his path of light that we should walk.

Yes, we are the shriveled flowers of an unseen, unfelt kiss of love . . . we do not yet know the full wonder of the creation. We look at our limbs and see them withered as flower petals. The fresh beauty of the cosmic kiss has faded in this life . . . and we are left on dry branches, hanging on to the frail tree of life which is daily destroyed to fill the needs of man . . .

And you ask why, Tortuga. Why were we transformed from blooming flower to withered petals? I will tell you . . . it is because we guard the new fruit of that kiss. We guard the new love which needs no explanation. We must search for the path of light and when we find it we must walk on it. And when the time is ripe the crippled, fragile shells will burst open and fly like the golden butterflies of summer . . . They will fly out across the desert to pollinate new flowers with love and beauty . . .

The next day Dr. Steel found out what the Nurse had done and he ordered her to move me back to the first ward, in fact I wound up in Mike's room with him and Sadsack and Jerry. Sometime later somebody asked about Salomón's story.

"Is that really what he said?" they asked.

I could only answer, "Yes, something like that—"

6

The sun is our father
I walk in his path
I walk in beauty . . .
He is the fiery rider
Who mounts the turtle
Day by day . . .

I opened my eyes to the words of the whispered song. The room was still and cold in the pre-dawn light. Mike and Sadsack were still asleep, snoring mounds in the eerie pearl light. The outline of a shadow stood at the window . . . Jerry, singing to the rising sun. When the first rays peeked over Tortuga and touched the clouds with fire, he sprinkled a yellow powder towards the mountain, then he cupped his hands as if to gather in the first strings of light to drink.

It was his prayer to the sun which had awakened me, a prayer he sang every day at sunrise. I closed my eyes and thought about this ceremony to the sun. I knew that as the winter days got shorter and shorter and the sun sank farther to the south the tempo and urgency of Jerry's song seemed to increase. His faith was woven into the journey of the sun, he watched it travel towards the lowest point in the horizon, and he waited for the solstice. On that day, if his songs were full of goodness, the sun would return. But would it return for us? It seemed we had lost faith in everything, even the sun itself had become the black sun of the wasteland. We saw only the frozen desert, and in it our faith had shriveled. Jerry kept something alive of his faith, something neither the walls of the hospital nor the despair of the barren desert could erase.

So each morning I listened carefully to his chant, tried to understand what he was saying and how it related to Salomón's admonition to walk in the path of the sun. I did my morning exercises while I listened, bending each arm at the elbow to build the muscles, rising them to my face to touch with trembling fingers my nose and mouth and forehead. I grunted and pushed every available bit of energy I could find into my legs. First I wiggled my toes, rotated my feet at my ankles, then I tried to bend the knees. So the morning chant was good for both of us. It filled us with a purpose. When Jerry was done he turned and looked at me, knew I had been exercising, and an unspoken communication passed between us, hung in the pale, cold air for a moment, then he slipped into his bed and retreated into his solitude. I lay trembling and sweating after my exertion, watching the sun burn the frost away from the hill and lift the cold haze in the valley. It filled our room with light.

Jerry never spoke to anyone, not even Mike's kidding could draw him out, still we had formed a silent friendship, one that needed no words. Mike had told me that Jerry belonged to a tribe of Navajos who lived beyond the Gila Mountains, the strange and distant serpentine range which lay to the west. I often wondered how many times he thought of home in those early hours of the morning before the hospital awakened. For me it was always the time for remembering home, and especially my mother because I knew my accident had been a heavy burden for her to bear. I knew the hardships the struggle of the people presented, I knew the poverty of the times, and so I knew there would be no visits from home. And there was nothing they could do if they came . . . like Jerry, I needed the silence, I needed to work my way out alone.

Still, Jerry had the sun, a faith, and an abiding assurance that his grandfather would come and take him away from the hospital. Yes, even here he kept his faith. Everybody knew it was he who had broken into the kitchen pantry and stolen a bag of cornmeal, the welfare government issue which they fed us, and Mike had kidded Jerry. "Hey," he had said, "I guess that old grandfather sun of yours is getting fed on government staples every morning, just like the rest of the poor people."

Jerry had looked down to hide his smile.

"How come Jerry gets up so friggin' early?" Sadsack had asked.

"Why don't you get up with him and find out," Mike had answered, "Tortuga does—"

"Ah balls!" Sadsack muttered, "I'm not going to get up that early just to see the sun rise!"

"He gets up early to sing to the sun," Ronco said.

"What's he sing?" Sadsack asked.

"Tell 'em the story about the old Indian, Mike."

Mike sat on his bed and said, "Well, in the village where Jerry comes from there's a very wise, old Indian whose job is to get up every morning before the sun rises. He saddles his horse and rides to the top of the highest hill, and when he gets there he faces the east and sings a song for the sun to rise. You see if it wasn't for that song the sun wouldn't rise and everything would freeze to death—"

"Well, whaz he sing?" Sadsack repeated impatiently.

Mike sat stiffly and beat the top of his night table to imitate a drum. In a deep voice and with great solemnity he sang the song of the old Indian.

> *"Grandfather, grandfather sun*
> *Oh hear me grandfather*
> *Listen to my prayers*
> *Oh great giver of life*
> *A song I am sending to you*
> *A song I am sending to you*
> *GET UP YOU OLD SON OF A BITCH!"*

We all laughed, and even Jerry cracked a smile.

Jerry was out herding sheep, Mike had told me later, and his grandfather was away at a blessing way ceremony, and that's when the Indian Health people grabbed Jerry and dumped him here. They never told anyone, they just picked him up like you would a stray dog and they brought him here. He didn't even come with Filomón, so he's got no way of getting back. Jerry's only hope is that his grandfather is tracking him down, at least that's what he believes, but damn Tortuga, how's the old man ever going to find him? They brought him here in a jeep, there are no tracks to follow. How in the hell is the old man ever going to find this godforsaken place?

I didn't know how Jerry's grandfather would find him, but I thought about it as I watched Jerry get back into his bed and withdraw into his silence. So he was waiting for his grandfather, always checking the window late at night when he thought we were all asleep. Maybe there was some hope in that, at least more than in my dead grandfather who haunted me only in my dreams.

Somewhere down the ward someone dropped a urinal and it clanged like a bell in the cold silence. Someone coughed and cleared his throat, a toilet flushed. The ward was awakening. Across the room Mike was still snoring, but he could be up in an instant. He slept with his levis on because he was sensitive about his burned, scarred legs.

He had been at a hospital where they had a special burn treatment unit for a few years, then he had been transferred here to see if his legs, which had been burned nearly to the bone, could be outfitted with leg braces so he could walk.

We were a big family, and poor, he had said, lived in a small, two room shack. We had an old kerosene heater to heat the house. Every morning I had to run up the road to the gas station and buy half a gallon of kerosene, come back and light the heater so the house would be warm when my father got up. He was a mean sonofabitch, ran us like slaves.

Each morning my mother got me up before dawn and I'd dress quietly and run out in the goddamn cold. I didn't mind it . . . it kept peace in the family, at least in the morning. And I got to see everything while it was still, before people were up. I'd run across a big field where they kept cows . . . I remember the way the frozen grass crunched beneath my feet, felt the cold air fill my lungs, saw the cows standing together, looking sad with their teats full of milk before milking . . . To make a long story short, one morning there was a new attendant at the station, just opening up, sleepy as me . . . I didn't watch while he filled the can . . . he filled it with gas. I went home and filled the heater as usual, then when I lit the match the thing blew like a bomb. I closed my eyes, but everything was so bright I could see right through my eyelids. The force of the explosion knocked me through the window . . . I must have passed out for a few moments. When I opened my eyes I looked down and saw my legs burning, sizzling the way pig fat sizzles when they're making chicharrones. My old man slept in a back room, so he got out through a window without a scratch on him, but my mother and sisters . . . He paused, breathed deep and continued. They didn't have a chance. I could hear them screaming inside as the house went up in flames. I tried to get to them . . . my legs still burning away, but I couldn't . . . Now I can still hear them screaming as they burned. At first I blamed myself, then I blamed the sleepy attendant who filled the can with gas . . . I blamed my father, then I blamed God. I didn't know why such a horrible thing had to happen. I couldn't explain it. I kept looking for a reason. All that first year while I lay soaking in my blood and juices and the doctors kept trying to take enough pieces of flesh from the rest of my body to patch up the burns, and they kept falling off, full of gangrene . . . well, they pulled it off, kept me alive, left me with a pair of the ugliest most burned skinny legs you ever saw. There's no place to fit the braces, a little meat around the knees and the feet . . . nothing else. I can stand on them a little, but I need the braces. So Steel's working on it. It's been a long wait. The nightmares are gone now . . . once in a long time they return and I wake up screaming at night, feeling I'm on fire, hearing the screams . . . I see the scene before my eyes again, as it happened then . . . so long ago. You can't forget the past . . . I found out you can't block something like that out. It stays with you forever. What I finally learned to do is to quit looking for a reason or an answer as to why it happened. When I realized that things just happen, that there's no reason, that there's no big daddy up in the sky watching whether you burn or not . . . much less caring, then it helped. Things just happen. They just are. Finding a cause doesn't change what has happened. They're working on curing polio, Dr. Steel told me, and he believes they're going to do it. In the meantime the kid that has polio right now has to live with it. He has to live with it and say to himself that's just the way it is. The rich get richer and the poor go on suffering . . . How do you change that, huh?

I didn't know. Somewhere down the hall Franco sang.

> *And I don't know, how long*
> *I can go onnn*
> *Cause it keeps right on a'hurtin'*
> *Every hour you're away*
> *Every moment of the day . . .*

I didn't know. I looked around the room and thought how each one of us had wound up at the hospital, and unlike Mike I was still asking why?

Opposite Jerry's bed, Sadsack mumbled in his sleep. He yawned and chewed at the bits of food stuck between his teeth. His long, bony arms flopped up awkwardly as he tried to scratch away the sun shining on his puffy eyes. "Aow, goddamn," he groaned and cursed. His long, limp legs hung over the side of the bed and he cursed because his feet were cold. He blinked his eyes open, scratched his balls and muttered, "Aw shit, another day, another dollar—"

Mike sat up, rubbed his eyes and looked around. "Complaining already, Sad?"

Sadsack farted. "Catch that and paint it red, Mike! Har, har, har . . . ." He laughed like a seal, flopping his arms up to scratch the thin hair that grew like scrub grass on his pointed head.

"I love you too, Sad," Mike smiled. He understood Sadsack's complaints, and they didn't bother him. "How you doin', Tortuga?"

"Great," I answered.

"Been working out already, eh?" he smiled. He knew I exercised in the morning. "Jerry, did you get the sun up this morning?" he called, and Jerry only nodded. "Damn, I was having a beautiful dream before Sadsack started farting. I dreamed I was back home, and it was Sunday, and we had all gone to the park to walk around and look at the girls, the way we used to. And I met a beautiful girl, I mean she was the most gorgeous chick I've ever seen! She had long dark hair, beautiful eyes that sparkled with love, juicy red lips, and skin so soft and brown it melted to my touch—"

"Did you touch her?" Sadsack asked.

"Yeah, that's what the dream's about," Mike answered.

"Bullshit!" Sadsack scoffed, "You didn't dream a chick like that, you're just making it up!"

"No I'm not!" Mike insisted. "I swear I saw her! I talked to her and went walking with her and I kissed her! Damn, Sad, I should know! It was my dream!"

"Aow, bull," Sadsack shook his head, "you're making it up!" He wasn't believing any of it. He cleared his throat and his thick, rubbery lips let fly a wad which fell short of the side of the bed and landed on his arm. He cursed.

"You're jealous, Sad—"

"God on, tell us about it," I urged Mike.

"Well, we met in the park," Mike said enthusiastically. "She just appeared, you know, the way people appear in dreams, out of nowhere. So there I am, walking down a path to the river. The birds were singing and the sun was shining in through the trees like golden honey, and the grass all around was green and soft. Suddenly I was holding her and kissing her and my head was spinning, but I wasn't pulling any fast stuff, you know, because I knew I loved her and I wanted to marry her. God, it was so real—" He paused. "Then she took off her clothes, just like that, she's naked, and I'm looking at the most beautiful thing I've ever seen in my life—"

"Aw, Gee-sus! Get off it, Mike!" Sadsack interrupted. "That's a goddamned lie! She didn't take off her clothes! You're just making that up!" He scratched his crotch.

"She did, Sad, I swear she did!" Mike crossed his heart and swore he'd die if he was lying. I believed him. It was too real not to believe.

"Bull!" Sadsack jeered.

"Let him finish, Sad," I said, "It's his dream, so let him finish it."

"Well, that's all there is to it," Mike looked at me and shook his head sadly.

"Geee-sus! Whadayah mean that's all!" Sadsack shouted. "For cryin' out loud, you brought us this far and now you're going to tell us you didn't get any!" He was really angry at Mike.

"It's hard to explain," Mike said. "The sun was shining like gold on her bronze skin, she was like a goddess who wanted my love, she was pulling me down on the grass, kissing me with her warm lips, begging me to make love to her—I wanted to make love to her, I wanted to hold her in my arms forever, even if it meant staying in the dream with her—but I couldn't. I couldn't make love to her because I was ashamed to show her my ugly, burned legs. I was afraid she would be frightened, or turn away—"

The room was quiet; not even Sadsack complained. I was sure each one of us had wondered in our secret thoughts about the love of a woman and how it would come to a cripple. Outside the room the nurses pushed beds towards the surgery ward.

"Surgery today," Sadsack said. Cries echoed down the ward.

"You should have taken a chance, Mike," I said.

"Yeah," Mike agreed, "it's not like me not to take a chance... that's not the way I think. But I had really fallen in love with the girl in the dream—"

49

"How can you fall in love with a dream," Sadsack spat, "besides, women are a pain in the ass. Who needs women?"

"What's this about needing women?" Ronco asked and pushed his chair into the room. "Are you horney toads discussing your wet dreams again?"

"Sad's a dirty old man!" Mike grinned and threw a pillow at Sadsack.

"Mike made up a dream about a real hooker," Sadsack complained, "and that's not fair!"

"Why not? It's all we have in this madhouse, our dreams—"

"Dreams of getting out."

"Dreams about walking, just getting up and walking—"

"Dreams about women, big, fat, juicy women who cuddle you up and make your tool wet with fire!"

"Eee-ho, I can buy that!" Ronco shouted. "I love the big mamasotas! The bigger the better!"

"The characters in your comic books are make believe, Sad," Mike pointed at the comic books that lay in a clutter around Sadsack's bed, "Wonder Woman's make believe, so why can't I make up a girl to dream about!"

"Ah! You made her up! You admit it! You made her up! Did you hear that? He made her up! She's not real!"

"Of course I made her up, I mean she was in a dream—"

"So she can't be real!"

"I said she was like real!"

"Hold it!" Ronco put up his hands. "This is getting me confused. There's only one reality: warm snatch. Rule two: if you need some you get some. It's that simple."

"Whores!" Sadsack drooled.

"Tom-catting," Mike smiled.

"No, no, you got it all wrong," Ronco shook his head. "Women don't have to be whores to get your little wand up. I'm talking about just plain women. A mamasota. A warm woman. A woman who knows how to love can solve any problem in the world. Ask Tortuga. He came in here stiff as a board and little Ismelda's been playing tricks with him and now he's squirming like a lizard!" He looked at me and winked.

"We've been through this before," Mike said, "what's the best medicine. As far as Ronco is concerned it's warm snatch, period."

"Right," Ronco nodded.

"So what else is new?" Sadsack groaned.

"Nothing. Let's go eat," Ronco suggested.

"Too early."

"Let's go for a swim at the pool then."

"They won't let us in this early," Sadsack complained.

"That's what I like about you, Sad, you got the power of positive thinking. It's more fun to lie around and feel sorry for yourself, huh?"

"It's easy for you to talk," Sadsack scowled, "you'd mount anything! You don't have to live with people when you get out!"

"Hey, my old man's people," Ronco smiled.

"Ronco's dad has a cabin up in the Black Range," Mike explained, "to the south of here. He says it's the most beautiful mountain in the world. And Ronco's been let out a couple of times to visit, cause it's close."

"Cause he's getting too old for this place!" Sadsack snapped.

"It's a beautiful mountain range," Ronco said, "it's not barren like the mountains around here. It's green, and in the summer when the sun comes up it sparkles on the dew like diamonds. At night the moon is so big you swear you could reach out and touch it. My old man says he's a rich man to have all that around him, of course the winters are tough, but in the summer it's like being in heaven. We sit on the porch all day, drink cold beer, and my old man plays a banjo he picked up in a card game, and when we get tired of sittin' around we jump in the jeep and head down for El Rito where we buy some booze, find us a couple of hot mamas and throw a party! Chingao, that's living! When I was there last summer we drank a case of whiskey, slept with every mamasota in town, started a fight in the bar and raised more hell than two mad bulls! My old man got half his ear cut off and I broke my arm, but damn! We showed them we could fight! It was worth it, cause we didn't start it. A couple of redneck cowboys started saying I should be home quilting and not drinking in a bar with men, cause I was still in my chair. But we showed them! And when we was broke and tired and the mamasotas who took care of us started talking about marriage we crawled back up the mountain and slept for a week. Damn, that's life!"

"You live like animals," Sadsack said. He sucked air and farted.

"Maybe," Ronco smiled, "but I wouldn't trade it for anything. We're not out to hurt anyone. We accept the world as it is."

"Yeah, maybe you're lucky," Sadsack muttered. "It sure as hell ain't that way when I visit at home. The last time I went home for a visit my old man was having a party for his clients. It was a con game. They brought a bunch of people from the east and were going to sell them some lots they had subdivided out in the middle of the goddamned desert! Anyway, he didn't want me around. Told me to stay outta the way, acted like getting polio was a sin! The sonofabitch. I stole a bottle and started drinking in my room, and the drunker I got, the madder I got until I pushed myself right into the middle of the party and started shaking hands with everybody. I was wearing only my shorts, and you should've seen their faces when I said, 'Hi ya folks, Sadsack here.' I went around and shook their hands and that scared the shit outta them.

They began making excuses and heading out. My ole man screamed his head off. 'You ruined my deal!' he cried, 'You ought to be ashamed of yourself! Why can't you stay out of trouble like your brother! Look at you! Just look at you—' "

Sadsack shook his head slowly. "Damn, how could I tell him that I have looked at myself, a million times I've looked at myself in the mirror and cursed myself for being deformed and ugly. A million times I've asked: why me?"

He thought to himself for awhile then said, "Getting polio was something I never dreamed of. Shit, when I was in high school I was flying high. I could've played college basketball after I graduated, I was that good. Every college in the state wanted me . . . and then what happened? I was walking down the street one day, and I turned to look at my reflection in a store window, and I saw myself falling down . . . I began screaming, because I was falling and I couldn't hold myself up . . . and that's all I remember. It was as if the image in the glass had broken into a thousand pieces—" He turned and looked at us. "But why me?" he asked.

"Because some little beasties got loose in God's experimental laboratory," Ronco said half-heartedly.

"My parents think it's something they did," Sadsack said, "they think they're being punished for their sins—now they drink a lot—"

"Ah, damn, what a way to start a morning—"

"Yeah," Ronco said, "it's depressing. Come on, let's go eat."

"Too early—"

"What about Tortuga? He never mentions his family."

"You got a family, Tortuga?" Ronco asked.

"Yeah," I answered. I thought about my mother. She would be waiting for me.

"Tortuga's not planning on any outside help to make him well, he's working at it on his own," Mike said. "He works out every morning."

"He wants outta here bad," Ronco said.

"That's rule number one, Mike's rule: get out." He jumped into his chair and pushed himself to my bedside. "You do want out of here bad, huh Tortuga?" I thought about going home, crippled like Ronco or Sadsack. It would be rough, but it was the only thing I wanted. "You'll make it," Mike nodded, then he spun his chair around and raced into the hall with Ronco on his tracks. Sadsack slowly climbed into his chair and followed them. At the door he bumped into old man Maloney.

"Watch where you're goin' you little punk!" the old man growled. "You little bastards think you own the world," he mumbled as he came into the room. He came in every morning before breakfast to collect the urinals and bedpans. He usually stayed long enough to run a cold wash

52

cloth over my face and to help me with my breakfast tray. He mumbled and cursed as he tossed things about, working his false teeth back and forth in his mouth, peering down at me through extra thick glasses and pausing from time to time to scratch the flaking dandruff on his thick, white eyebrows. When he was through cleaning up the urinals he set my tray on my nightstand and stuffed lumpy, cold oatmeal and dry toast into my mouth. "Least you're not trouble, not yet," he mumbled as he helped me eat, "but you'll get goin', like them, and you'll be a pain in the ass, I can tell, just a pain in the ass—" He made me wash the oatmeal down with orange juice then he grunted, cleared the tray and moved on, collecting bedpans and cussing the kids that used them at night, helping to feed those who needed help.

After breakfast there was a lull in the ward. The kids who could make it to the dining room usually went on to therapy or swimming. Some went to arts and crafts classes, classes which were supposed to teach them to do something useful for when they were released. Once a week the doctors visited the ward, but even they went quietly about their rounds, creating ripples in the monotony of our lives only when they announced a release or when someone was ready to get off the bed and get walking braces, crutches or a wheelchair. Those times were important, because they meant whoever could get up acquired a certain amount of freedom and they were milestones in the long process of complete freedom.

In the quietness of the morning I could hear Franco singing in his room. His sad words floated down the hall and mixed into the sounds of morning.

> *And I don't think*
> *I can go on*
> *Cause it keeps right on a'hurtin'*
> *Since you used your surgery knife*
> *Since you cut into my life . . . .*

53

7

On clear mornings the sun warmed our room. The ward was very quiet after breakfast. Jerry sat on his bed and braided beads into belts and pouches. I exercised then slept. I had a lot of time to think, and most of my thoughts centered around the vegetables in Salomón's ward. It had been a depressing place to visit. I wondered how long Salomón had been in the hospital, and why had I seen him in my dream before I knew him? Now, when I listened very carefully, I could hear his stories as they made their way up and down the ward. Salomón had sent me a stack of books, and I began to read some of the stories and poems which he liked, but reading reminded me of him and the eternity he would spend doing nothing but reading and sometimes in a rage I would toss the books away and release my energy in doing whatever exercises I could do by myself. But more and more I returned to them and read, and in them I explored a new kind of freedom, a freedom which didn't have anything to do with the movement of my muscles and nerves. The words struck chords and a remembrance of things past would flood over me and in my imagination I would live in other times and other places . . .

The words are like the wind, Tortuga, they sweep us up from this time and place and allow us to fly like butterflies to other places . . . When we think we are not of this time then we encounter absolute freedom, because we have created another universe, that's how powerful our imagination is. But wait, suppose it's not our thought that moves us. Suppose we are the very characters we invent in our fantasies? Then we have no freedom. Then we are only another group of stock characters in a crazy writer's notebook . . . then even the words cannot free us, even they are a trap. Then we must keep very still, not breathe, not think with words, not create disturbances or ripples, lie like my poor vegetables thinking without words, thinking about silence and the silent hum which is the rhythm of the earth, thinking silence until we think ourselves out of existence . . . then, that is freedom. Then we are characters who are not yet born! I think I like that better. Yes, I like it much better! For if we are not, then we can become, and we will become what you sing of us, Tortuga! How do you like that, Tortuga? Isn't that great! To become what you will make us in your songs!

Then he laughed and his laughter echoed down the ward. I found myself laughing with him, laughing insanely because he twisted my mind with his crazy thoughts then released me to think my own. His laughter was like the whistle of humming birds. When I heard it I turned to see if Jerry had heard it, and although Jerry said nothing I knew he did hear the laughter which shook us from our loneliness.

Sometimes I talked to Jerry when we were alone. I told him Salomón's stories and about the things I found in Salomón's books. He never spoke, but he listened. I thought he was tired of words, because he had been double-crossed by words. At the first thaw the false sounds had gone splintering to the ground, like icicles. They had taken his speech away. Now there was nothing to share except the whispers of butterflies, and so that's how we spoke, without promises.

The most important thing to look forward to in the mornings was the arrival of Ismelda and Josefa. They came to clean the rooms and make the beds. They were both working our ward regularly and so I got to see them every morning. I waited eagerly for them. They were my only contact to the outside world, a world which seemed to exist only in the accounts they gave of it. And Ismelda had become a strong link between my dreams and the mountain and what happened to me. Somehow she was always near me. She had been there to greet me the day I arrived, and she had been there when Mike found me. Most important, she was in my dreams. Every day as I recovered more movement in my legs the fire seemed fanned by that first meeting in the mountain's lake. She was a woman who haunted me, and although I could not tell her, I had fallen in love with her.

"Hey, Tortuga, how are you?" Josefa shouted when they entered the room, "look what Ismelda brought you, some real food! Not that hospital garbage which makes you skinny and pale!" Ismelda always brought me food she cooked at home. The smell of red chile with meat and beans and fried potatoes filled the room. I looked at Ismelda and she smiled. She was a handsome woman. She had dark features, with a smile that turned my night to day. Her dark eyes flashed with the fire of life.

"And you, Jerry, how you doin' this morning? Well, huh?" Josefa asked Jerry as she laid down her bucket and mop. She loved to take care of us. We were her kids. Every day she asked us how we were feeling and when she found one of us sick or in the dumps she appeared the next

55

day with a remedy from home. And her herbs and purgatives and food worked, because we felt better when she tended to us.

"It's the food," she muttered, "it's what they give you to eat that makes you sick. You gotta eat food from home, that makes you well!" And she fixed mutton and red chile for Jerry and me and we had it for lunch.

"How do you feel?" Ismelda asked as she changed the pillow cases.

"I feel good," I answered, then daring I whispered, "when I see you in my dreams you have green eyes—"

She smiled. "When I see you in my dreams you're a lizard," she answered. Then she explained. "My mother was living here in this valley when my father, a wandering gypsy, came one day. They fell in love, and I was born. He had green eyes; it's only in the dark that mine turn green," she laughed. I fell in love with the sound of her voice and her gentle touch. I looked into her eyes and saw the woman of my dreams. I wanted to ask her more, to hear her speak, but she turned to do her work. Usually it was Josefa who did the talking. She was a round, energetic woman who loved to tell stories.

Josepha was the real nurse for the ward. She loved to do things right and to keep the rooms clean. The Nurse took credit for our good health and tabulated our bm's with delight, but it was Josefa we turned to when we didn't feel well. Her only failure was Danny, but Danny was everybody's failure. The withering which had started in his fingers had now spread to his hand. The doctors couldn't do anything for it. Perhaps Josefa would have been able to help, but Danny never went to her. For some strange reason he stayed clear of her.

"Did you sleep well?" she asked me. "Good dreams, huh?" she winked and looked at Ismelda. She knew Ismelda filled my dreams. "And what did they feed you this morning? Oatmeal? Yuk! They want to give you empache the way they fix it—and look at you, Tortuga! Did old man Maloney make this mess? Look, there's oatmeal all over your face, and you haven't been washed in a week! Ismelda, bring a basin of hot water, and plenty of soap. We gonna wash the turtle. I won't have any of my boys running around dirty like that!" She pulled aside the sheets and sniffed. "Pee-you, Tortuga! You stink! When's the last time you had a bath? Doesn't that old man know he's supposed to give you a bath every day? Doesn't that Nurse check anything except for bm's?" She pulled off the sheet and left me naked on the bed. "Scrub him good!" she said to Ismelda. "I wanna see a pink turtle. Turtles aren't supposed to be afraid of water!" she roared with laughter. "You scrub him and I'll wash the floors," she nudged Ismelda, and Ismelda dipped the wash cloth into the warm, sudsy water and washed my face.

She worked in silence. Her firm strokes wiped away the grime which had accumulated. She scrubbed my arms until they tingled, then she washed my legs. Her touch sent hot fire rushing through my veins. I tried to speak but my throat was tight with the strange excitement of her touch. I closed my eyes and breathed deep, and I thought of the woman who had kissed me in my dreams. Ismelda teased me with her gentle hands. Under her care I wasn't the terrible turtle-man of the kids' rumors, I was a vulnerable, crippled turtle turned on his back. As she wiped me I could hear the soft jangling of her seven silver bracelets, and I could smell the clean, wild perfume of her body, an aroma that hinted of home odors and goat fragrances.

My body throbbed and grew under her soft, warm touch.

My flesh tingled.

In the warm sunlight I turned belly-up and dreamed of the woman who had led me into the mountain and who sang on a sea conch shell . . .

I felt her love smother me, and I wanted to cry for joy . . .

Then Josefa shouted and woke me from my dreams. I opened my eyes and she winked at me. "Look what a nice staff that turtle has! Perfect for working goats, huh, or for climbing in the mountains—"

Ismelda blushed but said nothing. She pulled the clean sheet over me and finished drying me. She took the dirty water away and when Josefa had finished washing the floors they sat and had coffee with us. Our room was their halfway point and they often had their morning rest here. Josefa brought sweet cakes, raisin bread or cinnamon covered biscochitos to share with everyone. She flavored her coffee with cinnamon and it was warm and sweet. She always told stories about the people and the land; today she talked about the village at the foot of the hill.

"—This village has been here as long as anyone can remember. It was a winter camp for the Indians, long ago, before the mangas largas came, before the sickness came . . . The Indians came to the warm baths, it was a part of their religion, and they planted prayer sticks in the caves and springs along the foot of the mountain . . ." She rocked her body and motioned toward Tortuga. "According to old stories I've heard, *the people* rested here on their migrations. This was a place they settled before they were told to go farther north . . . but who knows. On this desert time doesn't mean anything. It could have happened yesterday, or a year ago, or centuries ago, it's all the same . . . But we do know it's a holy place, because the water that flows from the mountain is holy. It's the only place in the desert that there is a chance for salvation—"

"But there's also suffering," I said.

"Ah, Tortuga, maybe that's your salvation . . . that you will learn to suffer . . ."

57

There was no salvation for me in suffering; nothing could be saved through the suffering of the vegetables which lay in Salomón's ward. But I said nothing. Instead I asked her who were the people that passed through here.

"The old ones," she said, "wanderers going north, people looking for a place where they could praise their creator and find spiritual peace—you are one of them," she said, "because you're from the north."

I didn't understand. "What about the mountain?" I asked.

"The mountain," she laughed, "why any fool could have named it, it's plain to see it looks like a turtle!"

We laughed with her, and at my side I felt Ismelda's presence. She knew something about the mountain, but she never said anything. I wondered what the secret was, and had I already found it in my dreams?

"When I was a little girl my grandfather used to tell us stories about the mountain. He said that once upon a time the mountain was a real turtle which had left the sea of the south to rejoin his brothers of the north . . . it followed the river north, and here at Agua Bendita it stopped to rest, and it fell asleep in its wandering. And that's all that old mountain is, a sleeping sea turtle which is going to wake up someday, look around then start its journey again . . . ."

So Josefa's story was where the kids' stories came from, that the mountain would free itself and move again, as we all wished to free ourselves and move again. I looked at Jerry. He pretended to be busy with his beadwork, but he was listening. I looked at the mountain through the window and saw the fringe of the lava flow around the base, and I shivered because I saw the dark clotted blood of Salomón's turtle!

"The mountain isn't dead," Josefa said, "it's just waiting . . . ."

"Waiting?"

"Waiting for the people to return to learn its secret . . ." We waited breathlessly. She continued. "The hot springs of the mountain cover a distance of seven miles up and down the river, and there are seven major springs . . . the water that comes boiling out of those springs is more than water, it's hot turtle pee. Yes, that's why it's miraculous and can cure sickness, because it's the hot pee of our brother the mountain. You've seen how a turtle struggles and pees in your hand when you hold it? That pee is so strong that some people get warts from it, same as from a frog, but it's good because it's strong!" She paused and looked at Ismelda. "Some curanderas use the pee of the turtle to cure—"

"What?" I asked.

"Paralysis," Ismelda whispered. I looked at her and saw the image of the mountain swimming in her dark eyes. I looked at Josefa and she winked.

"Sure," she said, "it's that strong! But the doctors don't know it.

They say it's the minerals in the water—Bah! If it's just the minerals in the water why don't they pour those minerals into their bathtubs and take their baths at home, eh? Because it's more than just the minerals!" She paused and looked out the window. "It's the power of the mountain . . . the power in our sleeping brother . . . just waiting . . . ."

Her words created a sleepy silence in the sun-flooded room. No one spoke. Strands of golden sunlight wove us together, wove us into the time of the hill and the river and the shell of the mountain. Over us the blue sky flowed like water, a palpable magnetic stream which spilled over its edges and flooded the earth with its intensity. We dreamed, each one of us woven into the same dream, dreaming of a time when the mountain would rise and walk and we would follow it north, saved by its holy water. The room buzzed with a quiet, summer madness, then the spell broke and Josefa stood.

"Time to move on, time to work . . . ."

I felt Ismelda at my side. She leaned close to me and I felt her warm breath on my face. "Take care of yourself, Tortuga," she whispered, "don't go play in the mud now that you're all clean—"

I smiled and her dark eyes filled with love. I wanted to say something to her, something about how I felt about her and what I was beginning to learn from my stay at the hospital, but I couldn't find the words and they moved on to clean the rest of the ward, lugging their mops and pails with them.

Later the doctors came on their rounds and I lay quietly while Dr. Steel probed and asked questions. Some of the pricks from his needle were beginning to feel sharper, and he grinned when I said so. He made comments on my progress, notes which the Nurse jotted down on my chart, medical gibberish which made the visiting interns nod and pucker their lips with hems and hahs.

"You're ready for some physical therapy," Dr. Steel said. He winked at me. I knew he was happy for me.

"Good," I answered, "I'm ready."

They turned and gathered in a group to discuss my case, the smashed vertebrae and the consequent paralysis, the slight movement which had returned, the treatment and the prognostication . . . and far beneath us the river of hot turtle pee gurgled as it ran under the ice which covered the land and the river.

8

Peeeeeeeeee-Teeeeeeeeeeeeee.

Ready for PT?

What's PT?

PT PT PT, you mean you don' know!

Oh my.

PT is prick teaser, get it?

PT is PT boat—

PT is the end of the line, or the beginning.

PT is physical therapy, that's when they start pulling your legs and arms apart and making them move. And KC is going to be your PT!

Oh, KC will rub you sooooo close, ooooooh soooo close. She'll put her big fat boobs all over you, she's a teaser, a real teaser. She makes your wand feel soooo good—

Then she asks you, you wanna little?

And if you can climb on she'll let you have it!

She'll do anything to get you to move. She'll torture you, threaten you, tease you, play with you, rub her boobs on your face, but she gets you to movin'—

I like the way she smells. Sweet sweat. She sweats with you while she's working you over.

Oh my—

Who's KC?

She's the physical therapist, the wonder woman of exercise who makes you wish you never got paralyzed! She makes you move even if you don't want to—she's kinda like Jesus, she pulls you out of the dead—who was the guy Jesus pulled out of the dead?

Laz-rus.

Yeah, Laz-rus. Laz-rus was dead, dead and buried, paralyzed cold, and Jesus said, Laz-rus, come out of the dead! I command you, come out of the dead! And poor ole Laz-rus had to do what the Lord commanded, but can you imagine how painful it was?

Oh mmmmy—

Yeah, I mean those nerves and bones were cold, and he had to move them again! And the heart started to pump again, and the blood shot into his dry veins and pounded in his head, and the juices started flowing into his empty stomach and burning everything, and the nerves started jangling like live telephone wires, shooting sparks and messages to the brain and the balls and everywhere! Can you imagine ole Laz-rus shouting, Stop, dear Jesus, stop! Oooooh, stop this friggin' pain! Oh God he was hurtin', and he probably thought he was better off dead, cause there ain't no pain like the pain of coming back to life!

Jesus is the patron saint of all the PT's.

Yeah.

They love to bring people outta the dead.

Yeah.

Especially KC. You can be burning with pain like Laz-rus, and all she says is come on, baby, give it to me sweet baby—

It's worse than being born.

Yeah, except when you're born you want it. Salomón said we can't help wanting to swim in the electric-acid of life. It takes only a while to suck air and feel its force in your lungs, and only a while till the acid burns you, then you're safe and warm sucking at your momma's breast. But PT is like coming back from the dead, and who in the hell wants to come back from the dead, huh?

Maybe we did come back from the dead, ever think of that. I mean, this place is like a dumping station between life and death. Our twisted bodies were dumped somewhere and Filomón picked them up to bring them to Dr. Steel to straighten them out . . . and where do we go from here?

Back to where we came from—

Or back to the dead.

Oh my—

I remember the pain. Oh God, I never want to feel pain like that again! Never. I'd rather stay dead! There's nothing to compare it to, unless it's Laz-rus. He knows what it's like to be born again, and I bet you all my comic books that if he had known he'd ah said no thanks Jesus, leave me alone, find somebody else to bring back from the dead. I'm happy here, it's quiet and peaceful, just watching the worms do their business, I don't wanna be an experiment, no suh. And he should've been left alone, right? Because what does the guy get for coming back? A pat on the shoulder, then everybody turns to the miracle worker and Laz-rus is left out in the cold, alone, to wander in his crumbling, stinking body forever, worse than a leper, a man no one will touch, they throw rocks at him, the dogs tear at his mouldy flesh, there are no friends left, who wants to have anything to do with a man who came back from the dead?

What about us? We will be born again in Jesus Christ. The preacher said we will be born again!

Listen, if it's going to be that painful then you can have it. I don't want anything to do with that being born again business. It's too painful. If St. Peter met me at the pearly gates and said before you come in I've got to work you over so you'll fit in heaven, I'd say screw it. I wanna be just as I am, even if I am a lop-sided freak. Send me where I don't have to face another PT in my life, ever—

What about Tortuga?

It's his time, man, he has to decide.

You know damn well KC's not gonna sit around and twiddle her fingers while he decides. When she comes in she's ready for work. She grabs ahold of an arm or leg and starts pulling. She's so mean she'll break open that friggin' cast if she has to! She's a mean, mean momma.

But she's good, don't forget that. She may be a bitch, but she does it for your own good! I mean she will beat the hell outta you to get you goin', but she does it for you. She pushes you to the end, I mean the goddamn living end!

This is the living end, har, har, har, our ward is the living end!

And when she asks you if you've had enough and you can't stand the pain anymore just say, give me more! Give it to me!

Why?

Cause if you give up, she gives up. If you get your it-hurts-too-much feeling into her, then she can't do her work, and you'll be the loser. Look at Sadsack. He cried and begged cause he couldn't stand the pain, and pretty soon she felt sorry for him and she began to lay back and so he never came all the way back from paralysis—

PT is like life . . . .

Hey, watch it! A philosopher loose among the cripples!

It is, man, you gotta commit yourself to it, and once you do there's no turning back and no excuses. You're either for it or not, right?

Raaaaght!

KC gets you hot but she stays cool. I mean, she knows what she's doing. When she did it to me she spread herself all over me. She spread her big, sweet boobs over my face and my little wand was waving like mad. She grabbed it and laughed. This is the cure, she laughed, as long as this pecker keeps tickling you've got the stuff to make it! I couldn't move an inch when I first got here, except my flagpole was sticking straight up for somebody to hang a flag on it, and the minute KC touched it it exploded. And now look at me, here I am running around! I swear she can do anything.

Yeah, and the first thing she's going to ask you is: Are you a turtle?

And the answer is: You bet your sweet ass I'm a turtle!

They all laughed, and their laughter was like the roar of a hurricane in the enormous white room.

"Hey," the dark woman laughed, "you look like a turtle! Are you a turtle?"

I looked at her and said, "You bet your sweet ass I am."

She laughed a deep, throaty laugh, and her big breasts shook. She leaned back and slapped her big hips. She had bright red lips and flashing eyes.

When she stopped laughing she looked at me and asked, "Hey, you're a smart one. Now tell me, sweet child, you wanna walk like a man . . . or you wanna stay a turtle?"

"I want to walk like a man," I answered, "I want to get up and get the hell out of here."

She smiled, then she nodded. "Good. We got a lot of work to do, honey—"

She pulled off the sheet that covered me, felt my arms and legs, told me to push and pull, feeling each muscle for its strength, jotting down her findings on a chart. She pulled harder than Dr. Steel had ever pulled and when I felt the first stabs of pain my legs drew back, like a turtle draws into its shell at danger. But she drew them out, slowly at first, warming up the muscles, cooing, "Push, baby, push, now don't that feel good . . . ."

She pulled and the feeling was a fire that went screaming down broken nerves and dead muscles. I screamed at first. Like a wounded animal in pain I heard my pitiful cry echo in the room, I saw Jerry turn momentarily, his eyes cold to the cry he hadn't expected, then he turned back to his work and I learned to hold the pain in check. KC paused, pulled again, waited for my response, and when I clenched my teeth she smiled and pressed her body closer to mine and whispered, "Give it to me, baby, give it to your momma—" And I gave it to her, one more inch of bending joints and muscles full of searing pain, one more grunt which popped the sweat at my forehead, then the relaxing and the massage of KC's hands as the rhythm rested, then the pull again, like two people making love, pushing against each other, learning to work together. She took as much of the pain as she could into her arms and body, but she couldn't take it all. I thought the exercises I had been doing on my own were painful, but that was nothing compared to the forced movement. The added pressure shot pain through the bones and blood and left me exhausted, sweating, gasping for air. White light exploded in my brain, exploded in each muscle that moved for the first time as the tentacles of pain reached out and suffocated me. Soon there was nothing but pain. I ceased to exist. I couldn't feel KC's hands on me. I felt swept away into the blinding, white light which kept exploding to the throb of the veins on my temples.

It ain't easy, Tortuga, it ain't easy, Salomón said to me. Nobody promised the electric-acid wouldn't burn you, and that's the beauty of it, that's the beauty of life–no eternal rose gardens, no repetitious sweet melodies, instead a search for the fragile flowers of the desert and a floundering to find our own voice to sing our own songs . . . It ain't easy, Tortuga, but being born ain't easy. In the spring there's a blind-green force that pushes to renew itself in dormant limbs, and as it forces itself to life it burns the tender marrow of the shoots with its acid . . . ah, pity the sleeping plant which awakens one day throbbing with the wet electric juice of life, Tortuga, pity it for the pain it feels–but celebrate its dance . . . .

Long after KC left I could still feel the piercing pain in my newly awakened, trembling muscles and tendons. I lay trembling and shivering, like a rabbit which has been mauled by a dog, gasping for breath. I felt limp and weak, but I felt exhilarated. The pain meant the muscles weren't dead.

"It takes time," Jerry said.

I smiled. He had shared the half hour of therapy with me. He had tried to weave as much of the pain as he could into the patterns of clouds and sky and thunder in the beads. "It takes time," I agreed.

At noon Mike and Ronco and Sadsack returned from swimming and we shared Ismelda's lunch. We were all hungry from our morning's work, and the flat, round tortilla bread was the only thing we had tasted of home in a long time.

"First time Ismelda's ever brought anyone a gift," Mike winked.

"She sure likes Tortuga," Ronco said.

"Better be careful with her, Tortuga, she's a witch—"

She is a witch, I thought, through the power in her fingertips she started to draw me from my paralysis. Now there was the new strength of KC. I wanted to shout. I wanted to kick my legs like a young foal to show the world it could not keep me down. Instead I smiled and tasted Ismelda's fragrance in her warm tortilla bread.

That night when lights were out Mike and Ronco celebrated my first therapy session with a party. Ronco mixed aftershave lotion, rubbing alcohol and orange juice, a drink he called the Ronco Lift and which he swore was stronger than bird farts. They had a little marijuana which Ronco had bought from Speed-o, so they rolled some and smoked and drank. Franco, in one of his rare times when he left his room, came by and played his guitar for us and smoked with us. I think he came because he was glad for me and because in the dark room we could see each other only as shadows. Outside, a storm whipped down from the north and rattled the hospital like an old tin shack, but inside the time was mellow and lazy in the heavy, sweet drift of smoke.

You scored a big one today, Tortuga . . . I bet KC's gonna bring you through . . .

I feel high on pain, like I'm floating out there, somewhere . . .

That's the way it is. I cried the first session I had with her, Ronco said.

I wanted her soooo bad, my pecker was aching, but I couldn't take the friggin' pain, Sadsack cursed and spit in the dark.

I never got my turn, Franco said sadly.

I tried, oh yes I tried
To satisfy, her wandering way . . . .

Ah, screw it! he mumbled and pushed his chair out of the room.

We were silent for a long time then Mike said, Pain is a high, and we try to replace that high with songs or women or booze. We never learned to live with pain, or we knew how once then we forgot. It's as natural as being born . . .

Or gettin' laid . . .

Yeah. But we're always running away from it. There's a whole ward over on the other side full of glue sniffers. Kids that ran away from all that pain out in the world. You pass by there and the place smells like a glue factory, and to come down they smoke some of this dope. Burned brains.

How many wards are there?

Lots . . . but let's not talk about that now, why man, we're celebrating!

Wheeeeeeeeee—

I'm sure getting sleepy, Sadsack mumbled.

The talk drifted slowly back and forth, soft words riding softly on the dark velvet of the night. Nobody got wild or loud. We talked about the memories of good times, and we made up stories about the things we wanted to do when we got out of the hospital. Silence crept into the long space between words as the rest of the kids got sleepy and wandered off to their own rooms. Somewhere Franco crooned,

A little love
That slowly grows and grows
Not one that comes and goes
That's all I want from you . . .

The rusty sand of sleep and the mellow memories of bygone times covered our eyes and we slept. I remember Mike getting up to throw a blanket over Ronco, who had fallen asleep in his chair.

That little evil smoke gets him every time, he mumbled in the dark, then he tumbled into his bed and was instantly asleep.

The room was warm and peaceful and quiet, but outside I heard the

65

screech of great warring owls as they swept across the valley; the feathers of their warfare swirled in the wind and turned the earth white. The wind howled as the storm worked its way back and forth across the empty desert. I tried to sleep, but the air was too charged with electricity, too full of strange sounds which cried like lost ghosts in the raging storm. It wasn't just the marijuana or Ronco's drink . . . it was something else . . . Something or someone seemed lost in the storm, working its way towards the hospital in search of one of us. But who? I wondered in my restless sleep . . . and suddenly my nightmare is alive with la Llorona, the old and demented woman of childhood stories who searches the river for her drowned sons . . . sons she herself has cut into pieces and fed to the fish . . . Now I see her again, as I saw her that day of my first communion . . . But where? On the trash heap of the town, along the highest cliff which dropped from the edge of the town towards the river below, there where the people of the town dumped their garbage, trash which burned perpetually as the coals crept beneath the rubbish and erupted in small fires and evil smelling columns of smoke. There on the narrow path which ran along the steep cliff . . . I walked, feeling my loss of innocence in the face of the first communion girls who had danced their spring dance for me while our parents picnicked down by the river. She appeared unexpectedly, dressed in rags, eyes streaked red from crying, fingers raw from tearing at her hair . . . You, my son! she cried as we met on the narrow path. She reached out to grab me, mistaking me for her murdered son, scratching at my face and eyes with long, black fingernails, crying like a wild witch . . . and I fighting back, driven by terror . . . No, no, I am not your son, I am my mother's son, I live, I believe in the holy Trinity which I now call to dissolve you, to make you disappear! But she is too strong, she has cried too many times at night along the river, and I have sat awake and listened . . . and she has filled my soul with the dread of her stories. You are the son I butchered for love, she cries, you are the son I lost at war, the babe forced into my womb by the power of your father, abandoned child. She reaches out and her long fingernails cut through my flesh as I struggle and cry for help in the smouldering darkness of the ash heap. Do not fear me, she cries, I am your mother, your sister, your beloved . . . I suckled you at my breasts, sang lullabies for you, wrapped you in rags torn from my skirts . . . I am all the women you have violated . . .

No, no, I cry and fight, pounding at her, stepping back and feeling the fires that burn beneath me and threaten to cave in and swallow us both. No, I am not your son. I am not your son. I step off the narrow path, totter at its edge, see the bright green of the river below, catch sight of the clean lines of corn fields which line the other bank, then I leap . . . tear loose of her grasp and leap off the cliff and fall and tumble into the air . . . fall until I can fall no more . . .

Then I awaken with a start, gasping for breath. My body is soaked with sweat. Only a dream, I tell myself, only a bad dream. The room is dark, outside the storm has let up. The small radio on Mike's nightstand buzzes with static. I lie back and catch my breath. In the silence I create I hear the room breathing. In the hallway all is quiet, but here in the room a strange presence breathes. My hair tingles, for a moment I believe that la Llorona has followed me out of the dream and into my room.

Who's there, I whisper in the darkness. There is no answer, but the cold night is heavy with a presence which is in the room or just outside the room. I cannot see in the darkness. I lie very quietly, listening for sounds which will explain the presence, waiting for a movement of shadows. I lie like that for a long time . . . and I think of Ismelda, is she safe, sleeping in her house by the river, does the wailing woman visit her dreams or is it we who are men the only ones tormented by that witch? Who visits Ismelda's dreams? Do giant snowmen awaken from the drifts of snow and move to her window to admire her beauty? Is her soft, smooth skin smothered in warm goose down . . . her heart beating in the middle of the tempest which covers the desert as heavy as the paralysis which infuses each of us . . . Her eyes are closed in peace, the long dark lashes undisturbed by the shadows of nightmares, her lips slightly parted, as if in a smile . . . Is she dreaming of me? Am I the man in the white turtle shell who swims nightly in the liquid of her dreams . . . hungry for her love and the touch which can melt the cold away . . .

Who's there, I call again . . . and wonder if Ismelda is sister to la Llorona . . . daughter of the same womb . . . companion to those young girls which shared the altar with me the last day of my childhood and who return to haunt every dream which seeks to tell me that in my innocence lies the answer to the question I seek now. Why me? Who was I then? Who am I now?

Where am I, I call . . . and thinking of the vegetables sleeping in their cold iron lungs . . . and Salomón, reading long into the night . . . dreaming what all of us will come to be . . . Salomón, I say, can you hear me. Tell me what will become of all of this.

Someone moves in the dark. A bed squeaks. Who's there? Who moves in the dark? Ghost . . . or man . . . or both?

I listen closely and hear a sound which is unmistakable . . . It is the same sound my grandfather's mules made as they thundered across the llano as he came swooping down on us, calling out his hello, slashing his whip and making it pop over the heads of the gray mules . . . Grandfather, I say.

I hold my breath and tremble. I hear the blue hooves chop into the frozen earth and turn the clods, then the rider pulls up outside, a rider with a remuda of horses, sliding to a stop, pawing at the ground, lathered hot with spume and froth, jerking at their halters . . . thick woven blankets of earth colors beneath the saddles . . . the air is sweet with their

67

lather and urine smell . . . Grandfather, I say again, I had not expected you . . .

I hear my cry mix into the heavy silence of the night, then a shadow moves to the window and opens it. Cold air bellows up in the room, icy snow explodes like a cloud, the horses whinny to be away, and overhead the owls are screeching . . . their blood and feathers fall softly on the white earth. The rider waits motionlessly. He has called, but in another tongue. It is not the llano Spanish of my grandfather, it is not his cry of vámoooooooo-nos! Away!

Who? I ask in the dark, and it's then I hear the sharp hiss of the well-thrown lariat as it snakes swift and deadly around the hump of the mountain. The rider on the red stallion has cast his lasso on the mountain, and now he is tugging at the huge hump, softly pulling the massive weight aside, slowly letting the streaks of light clothe the pre-dawn sky. I hear a song. Jerry sings at the window. It is his morning song.

Jerry, I whisper.

Jerry turns and stands like a warrior over my bed. He is dressed in buckskin now, rich and tanned buckskin which fills the room with its sweetness.

It is my turn, Tortuga, he whispers, my grandfather has found me. I leave this place forever. His voice is full of joy. His breath is warm as he speaks. His words are like yellow tendrils of light which reach out all around me to lift the dark rock of night.

A drum beats. He sings

> I walk in the path of the sun
> My grandfather commands
> I walk in the path of the sun
> He calls me to walk in his path
> As he once called the turtles from the sea . . .

Yes, Tortuga, long before his word was flesh the sea covered the earth, and men and turtles were brothers in the sea. Together they ruled the world of the fish . . . But the world was dark and so our grandfather called them forth from the sea. He opened a hole in the waters and for the first time man and turtle saw the bright sun and the clear sky. Man stood upon the back of the turtle and climbed into this world of light. Immediately he was blinded by the sun, he lost his golden scales and his skin turned dark and hard. But he was determined to walk upon the earth and to explore this new land of the sun. He called his new life 'walking the path of the sun' and he sang its praises. He wanted to share the new beauty with his brother the turtle, so he reached back to pull him through the hole in the dark water. But the turtle was afraid. Only a few came upon the land, and they were so frightened by the sun and the cold winds that they grew thick shells to protect themselves . . . and when frightened, they always retreat to the safety of the water. We cannot retreat into the darkness, Tortuga, we cannot build shells like the turtle . . . our commandment is to live in the light of the sun . . . to walk in the light of the sun . . .

"Jerry," I called.

"Goodbye, Tortuga," he whispered, "perhaps we will meet again, on the path of the sun . . ." He placed his open hand on my cast and with a black crayon he traced its outline on my shell. Then he turned and walked quickly to the window.

"Jerry!" I cried, fully awake, desperately, suddenly knowing that he was determined to go home. Outside I thought I heard the uneasy snorting and pawing of horses.

"On the path of the sun," he smiled and stepped out the open window. He disappeared into the morning shadows. I held my breath and listened for a long time. I heard the sound of horses riding away, shaggy horses crunching the thick snow, moving towards the river where they would turn to the west, towards the lost tribe.

The words of the morning chant echoed in the room, and hung like an incantation which raised the sun, because instantly the sun was a red, glorious stallion leaping over Tortuga's shell, and the rider was an old warrior dressed in brilliant head dress which sparkled and changed the pale pearl color of dawn into a fiery rainbow. He shouted his war cry and cast his burning spear which melted away the darkness and the ice.

I listened as long as I could, listened to the sound of horses breaking snow. The war cry was a cry which echoed all over the desert, far beyond its reaches, far beyond the serpentine Gila range, and into the last nook of every iron lung which provided the precious air for Salomón's vegetables. The cry and the light penetrated everything, even Ismelda's room, where she turned and moaned in her sleep . . .

"Mike!" I shouted. "Mike! Get up!" I suddenly knew Jerry would have to climb the mountain, and the passes would be covered and packed with snow.

Ronco stirred in his chair. Mike yawned and shivered. He sat up and looked at the window. "Who in the hell left the window open?" he asked and turned to look at me.

"Jerry," I said, "Jerry's gone!"

"Gone? What the hell—" Mike jumped into his chair and rushed to the window. I knew he was looking at the tracks which led from the window down the hill. He turned and looked at me and I wanted to tell him what had happened, but he already knew. He turned and raced his chair out of the room and I knew he was going for Dr. Steel.

9

A few days later they brought in Buck.

Ronco had wanted to move into Jerry's bed, but the Nurse wouldn't let him. She did her best to keep Ronco isolated from the rest of the ward. Mike said it was because in one of his horney moods Ronco had caught the big Nurse alone and had tried to put it to her. The Nurse came out of the wild attack with half her clothes ripped off and her legs scratched by Ronco's braces. She vowed to get even with him, kept him sedated for a whole month, but afterwards Ronco only laughed and said, "She almost gave in, too, she was hot to trot!" Now they kept an uneasy truce, but Ronco couldn't get any favors from her.

Danny asked for Jerry's bed too, but we turned him down. We didn't want him in our room. Mike said the only reason Danny wanted to bunk with us was to be closer to Sadsack's comic books. The story was that Sadsack had a treasure in comic books stashed in a discarded iron lung somewhere in the hospital, but nobody had been able to find it. The kids said Sadsack only went there late at night to check his cache and to count them like a miser counts his coins. Danny and his two cronies had searched everywhere in the hospital, but they never found it. Once, in desperation, they had tied up Sadsack and tried to torture him into telling where he kept his pile of comics, but Sadsack held his ground. They had tickled his feet with a feather until Sadsack passed out from laughing, but he didn't give away his secret.

So the new boy, Buck, was given Jerry's bed. He had been in a bad car wreck and was completely bandaged from head to toe. After they brought him in the Nurse and Samson took a long time getting the traction ropes and wires running in the right position across the two poles. Buck just kept moaning.

"He looks like an Okie TV antenna," Mike joked.

"Not funny, Mike," the Nurse frowned. Samson grinned.

"Bet every bone in his body's broken," somebody watching the hanging process volunteered.

"Oh myyy—"

"What's his name?" Danny asked.

"Buck—" the Nurse answered.

"Buckeroo! Yahoo! Bet he's a cowboy! Just look at that hat!" Ronco pointed at Buck's cowboy hat.

"Looks more like a ghost," Danny whispered. He had drawn close to my bed. He wiped his nose with his withered hand. The dryness was spreading from the hand up the arm, tormenting Danny with an itch which he scratched until the dry, scaly skin bled and formed blood crusts full of pus. "Jerry's ghost," he said and stalked away.

"Don't bother him," the Nurse said when she and Samson were finished stringing up Buck, "he's been in isolation and he needs a lot of rest—" They went out.

Mike nodded, but as soon as they were out of hearing range he was at Buck's bedside. "How you doin'?" he asked.

"Where's my hat?" Buck moaned weakly. Mike took the dusty hat from the night stand and placed it next to Buck; he seemed to rest easier with his hat in view. He sighed and moaned. "That was one bronc I couldn't ride . . . and I'm man enough to admit it—"

"A horse threw you?" Mike asked.

"First my girl threw me," Buck drawled, "then my horse throwed me . . ." he groaned with pain, "but I'm still a cowboy and a mean sombitch . . . and I can whip any mother's son that ses different—" He was still feverish. The Nurse said he had bled a lot inside, and a lot of bones were broken and bruised.

"Yeah," Mike nodded, "we know you're a mean-ass stud, but what happened?"

"I hated losing my hoss more than my woman—" Buck's lips trembled.

Mike shook his head. "Just wait till you've been here awhile, you'll change your mind."

"I hurt all over," he groaned.

"You want me to get the Nurse?" Mike asked.

"I'm okay," Buck mumbled. "Is this the bunkhouse?"

"Yeah, I reckon it is," Mike nodded.

"Well, I guess I'm in the raght place—"

"Yup. It ain't exactly home on the range, but it'll do for awhile," Mike winked at us.

"Hotdoggie, they got me tied down like a crazy bronc, don't they?" He smiled for the first time.

"They have all of us tied down like crazy horses," Mike agreed. "Every once in awhile one breaks loose, but they bring another one in its place—one after another to this crazy corral . . ."

I knew he was thinking about Jerry, we all were. There had been no word since he left.

"How did they happen to lasso you?" Ronco asked.

"Well," he drawled, "I was over to an FFA meeting in Gila Bend, jus' havin' me a grand ole opery good time, when a no account drugstore cowboy decides to throw his lariat on my little dogie—"

"Hey hold on!" Sadsack interrupted. "Would you mind translating what all that means so we can all know what you're saying? Damn, you sound like one of those cowboys on the radio! Har, har, har . . ."

Buck glanced at us, swallowed, then relaxed. I guess he realized we were all in the same boat and he didn't have to act the part of a big, mean cowboy.

"I lost my girl," he said meekly. "She double-crossed me for one of those city jocks that don't know the difference between a bull and a heifer . . . so I got drunk. I bought me a case of beer and I headed home. It had snowed the night before and the pass was as slick as a whistle with ice. There wasn't any traffic on it, the roads were closed, but I didn't know that. I was drunker than a skunk by the time I started over Flechado Pass. Anyways, to make a long story short, I fell asleep somewhere in the middle of a Hank Snow and went over the cliff . . . shoot, I'da made it if I hadn't fallen asleep. I spent all day at the bottom of that canyon, and it was cold as hell! I nearly froze to death. Lucky for me a search party found me—" He paused and looked at us. "Funny, one of them said something about looking for an Indian kid . . . and there was a doctor with them. They found me by accident. Any of you know anything about that?"

Nobody answered. We would tell him later.

"Anyway, it was lucky for me . . . I'da froze to death . . . oh, it was colder than hell . . . But Champ is dead."

"Champ? Who's Champ?"

"My horse," Buck explained, "my horse is dead and that's what hurts the most . . . I'd give anything to have him alive again, anything. I don't mind me gettin' busted up, I deserved it, actin' like a damn fool over that big-assed FFA gal . . . but oh damn, Champ is dead . . . I had to kill him . . ."

"What happened?" Sadsack asked.

"He was thrown from the trailer . . . broke his legs, and probably a lot of other bones. I passed out for awhile, and when I came to the first thing I could hear were his cries as he struggled to get up . . . course he couldn't. He'd rear up and just tumble back down. Then he'd rest awhile, look over at me, and I couldn't move out of the cab, I was just as busted up . . . I knew right away, the minute I woke up and saw him all busted up, that he wouldn't make it . . . that I had to kill him."

"How?"

"I had a 30-30 in the gunrack. I managed to get it out . . . then I said goodbye to Champ . . . aimed . . . fired. Oh damn I can still hear that shot

72

echoing down the canyon... like a bell. Some crows called, flew overhead, then it was quiet again. Only the wind moaned down that canyon ... and I had to sit there all morning, feeling the blood freeze where it oozed from some of my wounds ... watching the crows circling overhead ... It wasn't the cold I minded ... it was that I had to kill my horse ... I don't mind telling you, I cried ..." Even now his voice grew hoarse as he told us his story. His eyes filled with tears.

"You had to do it," Ronco said, "that's the only thing you can do when an animal's busted up that bad ..."

"Yeah," Buck agreed, "but it sure as hell ain't like the movies ... I found that out."

"No, it ain't the movies," Mike nodded, "nothing is. The movies paint it too easy ... Tom Mix shoots his horse with a broken leg, says goodbye Ole Paint, jumps on another horse and rides to catch the desperados who have kidnapped his woman ... it all comes out right in the end. Here it's different. But at least you came out of it alive, let's be thankful for that ..."

"Yeah, they can't keep a good man down," Buck tried to smile.

"That's the spirit!" Mike nodded and we smiled and tried to let him know we were pulling for him, even Sadsack who cut loose an explosive bomb cried out joyfully, "Yeah Buck, catch that and paint it red! Har-har-har!"

"My ole man always said I was full of piss and vinegar," Buck winked, "I'll be throwing a lasso on one of those chairs before long—"

"We got a whole corral of them," Mike said, "just waiting to be rode."

"Yeah," Buck groaned. "But it sure do hurt in the meantime—" He closed his eyes. He fell into a painful, troubled sleep, feverishly mumbling that he could rope anything that moved, including wild snakes, cyclones and hurricanes. He swore over and over that the horse hadn't been born that could throw him, and there wasn't a steer he couldn't toss on its back. He hated fancy drug-store cowboys who'd never rid' a hoss or roped a dogie and who'd never dirtied their boots in cow shit. Later he shouted that this sure as hell wasn't his last round-up and that he wasn't ready for Hill Billy heaven, and that ole JC, the toughest trailmaster of them all, could just trail boss a little longer without him. He sang parts of "Ghost Riders in the Sky," yodeled like a sick calf, then finally quieted down as his fever broke and he could rest.

The room was quiet while we watched over him. Someone whispered that it was a strange coincidence that the searchers had gone out looking for Jerry and found Buck, and that Buck had come to sleep in Jerry's bed.

The following morning they found Jerry's body. We had spent our time glued to the radio, waiting for news, but all we could get were the frequent sermons of a hill billy preacher who piped in from KRST, Del Rio, Texas. After that there was only garbled static and occasional snatches of music. We felt cut off from the outside world. There was a radio in the reception room, and that's how the news first came to us. It spread quickly throughout the ward, so by the time Danny and Mudo and Tuerto came running in with a newspaper they had swiped we already knew. The ward was very quiet.

"It says he froze to death," Danny said.

"He didn't have a chance crossing that mountain," Ronco said, "but it happens every year. Sooner or later one of us gets homesick, and when the call comes you don't plan on anything, you just go. There's nothing stronger than the call to be home. The time came for Jerry and he went. Home was his life . . . it was everything. He couldn't live in a hospital like this, damn, can't they realize that!"

"Yeah, home was grandfather . . . home was a place where he could have his religion without having to hide it," Mike nodded. He had taken Jerry's death harder than anyone, because he had tried so hard to talk with Jerry and understand what was going on in his mind.

"There was no way he could get over Flechado Pass," Buck said, "I know that. It was frozen solid. And all the other trails over the mountain are covered over too, either that or they're fenced in. I've been up in that mountain in the summer, and there's barbed wire everywhere. If the Forest Service isn't closing off trails then it's the big ranchers . . . Maybe Jerry didn't know that. He didn't know the old trails are wiped out . . ."

"In a way I'm glad he went," Mike whispered to himself, "at least he had the guts to make a break for it." Then he slammed his fist against the nightstand and cursed. "But he never had a chance! Damnit, he never had a chance!"

We all shared his anger and frustration, because we felt like he did, but there was nothing we could do.

"We should take this case to the Committee," somebody suggested.

"You're damn right we will!" Mike exclaimed. "The whole world should know what's happening here, and that creep of a director won't tell them!"

"Swanson? Shit, he doesn't know a damned thing!" Danny said angrily. "He never leaves his office. He's afraid of us, thinks we're freaks. Steel's the one that does all the work!"

"Did you hear what Swanson told the reporters? It was on the radio, somebody said. He told them Jerry was the Little Beaver of the hospital . . . and we were going to miss him, but we all knew he had gone to his happy hunting ground!"

"His real name was Geronimo," Mike said, "and he was Navajo—

We said no more, but later that afternoon someone asked how Dr. Steel had found Jerry and someone, I don't know who, said that when Steel came running to our room he looked out the window and he cursed. Seems like right then and there he knew Jerry would be heading west, into the Gila . . . and he also knew the mountain was packed with snow and ice and every friggin' pass was closed. Jerry would have to go over the top . . . even Flechado Pass was closed that day. By then the sheriff had already been called, he and the state cop were here, asking questions . . . and Steel just grabbed a jacket and told them to get going because they had to find Jerry before nightfall. He knew it had to be that way, because he knew that night it was going to be freezing cold as hell on the top of that mountain. So they went out in the jeeps, and first they found Buck . . . that's something ain't it? If they hadn't gone looking for Jerry they would never have found Buck, cause like I said, the road over the pass was already closed to traffic. Anyway, Steel climbed all day . . . and next morning he brought Jerry down. But what happened up there on the mountain is what's interesting. It took him all day to bring Jerry down, but he did it, and he did it alone because his own horse was frozen to death. He brought him down all the way, dragging him, carrying him over his back, anyway he could, down to the camp, down to the surprised men, never saying anything to anyone, just watched him loaded on the ambulance . . . then he came back to the hospital, and they say the first thing he did was to go over to Salomón's room . . . nobody knows why, but they say he talked with Salomón for a long time. Nobody knows why, but I got an idea. Know what it is? I think he knows Salomón makes stories, and it was important for him to tell him because one of these days Salomón is going to make a story of it. Yeah, just wait, one of these days you'll hear his story, maybe not right away, and maybe he'll change it a little, cause he's a good storyteller, but you'll hear it. He'll tell about the way Steel ran down to the river through the wet, frozen snow, how he was gasping for breath and how his eyes were burning with tears. And most important, he'll tell what Steel was thinking all that time, which I don't know because I wasn't even there. And he'll tell what he felt when he saw those tracks turn towards the mountains to the west . . . He will tell you exactly how Steel looked when he got back to the hospital, how wet and tired he was, how he didn't say anything as he put on the shoes and heavy clothes and finally the sheep-skin jacket. He'll tell you details like I couldn't, so you'll feel you're right there, with the searchers getting on the jeep and trucks, quietly kidding each other, checking their equipment, passing the whiskey bottle so the sheriff and Steel won't see, looking up at Solazo peak and somehow wishing they weren't going on the search, wishing they were back home sleeping late under warm blankets, getting a screw from their women, feeling the warmth of their homes. You'll see them drive up to where the tracks turned into the mountains, how they looked over the side and spotted Buck's tangled wreck and saw him waving and shouting where he was pinned in the cab, hear the murmurs of dissension when Steel wanted them to climb, listen to the hassling of the sheriff and the rancher over the price for the horses, hear the stamping feet of the packed horses, smell their sweet smell and hear the creaking of saddles and halters as the sheriff and Steel and the deputy mount up and head into the tall drifts, barely moving forward in the thick snow. The men at the camp rejoice inside that it's not them going, and they can settle down and play cards and drink all day, and joke with Orlando, the state cop, about the raid he made over in Santa Rita, and how he took one of the prostitutes home with him and she's been there ever since. He'll show you plumes of frozen breath marking the still, quiet air. Dots against the mountainside, dots which are the three riders making slow progress. You'll feel the cold wind coming down off the mountain, covering everything with the snow it's blowing around. Then you'll see two of the dots turn back as the sun dips over the mountain and it begins to get winter-dark very fast, and you'll hear them making up excuses to tell the others down at camp, excuses for turning back, the cold, the darkness, Steel's insanity . . . You'll see Steel get down and have to break the trail for his horse and pull him past the really thick drifts . . . and then he'll tell you about Steel's night on the mountain and how the moon grew so big and blue it looked like a giant balloon just within reach . . . and the silence and the peace of that frozen mountain top. And you'll realize that right in the middle of that cold beauty, right in that entire Gila wilderness on the back of a mountain that stretches a hundred miles, Jerry and Steel are sitting very close to each other, that's what really gets you, how Steel was right about the tracks that weren't there. You'll see the blue snow clinging to everything . . . and Jerry, sitting against the pine tree, looking down at us, waiting for the sun to rise, smiling . . . Maybe that's what Steel wanted Salomón to know, that in the midst of all that silence, with the ice cracking and groaning as the trees swayed in the wind, and with the moon so full and mysterious, Jerry was sitting so still and peaceful . . . .

"Did Steel get sick?" somebody asked.

"Yeah. Got a really bad cold, but he's okay now. Saw him going rounds yesterday."

"Best bones doc this place ever had!"

"You bet."

"He don't say much, but he knows—"

"What about the newspaper story?" somebody asked.

"That's all there is to it," someone answered. "The Director says he doesn't know why Jerry ran away. He told the papers Jerry had everything he needed right here: beads to work with, good food, the best medical care in the world. Everything!"

"Ah what does he know! He never comes out of his office! I saw him once and the guy looks like someone that's dead! The Committee hires him to direct this place, but he don't give a damn about us. Sometimes I don't think the Committee gives a damn! Damn old biddies, hired just cause they're friends of the governor, come here once a year and poke around! What do they know? Nothing. They don't know nothing . . . and they don't really give a damn!"

Maybe it was true that they didn't care, and thinking about Jerry didn't help the mood; we were quiet for awhile, then Mike said, "Jerry left us something, he left us his sign—"

"Where?" one of the smaller kids cried.

"On Tortuga's shell," Mike gestured with his chin.

They drew close and looked at the outline of Jerry's hand on my cast. Híjola, they whispered. It was his sign. He had been here. We had known him for awhile, now he was gone. But it was important that he had left his mark, like so many others before him had scribbled their names on the sand of the desert. Mike took a pen and wrote 'Algo es algo, dijo el diablo' under the outline of the hand. Ronco drew a screaming eagle. Other scratches and names appeared as the kids signed my cast.

"He's going to be a walking story!" someone exclaimed.

"But he can't walk!"

"Yeah, but it won't be long till he'll be able! I heard KC say he's the best worker she ever had. Then he'll tell them Jerry's story, and the story of anybody else who ever ran away from this madhouse."

"Tell 'em mine!" Danny interrupted and looked at me. "I've run away more times than anybody else!"

"Ah, Danny, all you do is go to the movies in town. They always know where to pick you up!"

"Nobody's ever run farther than Juanito Faraway," Mike said. "Jerry made me think about him, except Juanito made it—"

"Yeah boy," Ronco nodded and smiled. "He was from a pueblo up north, a place in the mountains—"

"I'd like to go north," Sadsack groaned, "see some green mountains with real trees, get out of this damned desert that boils in the summer and freezes in the winter— Hey! Maybe we could write Juanito and go see him! Maybe we could go hunting and fishing with him!"

"How in the hell are we ever goin' go huntin' wrapped up like Christmas packages as we are! How in the hell can you climb a mountain in a wheelchair, stupid!" Buck shouted. We looked at him. We knew he was nervous because of what had happened to Jerry. "I'd like to see you try to climb a mountain, or anyone of us! Did you ever see a goddamned cripple on a mountain? Fishin' and huntin' and havin' fun? No! No you haven't! And you never will, cause there's just some places we'll never be able to go!" He looked at us, realized he was shouting and turned to face the wall.

"I was just thinking out loud," Sadsack frowned.

We were quiet. I thought about the green mountains to the north and the foamy streams that cut down rocky canyons. Once we could have fished there, and chased deer up and down the mountain side, but like Buck said, the mountains were hard on cripples. I looked at Tortuga. Gray clouds washed across the empty desert and threatened more snow, but they were dry clouds. They would bring no moisture to Tortuga. There were no green, towering pines on the side of the old mountain, only the slag of old lava, granite boulders and the brittle grass and chamisa which clung to the harsh shell. Ismelda had told me that a huge, old gnarled juniper grew at the top of the mountain, and that there was a small meadow with grass. I wondered how she knew.

"Tell me about Juanito," I heard myself say.

"Juanito really missed his pueblo and he was always homesick," Mike said. "He kept looking at the calendar and telling us about the feast day he didn't want to miss. There was going to be dancing, races, clowns, lots of food and women, so one night he slipped out of here, went down to the bus depot and crawled into the luggage compartment of a bus headed north. He didn't know he got on an express bus. He fell asleep and never got out of that luggage place until the bus reached some small town in Montana. That's when they found him."

"Eeeeho la! Imagine us in Montana!" Ronco cried.

"Hot dog!" Buck yahooed, "there's good rodeos up there!"

"Maybe my arm would get better there," Danny said wistfully.

"And there's lots of mountains, green mountains," Sadsack moaned.

"When they found him they asked him what his name was and where he came from and Juanito pointed to show them he'd come a long ways and said 'Juanito, faraway' and they thought his name was Juanito Faraway and that's what they called him. They took care of him till they found out where he belonged and shipped him back here. But in the meantime their Chamber of Commerce came up with the bright idea of celebrating Juanito Faraway Frontier Day every year. So they drummed up a rodeo, Indian dances, fiddling contests, jeep races over the mountains and they made a fortune with it. They even have a Juanito Faraway museum! Juanito's crutches are there, and a picture of the Greyhound bus he rode up north. Now it's an annual attraction. Tourists go from all over the country. The little town that wasn't even on the map is now a city, and everybody makes a living from celebrating Juanito's day. Can you imagine that?"

We couldn't, but we laughed. Sadsack peered from behind a comic and said, "When I run away it's going to be farther than that!"

"How far?"

"It's not going to be anyplace you know about, brother. There won't be any wheelchairs or crutches or braces there. The sun will always be shining, and there will be lots of green grass and trees, and lots of food to eat, plenty of booze to drink, and nothing to do but play around with the women, who wear nothing but thin little skirts, like they did in Greek times—"

"There ain't no such place!" Danny protested.

"There is if I say there is!" Sadsack responded. "Why can't there be a place where there aren't any twisted bodies, no polio, no diseases, no cripples in dark alleys! Why can't there be a place where nobody has to work, and there's fruit on the trees, and the grass is always green, and everybody just spends their time making love, all day long, just making love . . ."

"Yeah, why not?" someone said, and some of us shut our eyes and imagined that paradise. Then Pee Wee, a small kid without arms and only stumps for legs, pushed his coaster into the room and said it was dinner time . . . And when I saw him I cursed Sadsack's dream and hated myself for letting it creep into the reality of the ward.

That night the ward was quiet. We listened quietly to Franco's sad lyrics.

They say a man should never cry
But when I saw your surgery knife
My heart stopped,
And my blood ran cold . . .

Now I don't know . . . how long
I can go onnnn,
Cause it keeps right on a'hurtin'
Since you sliced . . .

"He's in a bad mood tonight," Mike said, "sounds like he's cruising the halls and looking for Steel. He blames Steel for losing his legs, but there was nothing Steel could do. The disease was eating away the legs, something in the blood, nothing he could do to save the legs . . . ."

10

What did he tell you? one of the boys asked.
He told me a story about the beginning . . .
How does it go?
Let him tell it, I said, and Salomón continued his story:

I have spent most of my life on the wide beach . . . the beach which stretches into the dry and empty desert. I was drawn there to observe the sea turtles, those giant parasite-encrusted creatures which come lumbering out of the dark waters to lay their eggs in the warm sand. And I asked myself, what cosmic force draws them from the safety of the water to plant their eggs in the dangerous sunlight?

What force drives them to infuse their germ of life into the earth? And why am I the observer on the beach?

A drama unfolds. A drama which has no beginning and no end. The seasons swirl like changing sea clouds and the centuries are like the lapping of waves at my feet. I wait patiently. The sea breeze trembles, the ocean opens like a woman giving birth, and the giant turtles, slime and sea-weed clinging to them, come trudging out of the sea to deposit their eggs. Prehistoric creatures, some as old as the earth itself, some old enough to remember when the desert was an ocean, their home—giants of the sea, reptilian heads shining with sea water, eyes covered with the cataracts of time, sniffing the wind, blinking at the bright sun, feeling already the tremor of danger which the black sun brings to them.

What is that spot of light that burns so bright? they seem to ask, and why does it throb like the cell of light in my dark blood? Giant flippers dig the wet sand. The day burns on. The eggs drop in the nests, new forms which begin in the milky liquid of transformation eons ago, in the sea, in the darkness, guided only by one lonely cell which reflects the light of the sun.

Weeks later the sun breaks over the empty dunes in time to illuminate the beginning of the race. Again the breeze trembles with life; overhead birds cry; shadows race across the sand. The shells crack and break, squirming life breaks free to meet the electric acid of life, to breathe the air, to be blinded by the roaring sun. Some dark instinct fills them with the foreboding of death that greets all life A horn sounds long and mournful. There is safety only in the water! The race begins! The just-born turtles scramble across the wide beach to reach the safety of the water!

I watch dispassionately. The putrid smell of the egg shells invades the clean ocean air. The slimy, blind turtles fill the quiet beach with their squeals. Some struggle so hard to start their journey that they cave in the walls of sand and are suffocated in their own nests. For them the flight was short-lived. Those that escape the prison of the egg and the incubating sand begin their race for the sea. Overhead the burning sun drives fear into their hearts and drives them towards the safe, dark waters. There is no pause to look around, no curiousity about life on the beach . . . they do not see me watching them . . .

For miles and miles across the sands the fledgling turtles swarm across the beach, smelling out the water, blindly dashing towards the waiting sea.

They are driven by fear. Death stalks the beach. Suddenly there are shadows on the sand, loud, piercing screams fill the air! And the buzzards strike. Sharp beaks foul with lice and yellow mucous and downy feathers rip at the young turtles and tear at the soft limbs. The talons and beaks of the first enemy are deadly. There is carnage on the beach.

But the way is long and full of light, Tortuga, and it reveals life even in the buzzard's maggot stomach. That is why I watch without interference. Death squeals mix with the thrashing of wings and the shrill cries of the birds . . . fate is blind. Is it the strong or the crafty which survive the onslaught? Or is it those driven by fear of the blinding light?

The ocean heaves. The tide is going out. Safety now lies farther away. The race continues across the wide beach. Other enemies strike. Giant ghost crabs reach from beneath the sand and drag the little turtles down . . . another feast? Yes, there is a glimmer of hope even in turtle blood. At least I feel there is, else why would I watch the race? And why do I look on so indifferently?

Those which survive are attacked by the rock lizards, distant cousins of an ancient brotherhood, rough-scaled monsters who scramble to make a meal of turtle meat. Again the cries fill the air, shrill cries which turn my blood cold . . . What is more terrifying than your own kind turning on you?

The earth itself plots destruction! The receding tide has left long stretches of mud, quagmires which suck the little turtles down! Those that can't break free are imprisoned forever when the relentless sun hardens the mud. Still, some cross that wasteland of muck, driven by the acid which burns their soft skins, driven by the light burning in their blood! The sea calls them! While overhead, in the green-palm sky, a new danger

*threatens! Swift birds of prey swoop down and finish the job the buzzards
started. They turn over the small turtles and stab the soft undersides. The
yellow pee of death wets the sand . . .*

*A very few survive the dangers of the beach. They stumble forward,
gasping for life, needing the water . . . And now the most ironic enemy
appears on the beach. New hoards of mother turtles are coming out of the
sea to begin the cycle of spawning. Full of eggs and blind to the drama
before them they crush their own children into the sand, and some,
hungry from their journey to the beach, pick up the squirming young and
make a meal of the future they themselves deposited . . . It makes me
shiver, Tortuga . . . Is the light so dim that we don't recognize ourselves
on that wide beach? Is the sun setting on this game of life?*

*My body trembles in the evening breeze. The day is ending. The sun
is red as it drops into the sea. A few stragglers reach the tide and are
gathered into the white arms of the sea. I feel a sigh settle in my blood. I
am alone, and I feel very old . . . old and powerless. I watch the few
young turtles who disappear into the immense, lapping water. The cycle
is complete . . . the sucking ocean washes them away. But now the sea
itself is a new enemy . . . and to return to it is to return to live with the
ghosts of the past . . . to live in the sea-darkness. That is not our path,
Tortuga, that is not our way. If there is any hope it lies on the path of the
sun. That one glimmering cell of light which floats in our dark blood must
become a sun . . . it must shine on new worlds . . .*

11

So I pushed against the pain of the therapy sessions, because the pain was real and I would rather have it than the numbing paralysis. I felt like one of the little turtles in Salomón's story, I wanted to break out of my shell and sniff the air; I wanted a chance to run the race across the beach again. It wouldn't be easy, but nothing was. I had run the race before, I knew the joy and the pain in it, and I knew how it had broken so many of us, twisted our bones, exiled us—And why? Because we had dared to run? Perhaps we had loved the race too well, and had not been afraid? I didn't know, and I had no time to care. I only wanted to move. Already I could bend my elbows and lift myself to a sitting position, and eat by myself. My left hand was unbandaged now, but nearly useless, but I made do. Now it was my legs I worked to recover.

"You're a mean turtle," KC smiled. Beads of amber colored sweat rolled down her warm, brown skin.

"Yeah," I grunted, "I'm mean and I'm tough—" I closed my eyes in pain as she brought my knee against my chest.

"You're also kind of sexy," she teased, "in a mean turtle sort of way—" She relaxed the leg, massaged the muscles so they wouldn't tighten up.

"Yeah, that too," I smiled.

"You want some more?" she asked. Her painted lips were moist with perspiration. I knew she was tired too. Sometimes we got so wrapped up in the rhythm of the exercises that we worked beyond the set time.

"Let's do more," I said.

"Sure you wouldn't rather rest, baby?" she whispered. "I can shut the door and hold you in my arms for awhile, hold you like a baby against my warm titties, cuddle you awhile—" She laughed, a laugh deep in her stomach and throat, and I could smell the hot fragrance in her breath.

She was a beautiful woman, big and dark and sensuous. Everyone turned when she walked down the hall. She made the blood rush in my body, and sometimes I wished I was a dark, handsome man who could take her down. But I knew reality, and I knew her game, so I smiled and said no thanks, maybe some other time, maybe when I can walk, that's when I'll be ready to play with you, right now I'll settle for another dose of therapy, and pour it on double strong, please. She laughed and said that's how she liked her men, and we set to work again while she teased me about Ismelda and said she knew she was no match for Ismelda's magic.

She's a lizard woman, she said, and she sprinkled magic on you, and now she can come into your dreams every night, and she wants you to play in the sand with her, like lizards do. Don' worry none, honey, you'll be able to play with her, yes sir. One of these days I'm going to pull you clear out of that shell and then you'll be a lizard too! Then you can run and play in the sun! I can see it now, you running and trying to catch up with Ismelda, oh Lord! She laughed, and the laughter mingled with pain and the cracking of dry tendons. My muscles burned with sweet fire.

My, my, just look at that pecker, she smiled. Her pulling and pushing and her warm body rubbing over me made me grow with hot blood. That's a good sign, she said, then she added, for Ismelda! and burst out laughing. Pulling you out of a shell is just like pulling a little baby out of its mother's womb . . . those little buggers come out wet and dirty and squirming, shocked by a spasm as the cold air fills their lungs . . . and the best doctor is the one who will treat them rough right off. Whack 'em in the rump! Wham bam thank you m'am, now your kid ain't yours anymore, he belongs to the world and if the world wants to make an orphan out of him or her than it's up to you to change the world, not the poor kid who never had one bit of choice about coming to visit us here. Toss 'em in a rough blanket right away so they can feel the prickle of life! Let them go hungry for a little while before they find the warm titty, do 'em good later in life when they find out the world's a rough place to live in. Take those that wanna crawl back into the womb and give them a doubly hard swat and toss 'em in a basket and let them cry till they find out crying don' do no good and they have to start lookin' around and findin' their own way in this world, otherwise they just curl up into their fetal position which they're so used to and never move again—them's the Sadsacks of life. Those kids that are treated like dolls at birth are ruined for life. They'll always be timid about life, they'll grow slow, be consti-pated all their lives, never enjoy a decent screw—

"I can tell you weren't one of those, Tortuga—"

"One of what?"

"One of those brats that sits around and wants to suck titty all day long."

"Well, I never turned it down—"

She slapped her hands and laughed. "Oh no, you didn't get busted up sitting around the dairy! You were out sniffing life in the streets, I know. Come on now, pull that leg up . . . up, all the way, that's it . . ."

84

I lifted my leg as far as I could. It was like a lead weight. I strained more and felt the muscles rip away from the bones.

"A little more," she coaxed.

I grunted, lifted, farted, felt the sweat break out, felt myself wet the bed, swallowed the pain which raced through nerve and muscle.

"A little more, honey, just a little more," she whispered.

"Damn you!" I cried, strained to the breaking point, trembling from the tension my body was holding, wanting to cry and curse some more and knowing I couldn't.

"Good," she finally said, "good," and her strong hands grabbed my leg as it relaxed. The pain and the tension drained away. She massaged it for awhile, then pushed it back against my stomach, until she was almost on top of me, her sweating body covering mine, her brown-amber eyes looked into mine and she said, "You gotta suffer a little, to learn to love a little—"

Her cologne mixed with sweat and dripped on me; it was sweet and hot. She held my leg against her round breasts and stomach, and she moved her leg over mine. She moaned softly. Her hot lips brushed mine. "Now push, you little bastard!" she snapped, and I pushed as hard as I could and moved her to the side. "Ah, good," she smiled, "lots of strength there, just a whole hell of a lot of good muscle alive in that leg—" She sat on the side of the bed and massaged my quivering legs, and I could feel the tremble in her arms while she worked. "You're good to work with, because you're determined—" It was a good compliment and I was grateful because they didn't come easy from KC. "I bet you cut your mother plenty when you were nursing," she said as she worked.

We laughed.

"She didn't nurse me . . ." I smiled and remembered the story my mother told about going dry when I was born. She used to tell the story when we were all together, during good times when such stories fit easily into the slow give and take of the conversation, and she used to smile and touch my cheek, because I was her wayward son, but she loved me nonetheless . . . she smiled because she didn't think I remembered, but I did, because every time she told the story I could hear the tinkling sound of goat bells, and in the shift of the breeze I could smell the strong, pungent odor of the goats and of the old woman who came to nurse me. She was an old woman who lived at the outskirts of the village where I was born; my father said she was a witch. I only knew her milk was as bitter as the milk of her goats, and her smell was as strong as theirs . . . but she had been the second woman at my birth, she had been there to assist the midwife who cared for my mother. Later, no one spoke of her, she took no credit for the delivery, the birth which was so close to death because the umbilical cord came wrapped around my neck, suffocating me, drowning me . . . I came like a hanged man into the world, my mother said later, and it was only the swift fingers of the two old women which saved me . . . I remember the old woman's sour breath when she breathed into my mouth to pump up my lungs, I remembered her eyes staring at me, coaxing me to breathe . . . and then there was the scream that came from the pit of my stomach as I was startled into life. But I would never forget the eyes, the breath, the rough goat hands which swatted me and roughly brought me into life . . . I would never forget because she came again, when they knew my mother's breasts had not produced the milk I needed, they went to the old woman . . . and my father said she laughed, she laughed so the entire village heard her coarse laughter, and she said that she was like her goats, that she was never dry . . . So she came every day, in the morning and in the afternoon. First there was a silence. The wind seemed to die down, then I heard the tinkling of the goat bells as she came hobbling up the dusty street, her goats scurrying around her, running to the hiss which was her command. I waited breathlessly, patiently, filled with fear, gazing at the colors of the new world and knowing that to live I had to drink that bitter milk. My mother sensed my predicament. She would take me in her arms and rock me and say, my baby, my baby, it's only for a short while . . . Then she would take me outside, to the doorstep where the old woman sat on the steps in the sun . . . because she did not want to enter the house of a dry woman, afraid her goats would wither and go dry . . .

They didn't speak. My mother handed me to the old woman, and she unbuttoned her blouse and exposed her wrinkled but fruitful breasts. She held me on her bony knees while I drank. The goats gathered around her and nibbled at my blanket while they waited for their dam, and my mother stood quietly against the door, looking away, across the wide llano where dust devils were already dancing . . . she waited in silence. The old woman also looked into the distant horizon, but for her it was not space she saw, but a world that buzzed with life. She smoked, awful-smelling cigarettes which she rolled while I clung for dear life to her dugs, even while the ashes fell and burned my cheeks, I sucked her milk, in fear and in wonder I greedily sucked the bitter milk . . . while the wind clawed around the pitiful mud houses which clustered together for protection . . . protection from forces which rode the wind of the wide llano, forces which denied milk to a young woman who had just given birth and gave it plentifully to an old, withered woman . . . When she was empty she would look at me and laugh, gurgle a laugh like I gurgled the hot milk burning in my stomach, then she would hand me back to my mother, and my mother would reach for me anxiously and gather me in her arms and hold me to her breast, lend me her heartbeat to settle my trembling . . . and she would silently pray that I would not take a disease from the milk I had to drink . . . that I would not be wild like the goats . . . that I would not turn into a goat . . . Then warm and safe in my mother's arms I could hear the old woman moving away, laughing, calling to her goats with a sharp hiss, moving away into the open spaces of the llano ... while my mother's soft hands finally brought the hot, bubbling milk and gas erupting at my mouth ...

"I feel all wet," I said.

"You are," KC smiled and wiped away the milky sweat.

"But I feel good—"

"We're getting there," she nodded.

Then she walked away, swinging her hips to the rhythm of the song she sang while she worked me over.

> *Noooo-baaaady knows ...*
> *the pain that I've seen*
> *noooo-baady knows but me ...*

12

A few letters arrived from home. Friends wrote, my brother wrote, and always I felt that somehow their lives had not changed, that they lived as they had always lived, with the small, simple concerns of each day. After awhile I didn't read the letters, they had nothing to say to me. And after awhile the letters didn't come anymore and my separation from my past was complete. Only my mother continued to write, explaining that there was no way they could reach the hospital, still she could share her thoughts with me, pretend she was talking to me in her letters.

One afternoon the Nurse entered, looked at the crumpled envelope she held then placed it in my hand. It was from my mother. She wrote every week, and the letters were always the same. She prayed to the Holy Mother of God and all the saints that I would be returned safely to her. She had turned all the statues of her saints to face the wall and made a promise that they would not see her face until I was returned home. If I was absent from her sight then God and all his saints and archangels were absent from the world. That is why I offer up all my rosaries and prayers, she said, so that you may return. Each day I go to church and on my knees I make my way from the door to the altar of the Virgin, and there I pray for you. I tell the Virgin that you are a good son. I tell her I tried to keep you by my side, to protect you, but she understands that our sons become men and must follow their own destiny. She knows, she understands, she feels my agony. Her own son was crucified on the cross, she walked the streets towards Calvary at his side, she saw the nails driven into his flesh, she saw him mangled, crippled, taken down from the cross, torn and bleeding . . . and he died in her arms. She knows. She feels what I feel. She speaks to God. Forgive the sins of our sons, forgive the sins of the world, bring them back to us alive, well . . . She knows we die when our sons die, we suffer when they suffer, we die on the streets with them, in the jails, in foreign wars . . . our hearts bleed with their pain, our love is so strong it is a love which feels their anguish and suffering . . . I pray to the Virgin, and my Santo Niño de Atocha and all the saints to change this world which is crippling our sons, to make it a safe place for our sons and daughters, to stop the carnage in the streets . . . for that I offer up my heart, for that I turn the saints to face the wall and declare that God is absent from this world, and He will not return until the mothers of the world offer up their hearts and in an army led by the Holy Mother of God change the world, stop all wars, all diseases, all the bloodshed . . . for that I open my chest and tear out my beating heart and offer it to God so that he will send me your suffering, because I am strong and I can bear it . . . .

Mike came in, took the letter from my hand, folded it neatly and put it in my nightstand.

"How are things at home?" he asked.

"Rough," I said, "no jobs, no money . . . they had to sell the car just to get by, so they won't be coming for me . . . no way to make the long trip . . ."

"I know," Mike said, "things are hard—" he nodded.

"There was a big fight, a revolution or something . . . the people were trying to change things . . . there was so much suffering, so much despair, so many backs getting busted . . . the people were trying to change that . . ."

"Are your folks okay?" he asked.

"Yeah . . . but I get the feeling something's not right—"

"Look, don't worry about it," Mike said, "we don't get much news from the outside . . . and maybe it's better that way. You gotta concentrate on yourself, I know it sounds selfish, but you gotta get the legs going because that's the only thing that's going to get you outta here!"

"I know," I said, "it's just that sometimes I get the feeling that things are getting worse out there instead of better—"

"Ah, the friggin' world's never going to learn any better!" Mike cursed. "Everyday there's a new patient, a new battered kid. If it isn't polio or MD or palsy it's what we do to each other. That's the worst kind of sickness. Somebody out there is always cracking a kid's head: parents, cops, teachers, you name it, the name of the game sure ain't love. It's the opposite. And that's why we're here, in one way or another that's why we're here. We're in limbo, it seems, the only time we get news is when somebody new comes in . . ."

"And the few letters—" I thought aloud.

"Ah, you can't depend on the letters," Mike said, "they don't really tell us the truth . . . they can't. Now that big fight you said the people were having against the bosses up north, I'm sure there's going to be some people killed, but they can't tell us about it . . . news will trickle in as new cases come in from the north, but that's it. Damn, I'd like to be back there now! It seems like there's finally some changes taking place. I wouldn't mind getting busted up for that!" he smiled.

"How about your father?" I asked, "Doesn't he live up north?"

"Yeah," Mike frowned, "but that old bastard wouldn't raise a hand to help anybody. I haven't seen him since I landed here. When I was at the other hospital, the one for burns, he came by once, drunk as a skunk, had a whore with him, and they were living it up. He came in trying to act concerned, telling her I was his only son and how proud he was of me and asking me if I needed anything to let him know, he'd take care of it. He gave me a few bucks and told me to buy something. Boy, did that piss me off! I was burned clean to the bone, bleeding, the grafts they were trying to sew on weren't sticking . . . I mean I was just that far away from having the legs sawed off because the infection was spreading. I sat up in bed and I cursed him till my nose bled and I passed out. I swore I was going to get my legs in shape just to kick his ass! I got so angry it seemed the anger was a reason for living. I started telling myself I'm going to get better, I'm going to get better, and I did. The old bastard doesn't know it, but he saved my life. He forced me to be angry enough to live . . . Now I don't care about kicking his ass anymore . . . I don't care about him. I just want to get back home and make a new life for myself . . . find that girl of my dreams," he grinned.

At the same time Ronco and Sadsack came in, complaining about the visitors who had shown up for visitors day.

"I wish they'd stay away period!" Sadsack cursed and nervously fiddled with Buck's radio. We knew he was angry because he had expected his parents to come.

"Hey, don't mess up my station, Sad! Took me a week to get it right!" Buck grabbed his radio. Samson had wired the antenna wire around the traction bars so the reception improved, but the only stations we could get alternated between an evangelical hill billy preacher trying to save us from damnation and the cat-wailing of what Ronco called sad-ass western blues.

"What happened?" Mike asked.

"No one showed up," Ronco said.

"Little old ladies showed up!" Sadsack corrected him, "and they spent their time telling the kids that all this is God's will being done! Damn!"

"Take it easy," Ronco tried to calm him, "it's good for the small kids to have visitors—it's not our fault your folks didn't show."

"Ah! It's depressing!" Sadsack mumbled. He turned the radio dial and for a moment the radio whined, there was garbled static and a voice we had never heard before broke through. We held our breath. We thought he had found a new station. Then the voice faded and the hill billy evangelist shouted his Sunday sermon at us. "Screw you!" Sadsack said and turned him off.

"It's hard for poor people to make the trip," Mike said.

Sadsack turned and looked at us. "My mother used to come . . . she used to come every Sunday. She used to bring me candy, spending money for cigarettes— I didn't mind being sick then. Then she came only once a month, then she stopped coming altogether. We used to sit and look at each other. After awhile there was nothing to say. It's the same way with everybody here, I've seen it heppen. First they come to visit every week, then once a month, then not at all. They start looking at their watches, making excuses for not coming, then they forget—"

"Nobody comes to see me," Danny said. He had sneaked quietly into the room. He stood by the door.

"Who wants to visit a bunch of cripples?"

"They have their world, we have ours— Before I got sick I never saw cripples. Where were they? Did they stay home? Do they come out only at night?"

"They're ashamed to be seen," someone said.

"They don't feel ashamed!" Mike cut in. "Look at me. When I get out I'm not going to shut myself in a dark room. No sir! I'm going to walk the streets! I'm going to be proud and walk tall!" He said it for the few small kids who had gathered in the room.

"Bullshit!" Sadsack said, "It ain't that easy!"

"You gotta trust in God," Danny said defiantly. He looked at Sadsack and scratched his arm. It was encrusted with scabs and dirt. Danny had turned to religion in an effort to understand what was happening to him. He walked around reading the Bible, and he stopped kids in the hallway and read passages to them. He ordered *The Awakening*, a newsletter put out by a religious group, and he read it avidly. He was looking for a clue which would point to a cure for his arm. He knew in detail the stories of every cripple in the Bible. "Did you know that Job limped," he would say, or "Lot's wife was pigeon-toed." Of course he was making it up and nobody believed him.

One of the janitors had told Danny about a holy church up north to which people made pilgrimages to effect cures. He said they walked miles to that holy place, some doing the last two or three miles on their knees, praying rosaries and novenas. The miraculous thing about the small church was a small room near the sacristy where years ago a priest had dug a hole in the floor because he was told in a vision that the earth which came from that hole was holy. Since then people had been visiting the church to cover their sores and twisted limbs and every kind of infirmity with the holy sand, and many had been cured. Everyone who made the pilgrimage came away with a Kerr pint jarful of the holy sand, and after millions of scoops of sand the hole was still at its original level. It could not be emptied.

Danny believed the story. He got hold of the church's address and wrote the priest, and the priest said yes, for five bucks he would send Danny a pint of holy sand, with the understanding that when Danny was out of the hospital he still owed a pilgrimage to the church. So we all chipped in to help Danny buy the curing sand. The day the jar full of sand arrived Danny was ecstatic with joy. He praised the Lord and cried that surely now he would be cured of the strange illness which was withering his arm. He began to bathe his arm with the holy earth, but all it did was dirty up the scabs and sores he had scratched open. When Steel found out what Danny was doing he was furious, but by that time Danny had already been using the holy sand for two weeks and a strange mold had begun to grow on his arm, irritating the disease and spreading it faster.

"Trust in God?" Ronco laughed, "sometimes I think God doesn't give a damn about this place! He's forgotten it!"

"He sure doesn't visit here anymore!" Sadsack laughed.

"Not even on Sundays!" Mike cracked.

"Don't say that!" Danny pleaded. He looked at us with a worried expression. Then curiousity got the best of his faith and he asked, "Why doesn't He visit here?"

"Because He's afraid of getting polio!" Ronco winked.

13

"So it was Danny who spread the rumor that God doesn't visit the hospital anymore, you see, because God's afraid of getting polio . . . Can you imagine that? God afraid of getting polio! Oh wow, that Danny is one crazy bird! You gotta watch him. They got hold of the preacher, you know, the skinny one that comes up from town on Sunday mornings to teach Bible study; they cornered him and demanded to know why God wasn't visiting here anymore. Mudo and Tuerto held him against the wall while Danny stuck that ugly arm of his right under the Reverend's nose. Oh, they were mad. They were mad because they were afraid, right, afraid that if God's not coming around anymore then there's no hope for them. And the preacher knew they were mad because he got real red and began to shake . . . I would too, you know, cause Danny and those two monkey friends of his are crazy, bone crazy!

"You know what they did last year? They found the hospital's main switch and turned it off on operating day . . . On operating day, can you imagine? Damn, the whole place went dead . . . numb as a new polio case. The lights went out and Steel and his crew shit purple. I would too, you know, I mean it's no fun to be splicing nerves and have the lights go out, right? Course they turned it back on, but the doctors and everybody else around here went bananas for a few seconds. Danny was getting even with the doctors cause they wouldn't tell him why his arm is drying up, and of course they don't know. It's one of those strange things they can't find an answer to. Have you seen it lately? It's turning dry and brown like an old tree branch. First it was just his hand, now the damn curse has spread up his entire arm. And the more it crawls up his arm the weirder Danny gets; he says God has cursed him. So that's why he panicked when he heard God wasn't coming around anymore: no God no cure, right? Anyway, that's what Danny thinks. You know, he's spending all his free time in the art room, painting pictures of Christ, God-awful pictures. He paints Christ all twisted up and bleeding, and he even paints a withered arm on the poor man. You know why, don't you? Cause the preacher told Danny that if Christ had lived after they nailed him to the cross he would have been a cripple, like us. Can you imagine that? A cripple like us. Maybe then we'd get better food around here, I mean if the Christians thought we were made in the image of a crippled Christ. But it makes a little bit of sense, doesn't it? I mean, he would have been crippled the way those nails tore into his feet, and he'd probably have to lop up his food with his wrists, like Sadsack, cause his hands would be all broken. But the truth is the poor man didn't live. He died. There's the hope he will rise again, and if he does then so will all cripples . . . I think that's why Danny's painting the pictures, to find some kind of resurrection for the poor man. Now he's got the art room full of these giant pictures of the bleeding, crippled Christ, I mean the poor man is really torn up, mangled, surrounded by soldiers and people poking him with spears, cutting at his arms and legs . . . It's awful. I can't go in there anymore. I used to enjoy going in there and trying to paint by holding the brush in my mouth, and I was getting pretty good . . . but I can't go in there anymore. It's like a horror show. And Danny's like a madman who thinks he can give the painting some sort of life so his crippled Christ will just get up and walk . . . it's scary. Anyway, what was I saying? Oh yeah, about Danny and his pals cornering the preacher. And he finally came up with an answer . . . course those guys are trained to come up with answers, even if they're not true. He said Christ wasn't afraid of polio, in fact Christ invented polio! Yeah, he gave them a big sermon about how Christ was the first polio case in recorded history. He said it was a mild case, didn't need an iron lung, but he did have to go to a sanitorium, just like this one. He said right in the middle of the desert of Galilee there was a hospital like this one . . . and during those missing years in the Bible when nobody knew where Christ was, the preacher said Christ was really at the hospital getting over his case of polio . . . Can you imagine that? Christ crossing the desert with Filomón! Oh, it's too much, but that preacher had a theory . . . I mean, there must be a million theories to explain what Christ did during those years he's missing. But it makes some sense, right? I mean, if he was afflicted then that's why he chose to walk among the crippled and lame! He was their champion! He was their hero! I mean, here's a guy that's saying he is the son of God and he's hanging around with the cripples, the freaks, the dwarfs, the lepers, the prostitutes with VD, the real people, you know . . . I believed part of the preacher's theory, you know why? Cause I always pictured Christ as a poor man with a limp, maybe a club foot or a break that didn't heal right, I don't know why, but I did . . . Then Danny stuck his fingers under the preacher's nose and demanded to know why God wasn't visiting us anymore. They even threatened the man with the Committee—"

"What committee?" Buck interrupted.

"Why there's only one Committee, brother, it's the Committee for Crippled Children and Orphans. Don't you know, it runs the hospital.

Why even the Director and the doctors have to report to the Committee. The Committee is assigned by the state to run the hospital, to watch over us . . . it's really a bunch of old ladies who don't have anything else to do so the governor appoints them to serve on the Committee to run the hospital. They meet once a month . . . and we can go tell them about our problems, but it never does any good . . . it's just a little game to make us feel better. Once in awhile they make rounds with the doctors, pat the little kids on the head and tell them if they're good they'll be better in no time . . . bullshit, you know. Maybe you haven't seen them because they don't come around where Mike and Ronco sack out. They know those two won't stand for any bullshit. At Christmas they throw a big party for us . . . Hey? Weren't you here for the last one?"

"Nah," Buck answered lazily. "But what did the preacher do?"

"The preacher? Oh, he got scared. He trembled and shook. Anyway, Danny and his friends swallowed the preacher's story hook, line and sinker. By the time he finished his sermon they were beating their breasts and shouting hell-leh-loo-yah! I believe, brother! I believe if you believe! I believe Christ was a poor, orphaned cripple who died and will rise again to care for us! His chosen people! It was awful . . . They were beating their breasts, pulling at their hair, throwing themselves on the floor and squirming and rolling and shouting . . . I couldn't stand it, I left. Right when the preacher was shouting that we should spread the word that Christ is coming to free us all. He will enter every heart that's open to him . . ."

"Is that when Danny got the saw?" Buck asked lazily. He played with the radio knob, but nothing was coming in.

"Yeah, you know how Danny gets everything ass-backwards, especially now that he's got religion . . . so he and the gruesome twosome thought the preacher meant cut everybody free! They broke into a surgical cabinet and stole a saw, the kind that's used for cutting casts, and for a couple of hours they went around the wards cutting open every friggin' cast they could find! Then they started sending everyone who would go to the recreation room because by that time they really believed that's where the second coming would take place . . . and that's when the day Nurse got suspicious. Here were all these kids showing up in the recreation room without their casts! It was like a circus! Even Cynthia's bunch was there, and they only come out at night. I'm telling you, you gotta watch that crazy Danny! Boy were the doctors mad when they caught him. They gave the Nurse hell and she turned around and gave Danny the old castor oil treatment. She locked all three of them up for a week and pumped them full of castor oil. She was giving them that stuff in their breakfast cereal, in their milk, in everything! And when they wouldn't eat anything she had old man Maloney hold them and she forced the stuff down their throats. Oh, were they sick! They looked awful when she finally let them loose."

"Did Danny learn his lesson?" Buck asked.

"Hell no. You know Danny, never learns. Well, brothers, I've enjoyed rapping with you, but I gotta get to therapy. You know KC, she don't wait for no one. See you in the funny papers . . . ."

I heard the wheelchair squeak out of the room. "Who was that?" I asked Buck.

"I don't know," Buck answered, "never saw him before."

I had been listening to bits of the story, weaving them into my thoughts, thinking about Filomón taking Christ across the desert to a hospital with its adobe colored, cracked walls shimmering in the desert heat, the green of palms suggesting water, and to the south the dead salt sea. In every time, in every place, a desert, a sanitorium for those crippled by the pharaohs, a gathering of twisted bodies reeking sweat, sore feet cut by the desert, and the doctors and attendants waiting by the huge wooden door which sagged and weathered with age . . . there was an Ismelda there, at the door, waiting, smiling, her seven bracelets jangling in the cool breeze, tinkling to the tune of the camel harnesses and the squeaking leather of the donkey saddle . . . broken bodies of men, old warriors, young boys, the outcasts, Christ the cripple himself, slightly bent from the germ of polio, perhaps twitching with the fever of the desert or the epilepsy which at times fell over him like the wrath of God . . . What did it mean? Ismelda smiled. The date palm was heavy with fruit . . . bees buzzed in the sun. It was a journey, and I had come to one station, and this young woman of the desert who bathed me with the water from the springs and dried my broken body with her long, dark hair was mine. I would take her with me. Come with me, I said and reached for her hand . . . she was a desert bride, clothed in a flowing white gown. My white stallion waited nervously, pawing the wet earth of the oasis pool, anxious to feel my weight and the weight of my bride, ready for flight across the desert.

"Come with me," I said.

"What?" Mike asked.

"Tortuga's talking to himself again," Ronco grinned.

"He goes like that all day," Buck laughed, "and I have to be shut up with him. Sometimes I don't know if he's talking to me or to God . . . and he tells weird stories. Man, I sure do wish I could lasso me one of those chairs and take a ride . . . Hey! Where you two been?"

"Girls' ward," Mike smiled.

"But I thought that was off limits!" Buck cried. He could sit up now, but he was still completely bandaged. When his eyes opened wide in surprise he reminded me of the Halloween ghosts children draw in grade school.

"What's off limits?" Sadsack asked. He had followed Mike and Ronco into the room.

"The girls' ward! These two have been over there!" Buck exclaimed.

"So what else is new?" Sadsack scowled. "Ronco's girl is as ugly as a horse!" He twisted his rubbery lips into a grin. "And Mike's girl has only one leg! They're all like that over there!"

"Who cares!" Buck groaned, "We're no Hollywood heroes! Just seeing a woman would get my rocks off!"

"You see the Nurse everyday," Sadsack smiled.

"That's not a woman! That's a battle tank!"

"Tortuga's the lucky one, he's got Ismelda looking after him," Ronco teased.

"And he's got KC rubbing him every day!" Buck exclaimed. "Oh is she built like a brick shithouse! I can hardly wait to get to therapy with her! And I'd like to get me a chair!"

"You'll get there," Mike said, "but you gotta work at it—"

"Damn, this room stinks . . . Danny been here?"

"Smells like fish—"

"Get back to the girls," Buck cut in, "how are they?"

"They won't win any beauty contests, but they're real women. They take care of us and we take care of them."

I stopped listening and watched the sunset on Tortuga. Franco had a song which compared the color on the mountain when the sun set to the color of the blood of Christ. I never thought of the red color as the bright red of blood, for me it was the red of an ember which slowly turned to ripe apricot. The soft pastel lilacs grew mauve and seemed to glow from within the mountain, and as the colors changed the mountain seemed to move. He drew in his huge legs and head and settled easily into the earth. It was time to rest, and a time to remember home. The ward usually grew quiet at sunset. Sometimes someone would call down the hall that the mountain was moving, and that was always a good omen, because good luck always followed the movement of the mountain.

14

The Committee met one cold, gusty day. Our hunch-back, crippled mountain raised his head to look at the gaggle of old women that came yackity-yaking down the hall. He blinked his leathery eyelids and went back to sleep. There was no hope in the powdered, wrinkled faces and the thin lips painted red. Their cheap perfume mixing with the stale urine smell of the hospital made my stomach churn.

I wondered how they had crossed the desert . . . Did they come with Filomón, singing siren songs across the sand dunes which looked like sea waves? Or did they come alone, driving the large, black state cars which came from time to time to the hospital? They made the rounds of our ward, cackling like old witches, touching my cheeks with bony fingers, asking me what I needed, promising to deliver everything . . . I knew they lied. They were the same women I had seen in air-conditioned homes with rich carpets and expanses of lawns to break the monotony of the sand which drifted around the city. They drove their cars with windows locked so they could not smell the stench. They wore dark glasses and did not see the crippling of the orphans . . .

Tears filled my eyes. Ismelda was quickly at my side. She touched my forehead and I felt better. Oh, Tortuga, she said with her eyes of love, you were born to feel too deeply . . . Then she straightened my sheets and pillow to try to make me forget the bad memories, and she sat by the side of the bed and tried as best she could to ease the itching I felt inside the cast. She cooled it with alcohol. The inside of my shell was rotting, like Danny's arm. It itched inside and tormented me, a torment worse than pain, a punishment which couldn't be relieved.

Just wait till spring, Salomón said, in the spring all turtles throw off their shells and become lizards, like snakes sluffing off their skins, like butterflies leaving their cocoons, like the earth shuddering after a long winter's sleep . . . then the sun returns and warms the sand and the naked lizards run and play with each other, run in the sand and make love! Oh, just wait till spring, Tortuga!

98

"Do you know what Salomón said?" I asked Ismelda.

"About lizards?" she smiled. "He calls me a lizard woman because I'm thin and I like to run in the sun."

"I want to run in the sun too—"

"You will," she assured me, "you will . . ."

"In the spring—"

"Yes," she nodded, "in the spring." Her dark eyes grew sad. "Believe in what Salomón says . . . believe his stories."

"I do," I answered, "they come like whispers in my dreams . . ." She smiled, touched my cheek and was gone.

A few moments later Mike and Ronco came roaring into the room, cursing like mad hummingbirds.

"Hey! What's up?" Buck asked.

"Ah, those damn old biddies!" Mike swore and tossed the papers he had shown the Committee on the bed. Then he swung and hit the nightstand as hard as he could.

"What they do?" Buck asked.

"They didn't," Ronco explained, "they didn't do anything about Jerry. They said it was his fault. He ran away when he had everything he needed right here. One of them said, 'Runaways are inexcusable, you boys have everything you need right here. Runaways will not be tolerated'." He mimiced a shrill voice. "Oh, you should have seen the smile on the Director's face. Got him off the hook. Steel suggested a few things, but he doesn't count. He's only a doctor. He's supposed to cut and splice us together, but he doesn't have anything to say about the way the hospital is run. That's a matter for the state!"

"So whad you do?"

"We protested, but it didn't do any good. Everybody started shouting, but they wouldn't listen . . ."

"Danny jumped in front of them and shouted:

Order in the court!
Order in the court!
The judge is eating beans!
The Committee's in the toilet,
Making submarines!"

"The Nurse carted him off for another dose of castor oil . . ."

"That's the trouble with these people!" Mike cursed, "They think a bowel movement is a goddamned cure for everything! I swear I was nearly dead the day I got here, and the Nurse held my wrist, looked at her watch and asked me, 'Have you had your bm today?' Damn! I nearly fainted."

He made us laugh with his imitation of the Nurse. Ronco picked it up and sang, " A bm a day makes all your headaches go a-wayyy—Lotta doo-doo . . ."

"Regulars make better lovers!" Buck chimed in, "and better cowboys!"

Even Sadsack joined the chorus. His long, awkward hands beat the nightstand for a beat as he sang, "A bm a day will help us all walk away . . . yaaaah man!"

"It gets rid of acne, blackheads, club feet and sooo-rye-es-sessss!"

"It chases the blues awayyyy . . ."

" . . . and the long and restless lonely nights . . ."

"It helps us make it through the day . . ."

> *Adn when you get to heaven*
> *and St. Peter meets you at the gate*
> *The first thing he'll ask is:*
> *'Have you had your bm today?'*

We laughed at the crazy words and the improvised, snappy tune. Even Mike smiled.

"How in the hell do they expect us to be regular if they don't feed us soul food, huh? I haven't had a good meal of chile and beans since I got here! That's what Jerry was trying to tell them, there was nothing for his soul here . . . sure the medical care is the best in the world, but what good does that do you if your spirit is dying . . ."

"I can believe that," Ronco agreed. "When I go home my old man pinches me and says I'm too thin and pale, then he tosses me in the jeep and we go down to Hondo and buy a fat lamb from Casi, an old Indian who has a little flock there, and we take it back to the cabin where he hangs it by its hind legs, and I hold the bucket for the blood—sometimes we bring some big mamasan who wants to eat, drink and screw with us, and we'll fry up a batch of blood pudding, fried with onions, a little oregano . . . ah, that's living! And we throw the sheep's head in the oven so by late evening it's well done, and we sit around drinking wine and picking at the bits of meat, the eyes, slicing the tongue for sandwiches, and when that's done we split the head open and spread the brain on tortillas, salt it down and eat till it's coming out of our ears! That stuff is good for the pecker too . . ."

Sadsack twisted his face and spit. "You must be half Indian, Ronco . . ."

"No lie," Ronco smiled. "Ain't we all half something or other?" He winked. "And later we make menudo—"

"What's that?"

"It's a soup made with the sheep's tripe—"

100

"Aow, damn!" Sadsack gagged.

"Yeah, you clean out the intestines real good, cook them all day with some red chile, a little oregano, maybe some posole if you want it thick, and man, that's a meal for the gods . . ."

. . .Menudo was the meal of the dark gods, Tortuga, and in ancient times it was made from the flesh of young virgins, young women who had been sacrificed to the sun . . . man ate the flesh of his own kind, made the stew from tender pieces of the virgin's thighs . . . the priests misled them. They told the people the sun needed blood, and it wasn't true. The sun only needed love to speed it on its way . . .

"And we're still sacrificing each other—"

"What you say, Tortuga?"

"He's talking to himself again."

"Hey, remember the truck load of turtle soup that overturned on the highway just south of here? They were going to lose it anyway, so they donated it to the hospital and for weeks we ate nothing but turtle soup and stew! God, it was awful! The chunks of green meat tasted like it wasn't dead yet! It gave me the creeps . . . I felt like I was eating something alive . . ."

"I swore I'd never eat turtle soup again!"

"Hey, how do you feel about that, Tortuga? You're a turtle. How would you feel about getting cut up in little pieces and dumped into the soup?" They looked my way and laughed.

"That's what la Llorona will do if she gets hold of you. Snip, one cut and she makes soup out of the old tool."

"That old wailing woman's not going to get Tortuga, brothers, cause he's got Ismelda to take care of him. She's not goin' let no Llorona get her baby!"

They laughed.

"How do you know Ismelda's not la Llorona? She lives near the river, doesn't she? Some of the janitors say she and Josefa are witches."

"Hey, she's not a witch, ask Salomón."

"Ah, what does he know!" Sadsack frowned. "I'm tired of listening to his stories. What good do they do?"

"Pass the time," Ronco said.

They didn't know. They didn't understand what Salomón was working. Perhaps it wasn't affecting them, but I felt it was drawing me into a complex web. Somehow Ismelda and Salomón and Filomón and all the others I had met were bound together, and the force created was sucking me into it. When Ismelda sat by me I felt another presence hovering over us. When I looked into her eyes I often saw the outline of the mountain. When I asked her questions she would smile and tell me that my concern should be with getting well. But I had the vague, uneasy feeling that other things were in store for me.

" . . . You'll never change as long as you're meat eaters," Danny said. He had come into the room unobserved.

"So I'm a meat eater," Ronco shrugged, "what difference does it make if you eat meat or vegetables? Vegetables feel the same as animals. How do you know when you take a bite into a carrot that that poor carrot isn't going 'Ouch, ouch, here come the big, bad cutting teeth!' "

"Ohhhh my —"

"But that's besides the point. Everything gets used in one way or another, right? Salomón said it's *how* it gets taken in that's important. Does anybody remember what he said?"

I listened carefully. I thought I heard Salomón say, we're all bound together, one great force binds us all, it's the light of the sun that binds all life, the mountain and the desert, the plains and the sea. I listened, and the stories came clearly and vividly, as if I was there at the time the story took place, that's how good Salomón was when he told a story. I listened, and time ceased to flow; it became the light of the sun; it became a liquid in which we all swam. Sometimes I worried, because I found myself struggling to leave the vortex of time the story created. I worried because I was afraid to remain fixed forever in the story being told. Sometimes I looked around me and thought that everyone would remain forever in the hospital, that no one was ever really going to get out, that we had created our own time and place and nobody was breaking free. Were we one of Salomón's stories, and would he let us free when he was ready?

When I felt like that I pushed harder to get out, and I made KC push harder. I swallowed the pain and begged for extra time in therapy.

"You're working too hard," she said, and surprised me because I never expected that from her.

"I want out," I said.

"I know," she nodded, "but sometimes you work your body to a peak . . . then it drops. You have to know that there's highs and lows . . ."

"I've had my low," I said, "I want a high . . . and that's going to come the day I walk out of here . . ."

When she was done Ismelda would come in and bathe my sweating body. She massaged my tired muscles with a special ointment Josefa had given me. I was growing stronger every day. Dr. Steel said it was a miracle.

"You're going to beat a lot of these sadsacks out of here," he smiled.

"I have good help," I answered.

"It's more than that—" he nodded vaguely in the direction of Salomón's ward.

"What?" I asked.

He muttered something and walked away. He didn't know.

"It's your destiny," Ismelda whispered as she rubbed my legs. "Every person has a destiny which follows him like a shadow. And every destiny must be fulfilled . . ."

"But what is mine?" I asked.

"You will know when you meet it," she said, "you might try to fight it, at first you might not accept it, but you can never escape it . . ."

"Does it have to do with what has happened to me?" I wondered. Is coming to the hospital part of my destiny, and how do you and Salomón and the mountain fit into my destiny? I knew Salomón held the key to my questions; I had to see him, I had to talk to him.

You know, I said, my grandfather believed in the destiny. He said some men are born to a good destiny. He told me the story about a man he knew at El Puerto who was like that. It seemed that everything the man touched turned to good luck. When the years of drought came a spring appeared on this man's land, and his herds increased and he made money while others were going broke. In the summer the worms came and ruined the herds that were left, but his weren't infected. He took life easy, while others slaved just to keep their families alive, he gambled every night at the saloon and never lost. He became very rich, and he had many beautiful women. He was robbed once and left for dead by the bandits, but he recovered and in a few months he made twice over the amount he had lost. In other ways, he lost his fortune many times, but it always kept coming back to him. He bought worthless land and in a year the railroad was built on it and he was rich again. Some people said he had sold his soul to the devil, but that wasn't what my grandfather said, it was just that the man was destined to be lucky and he wasn't afraid of his destiny. That man met his destiny face to face, and he was in harmony with it.

So maybe destiny does hover over us, I said to myself, maybe Salomón's cosmic kiss is another form or a part of that force, maybe Jerry's path of the sun is the road to know your destiny. I thought and remembered that I had often felt a force directing my life. At first I thought it was God. The force would move, like the soft fanning of swirling wings, it would call to me, and it would lead me to see things I would otherwise have missed. There seemed to be a purpose behind the smallest incident. So maybe there was a reason for my stay at the hospital. But what was it? And who knew? Salomón knew. So I spoke to him about the afternoon Ramón's father was killed on the Agua Negra ranch.

A spring afternoon thundershower had just moved across the llano, leaving the earth cool and wet. Raindrops glittered on the mesquite bushes and on the snakeweed. A giant rainbow lit up the dark bank of clouds as they moved eastward. The rain had passed quickly, as it does on the open llano, coming suddenly without a groan, with the stillness, then the cool breeze, and then the quick deluge. It left a fresh silence in which meadowlarks called and mockingbirds answered them. Isolated raindrops still fell to the earth as I ran across the field toward Ramón's home. Ramón's father stood in the middle of the field he was plowing. Like me, he had not sought cover from the rain. We were drenching wet but happy because of the rain. I remember waving and running towards him to ask for Ramón. I ran on the damp, just-plowed furrows, feeling my shoes grow heavy with the red clay that stuck to them. I was only a few feet away from him when I heard my name called. I stopped and looked up in time to see the grey-flint clouds strike a flash of fire, then an angry, twisting snake flashed out of the dark clouds and thrashed its way violently into the wet earth. It was so close I could smell the fresh current of air it created, and I could see the blue sparks which sputtered alive. Ramón's father saw it too. I saw him frown, as if he knew some wrong had been done and a small mistake was about to catch up with him. His movement away from the plow shook raindrops from his tanned face. One hand moved as if to caution me away. Fear clouded his eyes and he tried to turn so I wouldn't see, but I was too close, I saw what I had never seen before in a man's eyes. He lifted one foot from the wet clay, but he never brought it down. Suddenly the earth stood still, a breeze stirred like a rattlesnake about to strike, the sun glistened over the edges of the dark clouds and made the light so vivid and alive I thought I could touch it, like one touches water or fire. Then the snake-lightning which had disappeared into the wet ground reared out of the earth in a blinding flash of fire and blew Ramón's father out of his shoes. He was dead when he hit the ground. He was dead before the scream could work loose from my frozen throat. The plow horses clawed frantically at the air, then bolted and ran. Now the fresh smell of earth after the rain was tinged with the odor of singed flesh, and my mouth grew sour with a sharp, metallic taste.

Later they said the only trace of how death entered were the two small holes burned at the bottom of his feet, but I had seen him glow with the fire of the lightning . . . and for a long time I couldn't forget the empty, mud-caked shoes. They said I had been lucky not to get hit.

For the first time since I entered the hospital I was remembering the past, trying to isolate those times when my destiny had hovered over me like my guardian angel . . . I had escaped the train which severed Sabino's leg the day we were laying pennies on the track . . . a thick tree had cushioned the fall from the river cliff the day we found Jason's Indian dead . . . I turned at the sound which exploded in my ears like a cannon to see Joey's surprised look, the smoking pistol on his lap, the bullet buried in the wall inches from my head . . . the nights in the streets, and the revolution which had swept around me like a fire on the llano, even the paralysis was a part of that, and still I was alive, for some purpose I was alive and my strength was growing day by day . . .

"There must be a purpose to all this . . ." I said.

"Yes!" Danny shouted triumphantly. "God's will be done! Glory be, brother!"

"Bull," Sadsack scoffed, "you find it and I'll believe it . . . but it's got to be in black and white, none of this spiritual crap Danny's into!"

"Be careful," Mike whispered, "find whatever you want to believe in, but don't go getting any ideas the Old Man upstairs is personally interested in what happens to you . . . it could mean trouble for you, none for Him, cause either way He is or He ain't, and it's us that suffer. There's only one rule: get out of here. Get out anyway you can, but get out!"

"There must be a reason for all this!" Danny insisted. "The Bible says not a sparrow will fall—" and he turned and looked at his withered arm and groaned as if in pain.

Somewhere Franco sang:

And where have you been my crippled son
And what have you seen my twisted, young one . . .

"He doesn't have the time to look over us!" Mike said emphatically. "If he did this goddamned mess would have been over long ago! We're on our own! That's all there is to it!"

"He sends us signs . . ." Danny whimpered and looked at me. I shivered.

"The only thing your arm means is you should quit playing with yourself!" Sadsack laughed.

"It's a sign!" Danny insisted and jumped up.

"From who? Answer me that! From who? Is God a crazy scientist working up there in his laboratory, mixing up batches of little germs and spraying them on us to watch us jump? Or is he still experimenting with life, trying to make us better? What kind of sign is all this goddamned suffering?"

"I don't know," Danny moaned. He twisted away and faced the wall. We were silent. No one knew the answer.

Mike finally broke the silence. "Look, I'm not saying for sure He's not up there, but if He is He just doesn't have the time to watch this little, god-forsaken place! I mean there must be thousands of hospitals like this scattered around the world! Millions and millions of cripples, orphans, deformed rejects, each with his own private story to tell God, each with his own reason about his disease . . . And I don't think God has the time to listen."

"The other theory is if he is everywhere, then he is us, and if he is us then we require no explanation. We simply are . . . and we happen to be here."

"Oh my . . . we are, just simply here, no reason . . ."

"I think he doesn't have the time to listen to us because he's too busy playing pool," Ronco suggested and winked.

"What's that supposed to mean?" Danny asked.

"I think the old man's a pool shark, you see, and the way this universe got started was when God chalked up and broke for the first time. Of course the game was billiards at first, cause they only had four suns to play with, but the minute he rammed that first sun which was his cue ball into the others then everything exploded and all sorts of universes were born . . . of course the game became eight-ball after that because now the sky was full of worlds. Well, it was a big surprise to God and his opponent when the whole sky blew up and became more complicated. God just stood back and laughed, and he lit a cigar . . . when you see a falling star that's just God lighting up his cigar . . . so he's chalking up and looking across the table at his opponent—"

"Wait a minute!" Danny interrupted, "Who's the opponent? Who's God playing pool with?" I looked sideways and saw that Danny was trembling. He was really afraid of the answer but he wanted it nevertheless. "Answer me dammit! Who?" he shouted.

"Take it easy, Danny, let him finish the story," Mike said. We were all interested in Ronco's story.

"Well, that's all there is to it," Ronco grinned. "It's his opponent's shot. The thing you have to remember is that shot was made at the beginning of the universe, and during all that time the balls have been exploding out across the table, settling into galaxies, universes, worlds which grew little plants on them then men like us . . . but for God and his opponent all that time has been only a few minutes, and they're so big they can't see us crawling around those little worlds that serve their pool game . . . it's just a game to them. They're standing across the smoke-filled room from each other, eyeballing each other, trying to hustle each other. It's big stakes they're playing for up there, control of all space and time, not just us little piss ants on this world . . . God tried to set up a few rules to play the game, but if that other guy outshoots him then it's the end, cause his opponent don't care for rules . . . He just wants to bring everything crashing down!"

"My, my," Billy mumbled, "I never thought of it that way . . ."

"You been reading too much science fiction, pardner," Buck grinned. "Why everybody knows God's not a city slicker, a pool hustler! Why he's a cowboy, and all those stars are his cattle. And when he starts the round-up, watch out! There's going to be hell to pay, he's going to put his brand on everybody, rich or poor, saint or sinner, there's going to be jangling of spurs for music and dust and turmoil . . . but God's going to watch out for all his dogies, you bet. Yahoooo! And I'm going to be riding with him!" He tossed his hat in the air, and because he was sitting up he came close to tumbling off the bed.

"Watch it!" Mike shouted. Buck balanced himself, put his hat back on and sat back in bed. He looked like a mummy with a cowboy hat on.

"I think God's an old guy just sitting on top of a mountain, all by himself, just watching us do our crazy things," Mike said and made up a story for the occasion. "Once in a while he gets lonely and he comes down to earth to mess around . . . that's where we get all these virgin births from. And as soon as he gets tired he hightails it back up the mountain to rest . . ."

"He's supposed to have everything he wants, right?" Sadsack asked, "so why should he come down?"

"Ah, a beautiful woman can draw even God off the mountain," Mike smiled. "Their little garden is what makes the world go around. Ask Tortuga . . . Ismelda's got him ready to climb out of the bed and get it on!" They laughed.

"Hey, Tortuga, what do you think of all these stories?"

I didn't answer. I didn't know or I wasn't ready to answer. I knew I had prayed and there had been no answer, that faith in the old powers was as dry as dust. I knew I had to find something to hold on to, we all did, but I wasn't quite sure what it was. The hospital and the desert which surrounded it seemed to be hopeless, and beyond that the world I had known before the hospital seemed to have only pockets of love fighting against a huge machinery which crushed everything. Here, at least, there was Ismelda, and Salomón, Mike and the other kids, and the doctors who helped . . .

" . . . You gotta remember, God doesn't think like us."

"Oooh my—"

"He doesn't see good and evil the way we do . . . in fact he doesn't care about things like that. He's more interested in just running the universe . . ."

"Then he doesn't run our destiny?"

"No. In fact, he's busy enough trying to find his own destiny—"

"He runs mine!" Danny shouted. He started shaking and scratching his arm furiously. "I don't care what you say, but I know God runs my destiny! He tells me what to do! It's like the story Salomón told about the visitors from outer space who came down a long time ago and wired all the peoples' heads so they could control them! Well that's how I feel about God! He planted a little radio in my brain and I can hear his signals from heaven! Glory be! Hell-a-loo-jah! Sometimes I hear ringing in my ears, and I stop whatever I'm doing and I answer, 'Is that you God? Is that you?' "

"Take it easy, Danny! Quiet down or you'll get sick!" Mike grabbed him and tried to settle him down, but Danny squirmed like a fish to get free. White spittle formed at the edges of his twisted lips.

"I'm his radio and he's calling me!" Danny shouted, almost hysterical. "I will do his will! Come in, God! Come in! I hear you! Glory be! Glory be!" he shouted uncontrollably.

Mike couldn't hold him. So he hauled back and slapped him then pushed him against the bed and held him down.

107

"Take it easy, Danny! Get hold of yourself!"

Danny quit shouting. When he saw he couldn't break Mike's hold he relaxed and slid to the floor, whimpering crazily that he could hear God's signals from heaven. "I can hear the ringing in my ears," he cried.

We were silent and he settled down. Then Ronco said, "Danny, you can't believe everything you hear. You hear wild stories and you twist them up inside, you twist them to suit you. Don't you realize, if things don't make any sense then maybe they just don't, but don't go around trying to change them so they fit your thinking. That's what's getting you in trouble." He turned to us. "Last year we saw a movie about atoms in science class, and this crazy teacher tried to tell us that there's empty space between the electrons and the nucleus of the atom . . . he compared it to the space between the planets and the sun. So, he said, if all atoms are mostly empty space, then you should be able to walk through a wall by squeezing your atoms through the empty space, right? Well, it's stupid, but not for Danny. He tried it. For a whole month he went around walking into walls. Broke his nose twice!"

"The worst part of it was that he had all the other kids doing it too," Mike added. "Man, once a weirdo starts believing in something watch out! They're dangerous!"

"Someday I will be able to walk through a wall, and nobody will see me," Danny said and stood up. He was still trembling. He raised his withered arm and wiped his nose.

"You okay?" Mike asked.

"Yeah," Danny answered and dusted his pants.

"I didn't mean to rough you up, but you were getting wild—"

"I hear things," Danny muttered.

"Well, an atom ain't space," Buck said, "it's just an electric buzz . . . that's what you're hearing, Danny, your own atoms buzzing with electricity."

"Could be," Mike said, "everything's made of electricity—"

"Our bodies, our bones, our blood?"

"Oh my."

"Sure, we're just a walking battery, charged up with a positive and negative pole. When your battery runs down you get sick. Then you gotta charge it up, get the flow goin' again—"

"That's what Tortuga's doin' with the mountain, gettin' charged up, and with Ismelda and KC?"

"Maybe . . . but you have to do it. You gotta find that opposite charge that will get you going. That's what love is, attaching like a magnet!"

"Híjola! I can believe that!" Ronco laughed, "I got a positive pole looking for a charge all the time! Last night I dreamed I was in a cathouse where all the mamasotas were big and fat and juicy!"

"Ah, you're making it up!" Sadsack interrupted.

"I'm not making it up!" Ronco shot back, "It was a dream! It was real!"

"Bull! Bet you played with yourself and now you wanna make a big story out of it!"

"Isn't that what we all do?" Buck grinned. "We make big stories out of little jack-offs!"

We laughed and they went on arguing if dreams were real or not, but I wasn't listening. I was thinking about my own dreams, dreams I couldn't share with anyone. In the empty days and lonely nights that flowed over me like water I had sketched out the dreams of my destiny, and they all led to Ismelda's door. She was the woman I had met in many forms since I arrived at the hospital, and in some strange yet unfathomable way she was all the women who had touched my past and forced me to become a man. My mother. The old goat woman who nursed me. The girls who shared their first holy communion with me . . . there was a power there which filled my fever, but which I couldn't touch. Ismelda seemed to know something of that past, and she knew about the mountain.

In my dreams we sat on the river bank and I sang to her. She smiled as the river gurgled past us. Her long, dark hair covered our naked bodies. Later I tried to remember the words of the song, but I couldn't. I only knew it was a song of love. And when she came with Josefa to make the beds and mop the floors I wanted to tell her about my dream, but I couldn't. She took good care of me, always giving of herself, never forcing what I could not yet offer. And that is why I was so bothered, because I had nothing to give in return. Sometimes when I wanted to explain my love a lump formed at my throat and when I shouted only angry screams came out.

"What's the matter?" Josefa asked me when we were alone, "Don't you know she has fallen in love with you—"

"I know," I whispered.

"But you're afraid," she said, "well that's natural. You are afraid to tell her you love her, because you feel you have nothing to give . . . well, for a girl like Ismelda that is not important for now . . . She knows you need time to get well, she realizes your wounds go deep, and just like the body builds scars and callouses around its cuts and sores so the soul must build an invisible shell in times of pain and loss . . . We know the acid of life burns deep and hot, my God, we have been here a long, long time, and we have been in all the wards—" She stopped suddenly and looked at me.

"But you have to be careful," she cautioned, "that you don't shut yourself away forever. Ismelda's love is not an acid, but a cool liquid which heals. Her love is like the curing water of the mountain and its magic can lift you out of that smelly shell of yours. She is a strong girl, that one, and sensitive. She's got magic in her fingers, and she can help

109

you break that shell you're building, but you have to help her, you have to meet her halfway . . . otherwise, it's no good."

I knew what Josefa said was true. Ismelda's touch was magic on my paralyzed nerves. She rubbed my numb muscles every day with the ointment she said was made of goat fat and sweet herbs, and the massages soothed away the pain I felt after therapy. But I had nothing to give her in return, because my only drive was a selfish one, and that was to get out of the hospital as quickly as I could. Franco's song interrupted my thoughts:

Chains of love are rattling,
And lonely hearts are humming
Here and there, and everywhere
There's going to be some loving . . .

And Salomón said, yes Tortuga, love can be as devastating as the straitjacket of paralysis . . . it can numb a person and make him useless . . . but as mad a force as it is, we must trust it. In the end it is the light of the sun, it is the path Ismelda walks, it is the melody of song . . .

"Look, Tortuga," Mike said sternly when he got wind of my budding romance, "I don't care what you do or how you feel, that's your business, but don't ever forget that there's only one rule you gotta keep in front of all the rest, and that's to get out of this godforsaken place! Don't let anything else get in the way of that! Get out! Escape! You owe it to yourself; you owe it to us!"

"But why me?" I asked, angry at Mike for reminding me of the one, strict commandment he lived by, and suddenly angry at myself for asking "why me" again.

"Look around you," he whispered, "what is it that all these people have in common? The doctors, the nurses, the aides and orderlies, the janitors, everyone! Look closely, and you'll discover their secret! They're all cripples, Tortuga, in one way or another they're all cripples! Samson can't talk, Maloney's nearly blind, the Nurse has a slight limp, you can barely see it, but it's there. Look at all the janitors, everyone of them either limps, walks with braces or has a missing arm like Corto. Even the Director is a former polio case, oh he tries to hide it with those fancy suits he wears and by staying locked up in his office, but he's got the polio hands all right."

"So?" I asked, "So what? What does it mean?" He drew closer to the bed so no one else could hear him.

"I began to wonder about it when I first came here," he said, "so I did some snooping. One day I sneaked into the Director's office, there's where all the doctors' files are finally stored. Just for the hell of it, I flipped through a few names I knew, like Samson's and Maloney's and Speed-o's, and I found that at one time they had all been patients here! I

110

mean, I was surprised! This friggin' hospital's been here a long, long time, right? So I began to wonder who in the hell has ever left it. I asked Dr. Steel why some of the patients are allowed to work here after they're released, and he said it was common practice in most places like this to allow a kind of rehabilitation time . . . if they're not ready to go home, if they think they can't handle it, then they can stay around and do odd jobs till they're ready to go. But I don't think any of them go . . . maybe some drift down to the town below . . . but I don't know how many try to cross the desert on their own. My guess is very few . . . that's why I made the rule. Right then I knew we had to get out, and so every new kid that comes in gets burned with the rule: Get out!"

I was quiet for a long time, thinking about what he had said. It was true, though, that everyone was crippled. In one way or another everybody in the hospital was marked.

"And who's made it?" I asked.

Mike shook his head. "I can't think of anyone," he said, "I can't truthfully think of anyone. Some have gotten home leave, like Ronco, he gets to go home every summer, but he keeps winding up back here . . ." He cleared his throat. "You know they make it easy to stay. Hell, we have everything we need! Good medical care, good food, school, swimming pool, entertainment, everything! It's like a holiday in hell, right? After a while you get used to being here . . ."

"How about Steel?" I asked.

"He's different . . . he came from the east, I think."

"And Josefa? Ismelda?"

"Josefa hobbles, arthritis, maybe rheumatism . . . she's been in the valley a long time. I don't know. Ismelda? She's the only hope."

"So she can help . . ."

"It's not that simple," Mike said, "don't you see, they all help us. Sometimes they help us too much! That's the point. They know we're in pain, so they try to make us comfortable, and the more comfortable we become the less we think about getting out. We've even lost touch with the outside world, and that's bad. The only times we think of going home we fantasize, make dreams and illusions out of cold, harsh reality. Why? Because that friggin' desert is a cold place to cross . . . and the mountains? The same. Look at what happened to Jerry when he made his break."

"And me?" I asked.

"Salomón's betting on you," he whispered and pushed his chair out of the room.

I lay in the twilight of the winter evening for a long time, motionless, thinking about what Mike had said.

15

The sun was a golden eye peering over the mountain's hump. I sat up in bed and watched the golden spears cut away the white frost on the hill. In the valley plumes of smoke rose from the nestling houses and I knew people were awake and stirring. I felt their tired bones cracking with old age and rheumatism as they moved about in the dark shadows. I thought of Ismelda getting ready to come to work.

The flaring light of the golden eye grew intense, sparkling. It seemed to dissolve away all shadows and horizons. My shell and the hump of the mountain disappeared, and for a brief instant the sun and the mountain and I danced and revolved around each other.

I sang to the sun, a crazy song. Not a chant, like Jerry, just crazy words. I laughed. Today was a special day.

Today I get my chair, I thought. It was one more step on the road to freedom. I flexed my arms. I knew I was ready for the chair, and I had kept after Steel until he gave in and agreed. I bent my knees and touched my legs, and at the same time old man Maloney came in, grumbling and cursing as he gathered the bedpans and urinals. I paid no attention to him. It was only a matter of time and then I would get crutches, and I would be free of the bed. I thought about all the things I wanted to do, and one strange, forboding thought kept pressing the others out of my mind.

*Come and see me when you can, Salom*ón had said . . . there's something you should see . . .

When I told Mike about my thoughts he shook his head and turned away, but he didn't say anything. I told Ismelda how I felt and she said that I had to trust Salomón, and then she added that there were no tears at the roots of sadness, that Salomón had said that tears are for the living, the lovers, and those who rage at life.

"Does he want to see me cry?" I asked myself. I touched my legs, stretched as far forward as I could with the weight of the burdensome cast, then lay back on the bed.

"I'm sick and tired of you little bastards making a mess in the bedpans!" Maloney cursed. He meant me and Buck, but he looked at me.

"Do you think I enjoy picking up your crap every morning, picking up the mess! Goddamned little bastards!"

"Ah, lay off Maloney," Mike yawned and sat up in bed, "Tortuga and Buck have to use the urinals at night . . . you know they can't get up. Do you think they like it any better than you do?"

"I'd give anything to be able to get up," Buck cursed from his bed, "my bandages are so wet and crappy they're beginning to rot."

"I can smell it," Sadsack moaned, "spare us the description. I can smell Tortuga, too. The inside of his cast smells like an old rotten pumpkin! Damn, the whole friggin' room stinks!" He cleared his throat and spit on the floor.

"Hey, Sad, you ain't no rose garden," Mike answered. "When's the last time you took a bath, huh? Sadsack won't even go swimming, he's afraid of the water!" he laughed. "But so what if it smells a little? Did you ever know anything that grows and didn't smell? No, cause everything needs a smelly compost pile to grow good and strong. Buck and Tortuga are just like vegetables, just stewing away, but wait till spring! Boooom! They'll flower like magic!"

"Spring?" Sadsack cursed. "What's today? What month is it? Did Christmas already go by?"

"All I know is today's a special day," Mike smiled.

"Doctors' rounds?"

"Somebody getting out?"

"Nah, none of that. Today Tortuga gets his chair," Mike said cheerfully.

"You're kidding!" Buck exclaimed. Even Sadsack smiled.

"No, today's the day," Mike said. They looked at me.

"Yahoo!" Buck shouted and threw his hat in the air. "Hot dog! I'm next!"

"So where do you want to go?" Mike asked when the Nurse brought my chair that afternoon.

Samson picked me up and placed me carefully in the chair. I felt the weight of the cast settle on my shoulders. For a moment I felt dizzy, then Samson placed my feet on the foot rests and I found I could brace myself. I pushed and settled into the chair. The nausea passed. I reached down and touched the shiny, cold steel of the wheels. I pushed with my right hand and felt the cumbersome weight move forward a few inches. A cheer went up from the kids who had come to see me get my chair.

"Tortuga's moving!" a kid whispered, and for a moment there was panic and a rush for the window.

"No, it's our Tortuga that's moving, our Tortuga," Ismelda said to calm them down. She placed a blanket over my knees.

"Ride 'im cowboy!" Buck shouted. "Spur that sombitch!" I spurred and the chair swung around in a wild circle.

"Yahoo! He got 'im now!"

I pushed again and the chair swung the other way. It was like riding a wild bronco in a corral of cheering faces.

"Go, man, go!" Ronco cheered, and even Sadsack shouted, "Give 'er the gas, Tortuga!"

They pushed me around and around the circle while Mike and Ronco sang:

La cucaracha! La cucaracha!
Ya no quiere caminar!
Porque le falta . . . porque no tiene,
Marijuana que fumar!

"Hey! Take it easy! Go slow on him!" the Nurse shouted and grabbed the chair. "I won't be responsible for one of your crazy chair christenings!"

Mike laughed and explained. "When Ronnie got his chair crazy Danny wanted to launch it like a ship, so he broke a coke bottle over the armrest and in doing it he nearly cut Ronnie's arm in half. Took twnety stitches to close him up."

"That's why Danny's not here today," the Nurse said coldly. "Let Tortuga get used to his chair . . . and when you get tired," she said to me, "call Samson." She marched out of the room, the giant Samson trailing behind her.

"She never gets off being a nurse," Mike shook his head sadly.

"With a capital N!" Ronco added.

"She didn't even act happy for Tortuga, but screw her, man," Mike turned to me, "this is one more step of freedom! Where do you want to go?"

"Let's take him to the girls' ward!" someone suggested.

"Yahoooo!"

"Hey! Let's race him across the recreation room!"

"Take him to the swimming pool!"

"For cryin' out loud, just take him to surgery so he can watch his buddy Steel at work!"

"Oh myyy—"

"Ah Sad, what would we do for laughs without you!"

"Why don't you let him decide," Ismelda said. She looked at me. "What do you want to do, Tortuga?"

"Damn right!" Buck agreed, "Giving a man a chair is like giving him his first horse! Let 'im do what he wants to do!"

"Yeah, make your move Tortuga!" Ronco nodded.

"Don't hold back," Mike said, "do what you wanna do!"

I had thought a long time about all the things I wanted to do when I got my chair, simple things, like getting up in the morning and going to the dining room to eat with Mike and Ronco. I wanted to be able to ride around after supper and visit the kids in other rooms, to go to therapy on my own, to explore the hospital and be able to get up at night and go to the bathroom . . . I wanted to do many things, but before I did anything I had to see Salomón.

I was strong, I was almost well, I had my chair, and I knew there was something he wanted me to see. I didn't know what it would be, but I felt a dread. He was waiting for me.

I mumbled, "I have to go see Salomón . . . alone."

Mike shook his head. "You ain't ready, Tortuga . . ." He looked at Ismelda.

"Tortuga," she whispered and held my hand tightly, "when you go to see Salomón you have to be very strong. The Nurse wasn't right in sending you the first time, you weren't ready. And now . . . maybe you should wait. You can see him later."

"What's she saying?" someone whispered.

"He wants to go see Salomón."

"Oh no . . ."

The group grew silent. Mike went to the window and looked out. "How can you stop the mountain from moving when it wants to," he said.

I withdrew my hands from Ismelda's. "I have to go," I said. I pushed and turned towards the door; the silent group parted to let me pass.

"Good luck, Tortuga," one of the kids whispered. Another added, "Nobody's been back there in a long time—"

I pushed myself into the silent hall. It was deserted and dark in the afternoon light. I breathed deep to screw up my courage and moved ahead. I pushed with my right hand and guided with my feet; the progress was slow but steady. Many thoughts kept tumbling through my mind, and I tried to sort them out and find some sense in what I was doing, but I couldn't find a clue. The vegetables were there, I knew that, and I would have to see them again, and I would have to see Salomón, but somehow the force which drew me down the dark hallways of the hospital didn't have as much to do with them as it did with other wards of the hospital. I had been asking since I arrived if there were more wards, and no one had answered me. Today I felt Salomón was going to tell me something that had to do with that nagging question and my reason for being here.

After some time I found Salomón's ward, the vegetable patch. The old nurse who sat at the desk by the door was asleep. Without disturbing her I made my way into the enormous room which housed Salomón's children. The whooshing sound of the groaning iron lungs greeted me. The air was musty; everything seemed covered with a fine, chalky dust. I wondered why whoever had built the hospital had built such an enormous room . . . and I wondered how many had been built.

I made my way slowly between the rows of beds and iron lungs. I held my breath. I didn't want to rouse them from their sleep, their sleep of death-in-life. I thought of the many times I had turned over large stones while playing along the river, turned them over to watch in fascination and with some repulsion the teeming life which lived beneath the stones. Pale bugs, colorless tendrils, white ants that scurried for the dark, insects that had never seen the sun . . . I remember squashing the bugs between my fingers, stepping down on the ants and insects that I had found beneath the stone. It was the destruction of a colony of foreign life . . .

So were the vegetables in the enormous room. They lived in the dark beneath the weight of the hospital. Their pale eyes turned to follow me. I couldn't speak, but I cursed them through clenched teeth. I cursed them because I could move and they couldn't. I feared them like I feared the bugs that lived beneath the stone.

Who would touch them? I wondered, who would feed them? Suddenly I felt like turning back, but it was too late, I was already at his door. I felt forced to call his name.

"Salomón . . ." It rang like the sonorous echoes of a bell.

"It's me, Tortuga," I said and entered. His small room was dark. The window was covered with dust, and the green vines I remembered were now dry. They curled around the bookshelves and clung lifelessly to the walls. Books were scattered on the floor; cobweb dust covered everything. I wondered how long it had been since I had seen him.

I called again and choked on the dry air which was as stale as a desert death. Over the bed one dim bulb cast a light on the book Salomón had been reading. Then he spoke.

Ah, Tortuga, so you found your way . . . good. You have a good instinct for finding your way in these dark and empty spaces . . . You look like a strange turtle riding that chair, he smiled. He laughed a soft laugh, then he coughed.

I was relieved to find him. For the first time since I began pushing the chair I rested. My arms fell to my sides and quivered from the exertion. My broken hand throbbed with pain.

I made it across your ward, I wanted to tell him, nothing can stop the progress of my destiny. I have found it flowing like a raging river. It has guided me across the wasteland to this god-forsaken place, but I swear I will leave here.

I felt elated with the sense of freedom the chair had given me, and so I wanted to shout that I was no longer afraid of the strange cries I heard at night. I wanted to tell him that my life was more than a mad dash for the sea. The emotions gripped my throat and I was about to spill everything when he spoke again . . .

Of course you want to shout, he whispered, that is why you have come here. You have found your destiny, but you have not yet found your song . . . That is why you must go farther, deeper, to the very last ward of the hospital . . . That is why you must see all there is to see. My friend, my friend, this is only the beginning of the nightmare we have made of life. Now you must see everything . . . You have only begun your journey. Today I will send you into the other wards . . . you must go to the very roots of sadness before you let out this shout of life that bursts in your lungs . . . yes, you too will have your butterflies, because you will be a singer, but your songs will be full of the sadness of life . . . Your destiny has become ours, Tortuga . . .

What am I to do, I asked.

Go farther into the ward . . . you must see the orphans of life.

But that isn't why I came to the hospital. I came to get well. I am not an orphan . . . I protested but I turned my chair and pushed it out of his room, down a dark hall to a door. Behind the door I heard the whimpering sound babies make when they're in pain. I shivered. I didn't want to enter this ward now that I had found it.

But I have already seen the vegetable patch, I said, I have already seen your cripples . . .

Ah, Tortuga, but you have not really seen what we have made of life. If you are to walk in the path of light you must first walk in darkness, if you are to sing you must gather the words for your lyrics . . .

I pushed the door open. The rusty hinges squeaked. I felt my body wet with sweat. I peered into the dark room and could see no end to it. Shadows moved from bed to bed, old women dressed like nuns who seemed to be the keepers of the ward. I entered and the door closed behind me. I struggled to turn my chair, to get out, when one of the nurses appeared over me, her wrinkled face so close to mine I could smell her putrid breath. I cried out in horror, suddenly trapped, deceived by Salomón.

"So you have come to visit us . . . Come," she nodded gently and pushed my chair towards the iron lungs which lined the room.

"No," I cried, "it's a mistake! I came by mistake!" Now I knew what Salomón had planned for me. This was another one of his wards, but it held even worse cases than his. He wanted me to see them.

"No!" I shouted again, but the old nurse paid no attention. She pushed my chair against one of the iron lungs. What I saw was burned into my memory forever. Even after I closed my eyes I could still see the comatose, shriveled body of the small child, and I could smell the putrid odor of the excrement that passed from the withered cocoon as it twisted with pain.

"They're all like this . . . helpless . . . more dead than alive," the nurse said, and she pushed me to another lung. The scene repeated itself, down the long line of iron lungs which lined the room, the scene repeated itself. In each lung lay a twisted pretzel, kept alive only by the forced air of the lung and the i-v tubes which fed them. Except for an occasional spasm of pain there was no sign of life, and yet they were alive. One thin filament of life ran in their bodies, made the heart beat, created dreams in their burnt brains.

"No!" I pleaded, "Salomón! No! Please no more! I've seen enough! I've suffered enough! Let them die! Dear God, please let them die!"

I closed my eyes and gritted my teeth. I would see no more. I had seen enough. I had not asked to see the awful sight of this ward. I kicked with my feet and pushed the nurse aside.

"There's more," she said, startled that I had broken loose. "See." She pointed, and at the end of the room there was another door which led to another ward. "There's more —"

"Oh, God, no," I cried. I felt my teeth splinter as I gritted them. A terrible anger swept over me. I heard myself curse. "Damn you!" I shouted. "Damn all of you! You're all crazy! This is a hell you've created! Pull the plug and let them die! Let them die! Please . . . dear God, let them die . . ."

I whipped my chair around and raced out of the room, still cursing, still hot with the rage which made me push like a madman. Damn you, I cursed myself, how stupid of you to think that there is a special destiny! It's only a nightmare! Life is a nightmare! And part of that nightmare is shared by these freaks which lie suspended between life and death! Better to pull the plug and let them die! Better to end this perversity! Even for us the end should come! There is no meaning! There is no special destiny! Nothing! Nothing! Only the stories! Only the empty words which try to give meaning to this hell!

I raced out of the dark wards, gasping for breath, feeling the terrible erosion of everything I had pieced together while I had been at the hospital. Now it meant nothing. Now only my anger could keep me alive. Faces rushed past me, hands reached out to stop me, and I cursed them all and fought them. The weight of the mountain was falling on me, darkness was settling over me as I burrowed into my shell . . . but first I wanted to see Salomón, I wanted to tell him that he had deceived me and his stories were false . . . I wanted to tell Ismelda that even she had been unfaithful . . . She hadn't warned me, she hadn't told me that it could be that terrible in the wards which lay like a labyrinth in the subterranean tunnels beneath the earth. No one could stop my mad rush until one face came into focus, and I recognized Mike.

"You sonofabitch!" I snarled, "Why didn't you tell me!"

Then I swung as hard as I could and drove my fist into his face, sending my chair crashing into his, sending both of us toppling over into the frightful darkness which opened like a monstrous mouth to receive me.

16

When I awoke Mike was sitting by my bed. I tried to move but my arms and legs were tied down.

"I'm sorry—" he said.

"How long have I been under?" I asked.

"A few days . . . they had to tie you down and drug you, because you were kicking a lot . . . they were afraid you'd hurt yourself."

"Those poor slobs," I mumbled through gritting teeth, "those poor sonofabitchin' slobs—"

I looked around me. I was back in my room. An i-v bottle hung over me. Around me the oxygen tent shimmered with light. I looked at Mike through the plastic. His face looked grotesque in the refracted light.

"It's good for you to stay angry," he said, "at least for awhile."

I had been angry, but it had passed, like a wave of nausea sweeping over me, it had emptied itself. And I had retreated from the anger as I had retreated from the pity I first felt when I saw the ward of comatose orphans . . . the images of the twisted, dying bodies which had filled my nightmares were burned into my brain, I saw them now, reflected on the slabs of light on the clear plastic. They were a part of me; I would never be free of them. But they would only live in the farthest niche I had found in my shell, the shell which would protect me from the searing acid of the damned path of the sun and the pain of the bitter songs, which were really not songs, but the whimpering of the babes of limbo, the living dead . . . I was empty . . . that's all I felt, emptiness.

"I'm not angry," I said. "I just don't care . . ."

"Hey, don't say that," Mike answered. "You got to care. If you don't care . . . then it's all over. You have to care! That's the first rule, remember! Care enough to get out! That's what you have to do! Get angry! Strike out! Hit me! Come on, hit me again like you did out there in the hall! Hit anyone, but just hit! Don't give up on us, Tortuga, don't give up . . . Don't you see, we're all depending on you? Don't be a Sadsack . . . Get mad at what you've seen and stay mad!"

I wasn't listening . . . I was retreating, moving deeper and farther into my shell, covering my hurt and pain with layer after layer of silence . . . meaningless silence.

We don't know what you saw. Most of us have seen Salomón's ward, but we never went any deeper . . . There's only rumors of the other wards and the kids that are in there, but most of us mind our own business. We don't want to know. We can't take it. But Salomón had to send somebody, someone had to see . . . I don't know why . . . hell, nobody knows why he does things like that, why he picked you. Maybe it's just the way you are, Tortuga, just the way you are . . .

I closed my eyes. Tell Salomón to shove it, I thought. Tell him to take his stories and his singing and his path of the sun and shove them up his ass. And you take your number one rule, which you're always preaching and which you never obey, and shove it. All of you, leave me alone, go away, I have no need for you. Go and show your cripples and your mummies and your living dead to someone else. I've broken loose from you. I don't believe in anything anymore. I am free. I am nothing. I won't be responsible for anything. I denounce my destiny. There is no destiny . . . there is no fate . . . there is no God, no universe . . . only my thoughts, and I can learn to silence those. I have given up sadness, because I can't understand the reason for the existence of those poor slobs, those poor withered vegetables that look like plucked carrots and turnips drying and shriveling in the sun . . . and I couldn't love them or touch them . . . I hated their depravity, the cruel, obscene joke which allows them to exist in that plane of life, that shade beyond life, that first circle of hell where pain is still felt, where love is dead . . . and they don't know they're alive; and they don't even know who's feeding them the juices which keep them alive . . .

Beyond the last ward, where the shriveled infants slept, there lay the wharf. In the mist I heard the slapping of the water, looked and saw Filomón's boat. I waved and he drew close for me. I am ready, Filomón, I cried, and pulled my shroud around my shoulders and stepped onto his rocking boat.

Return to my love, Ismelda called from the shore.

Fight him! Mike shouted. Rule number one is to fight! Get mad and fight!

Spur the sonofabitch! Buck yahooed. That boat is death itself! Spur him! Treat 'im like your first hoss!

Fear death by drowning! Ronco cried. Head for the mountain! The top of the mountain!

The green fields! Sadsack laughed, where there are no cripples and all we do is make love all day . . .

Dr. Steel jolted me with stabs of electricity, forced air into my lungs and cursed, Don't give up on me now. He slit my throat and pushed his tubes into my lungs.

KC mounted me and covered me with her hot flesh to drive away the chills.

I cannot fight their power, Filomón cried, and he returned to the decaying beach where the rotting bodies of the vegetables lay scattered. With Clepo's help he tossed me on the sun-baked beach with the rest of the suffering turtles.

You must run again, he shouted above the crashing waves of the sea, and he pointed to the gray figure of Salomón who stood on a bluff and watched the race.

The paralysis seemed to return . . . my muscles went limp, my bedsores opened again and bled. Time cradled me with its patience and allowed me some rest. Outside the window the earth changed her colors, and the months of the calendar fell like leaves. The dry winds came from the west, rattling the hospital with their fury. Great dust storms rose over the land and hid the sun. The empty rooms moaned like the wheezing of the dying bodies in their iron coffins. Ismelda called me in the storm . . . and her cry was the cry of la Llorona seeking her lover. When I opened my eyes I looked for Tortuga, but the howling winds and dust obscured everything. Tumbleweeds moved across the bleak landscape, the dry souls of the vegetables, lost and by the wind grieved. Dry electricity plagued the air and burned the desert dry. The thunder cracked and bolts of green lightning seared the sky. Nothing grew. The land was burned raw. Trails vanished. The springs went dry. The carcasses of Josefa's goats littered the dunes of the desert. I saw my mother lost in the storm . . . praying to a God who didn't answer . . . Then the cold weather came and I shivered in my nakedness as the great horned owls struck, screeching as they hunted us down, grasping us in their talons and uprooting us from the meager earth which held us, covering the land with a shroud of ice and blood as their feathers fell . . . their mournful call silenced the nights, the never-ending nights. Dread and nausea drove itself into our souls . . . I withdrew into my shell, dug into it like a root burrows for protection after the stalk has been cut . . . nothing mattered, shadows moved around me, spoke, wiped away my vomit and ex-crement . . . racking fevers shook my withering body . . . My rage and anger were dead . . . the hoax of life no longer concerned me . . . I gave up everything . . . only Salomón's perverse and stubborn flame kept my heart beating, kept my lungs sucking air . . . that much I shared with his vegetables. I thought of dying, but I was beyond death. Inside my cast my body dried and shriveled like the nut of an old peach pit . . . maggots gathered in the stench and mold and consumed my flesh . . . sometimes in the dark I awoke, and I heard my laughter echo in the room, and I heard my curses hurl themselves into the dark wind . . . I felt the eyes of the vegetables on me, the pitiful eyes, the mournful eyes. Sometimes I was awake long enough to hear the rushing of water as Tortuga's underground springs washed and refreshed the thin roots and tentacles which kept us clinging to the dry earth. I imagined the water bitter and hard with

121

crystalline minerals which washed over my soul, leaving layer after layer of calcareous material which dried and formed a shell, a white shell which protected the frail body . . . and inside I felt the constant throb of an aching heart.

Perhaps it was that ache which I could not dissolve and which I could no longer beat that made me say yes to Danny when he asked me if I wanted to die.

He had been my constant companion. Whenever I opened my eyes he was lurking nearby, like a vulture waiting for death to peck the answer from the riddle of life. He stood waiting, yellow eyes burning with the insanity which drove him to mumble God's phrases over and over, his dry arm hanging uselessly by his side, bent over by the hump that was beginning to develop on his back . . . Sometimes he talked to me, wished me to die, confessed his fears, cursed the vegetables, blamed me for listening to Salomón and not to God . . . I never listened . . . not until that afternoon when he drew close and whispered his story.

"It was a story on TV," he said, "about a woman who had been in a car accident, and she was crippled, and she couldn't talk. She was a beautiful woman, but she couldn't move one muscle, just like you when you came here, Tortuga. All she could do was smile. Her husband took good care of her, because she was so beautiful and he loved her . . . and he would sit and talk to her and she would smile, so he thought she was happy. But in her thoughts she wanted to die . . . Wanna know why? She had a friend, and she was a beautiful woman. They had grown up together. When they were young they had both been in love with the husband, but this woman married him. Now she knew she couldn't make him happy, ever again, so she wanted her friend to marry him. She wanted her husband to be free and marry her best friend, and to be happy ever after. But she knew her husband was loyal, and he would never do anything. So she wanted to die because she was only in everybody's way. She was like one of those damned vegetables Salomón takes care of, she couldn't do anything! She couldn't even kill herself! She tried to tell her husband she wanted to die, and all she could do was smile, and so he thought she was happy and he went on taking care of her. She was trapped to go on living like that; they were all trapped.

"But one day the husband hired a gardener to take care of the lawn, cause they lived in a great, big beautiful house, cause they were rich, but even the money he had hadn't been able to cure her even though he hired the best specialists. The gardener saw the woman lying in her bed, and he came in and brought her flowers, and every day he came in and talked to her and brought her flowers. Soon he fell in love with her. He told her he loved her and he would do anything for her. One day he kissed her and he realized she wasn't happy and she wanted to die. That's what she was trying to say when she smiled. He knew what he had to do, so he got real

122

close to her and told her that if she wanted to die she should blink her eyes twice, like this. And she blinked twice. He got real sad and started crying, and he was kinda hunch-back and ugly, but he loved her and he knew he had to obey her wish. So that night he covered her face with a pillow until she suffocated. Then he took her to the garden and he buried her in the middle of all the roses, and at the end of the movie he picked up one rose and put it over her grave . . ."

Then Danny bent close, so close I could smell the decaying smell of his arm and his bad breath. "I think you want to die," he whispered in my ear.

I blinked twice and it was done.

Late that night he and Tuerto and Mudo came for me. Like three grave robbers they stole into my room and quickly and quietly lifted me into a chair and carted me away. I didn't know where we were going and I didn't care. As they pushed me down the dark hall I had the feeling they had done this before. Tuerto went ahead of us to watch for the nurses. Mudo and Danny pushed the chair. They kept to the shadows.

The wheelchair sounded like rats squeaking in the dark. Outside the wind had stopped; the moon bathed the hill with its light. Across the way I caught a quick glimpse of Tortuga sleeping in the moonlight. It was the first time I had been aware of my surroundings in a long time. I rubbed my arm and felt the soreness where Danny had pulled away the i-v needle. I had no sense of direction, so I didn't know where we were going, but I could hear the sound of water, and I thought I heard Clepo's gurgling laughter.

"Where are we?" I asked. In the mist which rolled over the lapping water I thought I recognized Filomón. I called to him. This time he could not deny me, Danny would see to that.

I shivered. The fever had returned quickly, enveloping me like a thick fog. Water gurgled at my feet. Its sharp smell filled my lungs. On the other side of the lake Filomón's boat tossed gently on the swells.

"Where are we?" I asked again. I didn't remember the lake, but I was sure I recognized Filomón. A woman stood at his side. It was Ismelda.

Why are you here? I asked them . . . and they waited, patiently, in silence.

"We gonna throw him in?" Tuerto whispered.

"Yes, we're gonna drown him," Danny answered.

I smiled. So Danny's insanity would return me to Tortuga's water. I laughed. I was ready.

"Why he laughin' Danny?" Tuerto asked nervously.

"He's crazy," Danny answered.

"We-we, r-ready, Da-Dan-ny," Mudo stuttered. He held the chair at the edge of the water.

Through an opening in the sky I could see the moon. It was full and blue, like the moon Steel had seen. Its light danced on the waves like mermaids dancing on the water. I felt happy with myself, at peace, unafraid . . . I had run the race and come to the edge of Salomón's sea . . . I was rejoining Filomón for another journey . . .

"Can he swim?" Tuerto asked.

The spray of the sea washed across my face and startled me from my reverie. I looked for Filomón, but his boat was gone. The singing of the siren at his side had ceased. The chlorinated water of the swimming pool pierced my nostrils. The huge room was deserted except for the four of us standing at the edge. The only light was the light of the moon as it shone through the skylight and illumined the room. Suddenly I felt panic fill my lungs; I gasped for breath and pushed back. No, I heard myself whisper.

"Can-can, h-he sw-swim?"

"No, he can't swim," Danny laughed, "he's a turtle, but he can't swim! But a turtle should die in his home!"

"Filomón!" I called, but there was no one there. "Ismelda?" Still no answer. They were gone. They weren't going to make the journey with me. I looked closely into the water and churning in the dark depths lay Salomón's headless turtle. The water was wine-colored with its blood.

I turned to Danny. "No. I'm not ready. I can't make the journey alone. Can't you see! They're not there!"

"Shut up!" Danny shouted.

"Let's dump him and get outta here!" Tuerto cried.

In front of me the headless turtle thrased angrily and made the water boil. It was waiting for its brother to return. But then I heard Salomón speak, and he too said I was not ready.

Ah, Tortuga, Tortuga, I heard him say, *you have come to the edge of the sea . . . you have run your race and suffered as much as any man . . . but you must turn back, you must face the blinding sun . . . you must cast off your shell and come to sing the songs of man . . .*

"Ready!"

"Okay, push!"

"No!" I shouted and dug in my feet.

"Push!" Danny shouted, and the three of them heaved and sent me plunging into the cold, clear water. I closed my eyes and screamed as I felt the shock of the water. A choking mouthful of burning water filled my lungs. The chair tipped sideways and sank, but I remained afloat on the tossing water, buoyed by the cast.

The momentum had pushed me towards the middle of the pool. I struggled to right myself, but it was useless, I remained face down, unable to turn. I held my breath and settled into the gentle, rocking motion of the water . . . the waves drummed against my ears. I flopped my arms and kicked with my legs until I was exhausted, but I couldn't turn over. I realized I was going to drown, like a crippled turtle reaching the sea only to discover it can't swim, I was going to drown in a few minutes . . .

I opened my eyes and looked into the water . . . strands of moonlight swayed like golden seaweed in the dancing water. The light was gold, like the notes of a gentle melody . . . Knowing that I was going to die filled me with a sense of peace, as if after the momentous struggle and rage I had suddenly been taken into my mother's arms, and there was no more care or need to fight . . . I felt as if I was falling asleep, until even the piercing pain in my lungs and the swollen veins along my neck throbbed with a gentle dull feeling.

I thought I heard Salomón calling to me . . . and somewhere Filomón's oars pushed against the water, then receded and left the silence of the water and its gentle massage. My grandfather appeared before me and told me to awaken slowly, because I was entering a new dream . . . my mother prayed to her saints, the lifeless, plaster statues that would remain forever with their backs to her because I hadn't returned . . . and in the blinding light which flashed around me the girls of my first holy communion entered the water and swam like mermaids around me, singing a song of life, singing the song Ismelda whispered from the shore . . . I smiled and breathed the thin strands of golden water . . . and the water pushed through my nostrils like the bony fingers of la Llorona and crushed my lungs. I breathed for air and sucked in the sweet water, Tortuga's pee, Josefa's medicine . . . The lights flashed brightly, like thunder from the heavens, and the song of the innocent mermaids flourished like a choir of angels around me . . . Fragile bubbles of air escaped from my mouth and exploded on the calm surface as the strong liquid fingers of the water pried my mouth open . . . butterflies wove a song upon the tossing water . . .

Then suddenly the water churned and bubbled madly around me, and someone shouted, Tor-tuuuuuuu-ga! Then strong hands lifted me out of the water. I gasped for air. I smiled. Rough hands lifted me over the side and stretched me out.

"You crazy sonofabitch," Mike muttered, breathing hard, wet . . . Before they pushed me on my stomach I recognized Ismelda in the faces which swarmed over me. I felt a terrific pressure on my back, felt the cast crunch, saw chunks of the wet plaster fall away, and I heard a lot of shouting as the foam and froth of the water came spewing from my mouth . . .

"Is he all right?"

"He's breathing!"

"Let's get him into the other room!"

"Easy now! Watch it!"

"Breath in!" Dr. Steel shouted and placed the oxygen mask over my face.

They lifted me and carried me into a small room across from the pool.

"He's going to be all right!" I heard Mike shout.

"Get those goddamned kids outta here!" Steel shouted.

"Hey, watch it! We could report you for cussing!" one of the kids shouted.

"Yeah! Just cause you saved his life don't mean nothin'!"

The door closed behind me. I heard Mike shout that it was all over, I was fine, it was time to get back to the ward, and I heard a big cheer.

Someone began singing, then the whole troop sang as they marched back to the ward:

> *Poor ole Tortugaaaaa*
> *He never got a kiss*
> *Poor ole Tortugaaaa*
> *He don' know what he missss . . .*

The nurse held my wrist and looked at her watch, and I had to smile because I thought for sure she was going to ask me if I had had my bm today. Ismelda massaged my wet legs and arms with a warm towel. Dr. Steel looked at the dripping cast and cursed. "I won't even need a saw on this one," he shook his head and pulled at the wet plaster. He cut through the wet cotton and gauze and tore apart the cast, ripping with a carelessness I had never felt in his hands before. He seemed to be looking for something, something hidden in the core of the cast. Ismelda helped him, snipping the cast away very carefully, as if she was helping a baby chick tear through its shell.

When they were done I lay smeared with wet plaster and the filth which had coated the inside of the cast. Steel pulled the oxygen mask away and asked me how I felt. I nodded. The worst was over, I felt all right.

"He sure looks like a wet turtle," the nurse said to ease the tension.

"What?" Steel asked. Beads of perspiration covered his forehead. He placed the cold stethoscope on my chest and listened. He looked at me, questioningly, and I knew what he was thinking but he didn't ask anything.

"Yeah," he nodded and breathed a sigh of relief. "You look like a bloody mess," he smiled weakly, "but you're okay. How do you feel? Any pain?"

"No," I answered.

"Well, the cast is gone," he said. He looked at me and then at Ismelda, then he went to the sink and washed his hands. "I don't think we'll have to replace it—"

"Good," I answered and felt Ismelda touch my shoulder.

"Clean him up," he said to the nurse, "and get him back to the ward . . . Are the kids gone?"

"Yes, doctor, Mike took care of that. They're all back in the ward," the nurse answered.

"Damn kids," he muttered. He took a cigarette from his shirt pocket, put it to his mouth, then he crumpled it and tossed it away. "It could've been worse," he said. "You're damn lucky, Tortuga . . ." He went out shaking his head.

"You crazy turtle," Ismelda whispered. Her eyes were wet with tears. "Why do you want to go swimming in the middle of the night— Thank God you're safe . . ."

She took the basin of hot water and soap from the nurse and said she would clean me. The nurse nodded and went out, but not before she gave me the shot the doctor had ordered. That and the drain of fatigue I felt in my muscles made me sleepy. I closed my eyes while Ismelda scrubbed away the crud which had built up beneath the cast. Her touch was like the reawakening of nerves, tender fingers touching flesh so long dead, a liquid fire spreading down my arms and legs.

"I was staying in the girls' ward when I heard the commotion . . . I don't know how Mike found you but he did. The screams awakened the wards, you should have heard the kids . . . Look," she said, and ran her fingers through my hair, "your hair has grown. Tomorrow I'll come early and wash it . . ."

"I couldn't drown—" I murmured.

"No, you can't drown in Tortuga's waters," she smiled. "It's not your fate . . . and now that the cast is gone you look like a lizard, so you'll have to think about living on dry land," she smiled.

I nodded. Yes, the water had spit me out. I couldn't drown in it. The water had rumbled and the mountain had groaned in the night and its tremors had moved Mike, moved Ismelda, drawn the screams from their throats, cried the alarm and awakened the ward. I remembered hearing Salomón's voice, too, so he had had something to do with Filomón rejecting me . . . Now I would have to return and see him, but now I could, because the dread had passed and I had discovered that I was afraid to make the journey across the ocean alone . . . I had made some connections which I needed to understand before I could travel with Filomón again . . . it was my fate, it was my destiny . . .

But I had to create it, to create it out of Mike and Ismelda and Salomón and all the rest . . . that was the clue . . . to make some sense out of it . . . just like so long ago when the paralysis came I hadn't died, and the movement had returned, for some purpose . . . but it was to be my purpose, not God's purpose, not Mike's, not Salomón's, not the past which haunted me in my dreams . . . but my purpose . . . alone . . . sharing it with Ismelda . . .

Her fingers washed away the layers of pain and sorrow and despair which had separated me from her and the others. She reached deep into the core of the invisible shell and shared my pain, the roots of sadness, and her touch let me know that I wasn't alone . . . her touch was like the ripple on still water, the ripple which duplicates itself and reaches out . . . into eternity, touching all, encompassing everything with its gentle love. Her touch was magic. Her supple fingers rubbed life into my tired nerves. She sang a song and made my eyelids heavy with sleep.

" . . . You are a lizard woman," I remember saying.

"Yes . . . we'll live together in the sun," she whispered.

"Forever?"

"Forever."

She lay her head upon my chest and sang a lullaby, a song of love:

> *Sana, sana, colita de rana*
> *Si no sanas hoy*
> *Sanar*ás mañana . . .

It was a song of peace . . . of love, a song which erased the dread of time and the past which had haunted me . . . Her long, dark hair wove a web, a web of dream in which I rested . . . from which I could see the waters of the mountain flowing into the river and winding their way south towards the sea . . . and the people of the water and the golden fish played in the gentle water . . .

On the shore of the river Salomón stood . . . and all his children stood around him, dancing like leaves in the wind, dancing like seaweed dances in swaying water . . . and he sang this song . . .

Once beside the stream of time and memory, Ismelda found a magic flute . . . the flute of a man who had crossed the desert to climb the magic mountain . . . She rested in the shade of the green juniper, and she sang a song of love . . . the wind played through the flute and made her moan . . . her lips were red and sweet with the juice of the prickly pear, the cactus fruit. The goats stood still and sniffed the air when they heard Ismelda's moan . . . the lizards sat quietly in the sun. Ismelda shuddered in her dream, a pleasant tremor of magic and love, a liquid-dream which made the mountain smile. She moaned again, covered herself with wild oak leaves and rested on the juniper needle bed, and slept and dreamed again of the lizard-man who came to lie by her side and taste the sweet, red juice on her warm lips . . .

17

Mike and Ronco came in early the next morning.

"How's it goin'?" Ronco asked.

"Okay," I answered. Ismelda had come earlier in the morning and washed my hair and shaved the fuzz off my cheeks. I was still groggy from the drugs, but I felt good.

"You look skinny without your cast," Mike said. They tried not to look directly at me, so we wouldn't have to talk about last night.

"Hairiest looking turtle I've ever seen!" Ronco laughed then cleared his throat. My hair had grown almost to my shoulders.

"Well, we'll see you in the ward tonight," Mike said. "We'll have a party, celebrate—" They nodded, told me to take it easy, then raced out, shouting, "Algo es algo dijo el diablo!"

The nurse who worked the isolation ward came in with a breakfast tray and I sat up and ate. She placed a valentine card on my tray and smiled. "The girls in the ward sent you this . . . they hope you get better," she said.

I had lost track of time; I had slept through Christmas and the new year, which meant the days were growing longer and we were headed into spring. I looked out the window and saw the sun shining. I ate the big breakfast, like a man who has not eaten in months, stuffing everything into my mouth at once, smacking the food with gusto, feeling the juices of my mouth mix with the eggs and bacon and cereal, feeling the hurt along the side of my jaws as the juices spurted and feeling the warm mixture which I washed down with milk grumble in my empty stomach. I ate ravenously, like a bear that has awakened in the early spring. I ate until my stomach bulged with food. When I was done I lay back on the bed and closed my eyes. I ran my hand over my chest and remembered the excitement of Ismelda's touch. My sensitive skin still tingled with her touch. I had lost my shell and now my skin was exposed to the acid in the air, as it had been exposed to her, and it felt good.

Ronco had said, he lost his shell and all the stories written on it . . .

Don't worry, he hasn't forgotten what he's seen and felt, Mike had answered.

"Salomón said I'd learn to sing, and I don't know what in the hell he means by that," I said.

"What?" Dr. Steel asked.

I opened my eyes. He was standing by me. I smiled. "I was just thinking aloud," I said.

"Well, you look pretty spruced up," he winked. "Feel up to an x-ray?"

"Anything you say," I nodded as he felt the muscles along the side and back of my neck and made me turn my head. The freedom of movement was exhilarating. I felt weak but there was no pain and there was enough strength so I could control the movement.

"Looks good," he said then paused, sat by the side of the bed and looked out the window. "I have to write a report about what happened last night," he said.

I thought awhile and then I said, "It was an accident. Can you just say it was an accident—" I didn't want to make it hard on him, but I didn't want to go into it. It had been my doing and now I wanted to forget about it and I didn't want crazy Danny to pay for what I had chosen to do.

"Okay," he nodded and slapped my leg, "it's up to you . . ." He called Samson and Samson came in and lifted me on to the gurney and pushed me to the x-ray room. Kids on their way to therapy shouted greetings.

"Hey, Tortuga! How you doin'?"

"He don' have his shell anymore!"

"Oh myyy—"

"Shhhhh!"

"Hey, honey, when you goin' come and see me?" KC waved. I turned and waved back. She looked beautiful standing in front of the therapy room in her crisp, freshly-laundered uniform. There was a buzz of excitement in the air which I had not felt before; the air and the sounds were alive. Even the doctors on the way to surgery waved, one reached out and patted me. The hall was bright with sunshine.

The technician whistled while he shot half a dozen pictures, but one was all Steel needed to tell him I didn't need another cast.

"You're a free man, Tortuga. Bones have healed nicely . . . you don't even need a brace. How do you feel?"

"Great."

"Ready to get back to therapy?"

"Anytime," I answered.

"Let's start with a whirlpool bath . . . it'll get the soreness out." He called KC and she and Samson took me into a small room with a big, stainless steel tub. They picked me up and sat me down in the tub. Then KC turned the tap and the hot, yellow pee of Tortuga came gushing out.

"How does it feel?" she asked as the water rose.

"Hot!" I shouted.

"It's nice and warm," she smiled and ran her hand in the pungent mineral water. I inhaled the steam which rose up and felt it open up my lungs. "Breathe deep," she said, "it's good for you." She splashed the water on my chest and back and ran her dark hands up and down, carressing me, helping me get used to the strong water which filled the tub. "I like you better without your turtle shell," she teased and massaged my neck and back muscles. She flipped a switch and the vibrator sputtered alive. The hot water boiled and churned around me. I went rigid and resisted and she whispered, "Relax, honey, relax. Flow with it . . . let it caress you, let it carry the weariness away . . ."

I relaxed and sank into the swirling water, leaving only my head above water to breathe, allowing my arms and legs to float up and down in the churning water. K C kept massaging until I closed my eyes, felt safe in the water, worked with it and let it ease the soreness out of my cramped muscles. She sang while she held me, sad and blue, but full of love.

> *I once had a lover*
> *Who left me for another . . .*
> *So I'm sittin' by the river,*
> *Just starin' at the water . . .*

Her song became a part of the water . . . a part of memory. I, too, had been at the river, I too had seen the innocent girls of my childhood scatter throughout the land as they grew into womanhood . . . and that same Sunday I had met la Llorona along the river, on the path beneath the cliff . . . and in meeting that poor, wretched creature who filled my life of fantasy with dread I had discovered the other half of my dark soul . . . and I had realized that the loss of innocence belonged to me as much as to the first communion girls . . . and last night I had seen Ismelda by the edge of the water. She had stood on the beach and called me back from my journey . . . and that's why Tortuga's water had spit me out. I could not drown . . . I could only live, with the woman and the water, with the siren who always sang in the moonlight by the edge of the water . . . a thousand stories flooded by memory, I saw my past flash before me for the first time, and it was a past of whispered stories, cuentos told by the gaunt men and women of the sea of land, history and tradition wrapped in words which moaned with the terrible urgency of the wind, moaning my past and my destiny . . . words tying together past and present in the magic of the moment . . . holy water caressing the cripples of the desert we had created . . . forcing us to live not in its depth and darkness but in the light of the sun . . . water a million years in the making, full of the earth's strength, water from the heart and core of the earth . . . water as old as the earth, trapped in the dark bowels of earth, heated by the burning heart, gushing out in Tortuga's pee to cure us . . .

I laughed . . . loud and throaty . . . feeling alive and new, and I prayed for the water to wash into Salomón's wards and bathe his cripples . . . his vegetables. I gurgled with joy and laughed and wished they were with me, riding the crest of the waves, inhaling the salty, mineral fumes of steam, floating on the white foam which held me like the arms of Ismelda . . .

"That's it honey! Get it on! Get it on!" KC cried and pointed at my swollen tool, and we both laughed above the roar of the vibrator and the churning water.

18

Perhaps I can never love again   never hold Ismelda in my arms
again without holding the girl who lies wasting in the iron lung
Perhaps the shadows which pursue me will drag me down   into the pit
of shrunken bodies and withered souls   Never see a child run and play
again without seeing the endless rows of crippled orphans   the orphans
of a world without love   the innocent tortured by the hatred which
lurks in all souls   and pursues me in my nightmares

Perhaps not even Ismelda's magic can erase the memory of the dark
wards   the stench of the living dead   the helpless creatures dying
breath by breath

Perhaps I will never dance again   Never laugh again
Perhaps I will never run and play again
Never love again
Never be free again

Perhaps the sun will never shine again   never see the path again
Only the black sun of Salomón's wards will guide me through the air
stale with death   cries of death

Perhaps I will never turn again, to see the shimmer of light on green
leaves, to feel the cool breeze of summer touch my forehead, to learn to
love again

My love is the love I brought with me from the dark wards   a love
unknown to you   a love which you fear to draw into your heart

I will sleep eternally with the cripples of the desert   share their
bed   eat their bread   drink their water   I will lie by their sides
all my life   as I touch you and caress your glowing skin

Perhaps that is my love   a growing love   a love you must reach
to share

Perhaps you cannot love and touch our crippled bodies

Perhaps it is you who cannot walk in our dark wards and reach out to
touch . . .

133

"God! Oh, God!" I panted and gasped for breath.

"You okay? You okay, Tortuga!" Mike shouted and shook my shoulders. "You were having a nightmare, that's all!" He rubbed my back; my hospital gown was soaked with sweat.

"A bad nightmare," Ronco said and held out a glass of water. The water calmed my trembling.

"You were shouting about the ward—" Buck said and nodded in the direction of the garden. He was still bandaged like a mummy but he was sitting in a wheelchair, twirling a short rope and smoking a cigarette.

"Don't talk about that place!" Danny interjected. He was sitting in the corner pretending to leaf through comic books—he was still watching me carefully. He kept his rotten arm turned away from me because the disease was spreading up his neck and on to his face.

"We can't pretend they're not there," Ronco said and looked at me, "not any more—"

"They're there, all right," Sadsack spit, "and some of them have been hanging on to dear life for longer than any of us—"

"We knew they were there all along . . . we just didn't want to face it," Mike said.

"Well it was better that way!" Danny shouted. "It was better to keep them hidden! They're nearly dead anyway! So why did he have to come along and remind the rest of us, huh?" He pointed an accusing finger at me.

"Maybe he didn't wanna go," Buck said, "maybe he had to go—"

"That's true," Mike agreed, "the way I heard Salomón tell it Tortuga *had* to go. He never made any of the rest of us go back there . . . for some reason he picked Tortuga . . ." He looked at me. I knew he understood part of the reason Salomón had chosen me. There was something in me that he could force to become the singer, the man who would not only feel the misery of the hell we lived in, but also return to sing about it.

"Anyway, why in the fuck do they have to keep them around?" Danny cursed. "They're better off dead!"

"I think they're here to tell us something," I said, "to remind us of something—"

"What?" Danny exclaimed. His eyes bore into mine.

"I don't know," I answered. "All I know is they're here to remind us of something . . . something we've almost lost . . ."

"You don't make any sense!" Danny scoffed.

"It makes some sense," Ronco said, "because at least Tortuga went to see them. We had pretended they weren't there, then Tortuga came along and reminded us of all those poor vegetables. Now that's what's bothering us. We're blaming Tortuga for bringing all of this out in the open again—"

"Bullshit!" Sadsack protested.

"Yeah we are," Ronco continued. "Listen, most of us weren't even listening to Salomón any more, then when Tortuga came we had to start listening to him again. A lot of the times we didn't like what we heard, but we had to listen. And Tortuga trusted Salomón, maybe he realized how smart that little bastard is . . . anyway, Tortuga at least was listening. He wanted to know about the wards; he kept asking—"

"And he got what he deserved!" Danny shouted.

"Yeah, but he shouldn't have to be in it alone . . . we're all in this together—"

"Bull! Leave me out!" Sadsack complained.

"Me too!" Danny shouted. "I don't wanna have anything to do with those vegetables! I think they should be dead!"

"Why are you afraid of them, Danny?" I asked.

"I'm not afraid!" he jumped up and faced me. The withered tissue was wrinkling the entire side of his face. His eyes burned yellow. "I'm not afraid of them! You're the one who was afraid! You went bananas when you saw them! Don't tell me I'm afraid!"

"Take it easy!" Mike shouted, and Danny looked around then backed off. He sulked to his corner and slumped down.

"Maybe we're all afraid of them, in some way," Buck said when the air had cleared.

"But why?"

"It's not just because of the way they look . . . man, I know they're nothing but little shriveled stumps, but a person can get used to that. It must be something else—"

The room was quiet. Perhaps we all knew why, but the silence forced me to speak.

"Maybe it's because we don't know whether they should live or die—"

They looked at me, glanced away, tried to pretend I hadn't asked the question, then Mike finally admitted the possibility of this question which nagged us all.

"You can't be serious," he said, then he added, "you mean if they had a choice would they rather be alive and hooked up to those machines like prisoners, or would they rather be dead?"

"It makes sense," Ronco nodded. "And the thing is we don't know! They can't talk! They can't move! They can't make the choice—"

"So it falls back on us," Mike said gloomily. He pushed his chair to the window and looked out. "Damn," he whispered. We were quiet for a long time.

"They can't talk but they can move their eyes," Danny whispered and looked at me with a sneer on his face.

"What does Salomón say?" Mike finally asked.

"He says it's up to us," I answered.

"I've already said, leave me outta this!" Sadsack grumbled. He buried his face in a comic book. Buck worked on his rope tricks and pretended not to listen.

"Why us?" Mike asked.

"We decide for animals, don't we," Ronco told him. "On the mountain when a horse breaks a leg we have to shoot it. It's that simple."

"So they won't suffer—"

"Yeah," Ronco nodded, "death should come quickly. Nobody wants to linger in that twilight zone between life and death. If you leave a wounded animal out there the buzzards will be pecking at it for days; if its lucky maybe a cougar will finish it off quickly. Everybody wants to die quickly. Most of us know what it's like being shackled to a bed, and we could put up with a year or two or three . . . but the vegetables are there forever, with nothing to look forward to . . . like wounded horses out on the desert." He turned and looked at me. "You know, we do it for ourselves too. That's what my old man said. We do it because we don't want to hear the cries of a wounded animal in the night. After you shoot an animal that needs shooting you can forget about it. You've done that animal a favor, you can go home and sleep. But if you had left it to suffer then its cries would sound up the canyons for miles, you could hear it at night and you wouldn't be able to sleep . . . My dad once climbed down a sheer two hundred foot cliff to shoot a mule which had slipped over and was still kicking and crying. The mountain people are kind, he said. They'll go out of their way to kill a wounded deer, or a wild pig, or a dog . . . and they also know about the cries in the dark . . ."

"Same cries we hear from the vegetables," Danny mumbled.

"Shhhhh. Listen!"

We stopped talking. We listened in the darkness. Outside the sun pulled a mantle of gray shadows over Tortuga as a new storm bore down from the north. Doves cried at the ponds by the river. Then we heard the whimpering, the soft, painful groans which came from the garden. The orphans were crying, sadly crying. I thought of Salomón, lying quietly in his dark room, his eyes moving in the cold darkness as he tried to catch a glimpse of Tortuga before the night covered him, listening to the sound of his cripples.

"Ah damn!" Mike cursed.

"What are we gonna do?"

"We're not goin' to do a goddamned thing!" Sadsack shouted and tossed away his comic book. "I'm sick and tired of all this talk! Somebody turn the goddamned lights on!"

"It's not our responsibility," Buck added.

"Salomón said it was! We can't escape it!" I shouted back. "We can't just pretend they're not there!"

136

"It's your fault!" Danny shouted at me, "It's your fault because you went and brought all this up!" He rushed towards me.

"Don't blame it on Tortuga!" Ronco yelled and pushed his chair in front of Danny. "He didn't create the goddamned mess!"

"Well then whose mess is it?" Danny yelled. Spittle spurted from his mouth, his eyes bulged out. He pulled himself up as straight as he could and exposed the dry rot which spread up the side of his twitching face.

"Blame it on God!" Mike cursed.

"Then it's up to God!" Danny turned on him and slashed him with his words. "God will decide! Not us! It's his mess so let him take care of it!"

"You're crazy Danny, crazy . . ."

"God's always the easy way out for Danny!" Ronco shouted and grabbed Danny. He held him close and cursed in his face. He was angry. Even in the dark I could see his veins bulge and throb along his neck and temples. "Listen you little shriveled bastard! It's God that's keeping the vegetables alive in their machines! That's his decision! Don't you see that! We have to decide beyond that! We're free to do something on our own!" He hurled Danny into the corner. I thought he was going to go after him, but suddenly the lights came on and the room flooded with light. We blinked, shocked by the bright light and the immediacy with which we saw each other, then we turned away awkwardly.

"Oh boy," Sadsack smiled with relief, "juice time—"

Ronco glared at Danny then pulled away. "Big deal, juice time," he muttered, "live a whole day just to look forward to a glass of juice at the end of it. Shit!"

"Well, if we're lucky it'll be pineapple," Sadsack mumbled then grinned. "That's my favorite—"

"What Ronco's saying is there's got to be more to life than that!" Mike said and threw a pillow at him.

"I feel like a snort," Ronco said nervously, "What do you say we spice up the juice with a little rubbing alcohol . . . I got some left." He rubbed his hands. What we had been talking about had really affected him. I felt sorry for him because I knew the question bothered him as much as any of us, but there didn't seem to be anything we could do about it . . . we had to go on living and looking for an answer.

"Ah, I'm sick of that too," Mike shook his head. "You know there's a whole ward of goof-heads back there, kids that have dried their brains out on glue and alcohol and anything else they can chew or sniff! Poor bastards, they're worse off than we are. They don't know what day it is. Most of them sit all day and stare, they mess in their pants and have to be fed like babies— They don't know anything. Hell they've even forgotten who they are! Their heads are so screwed up not a one of them remembers that the only reason he's in here is to get out!" He paused, looked at us and said, "Hell, I don't ever wanna forget that—"

"If you're so hard up and dissatisfied why don't you sneak over to the girls' ward and let Sandra settle you down," Sadsack grinned.

"I'm tired of that too!" Mike shot back. "I'm tired of anything that's too easy! For cryin' out loud! We're not supposed to be enjoying ourselves here! We're supposed to want to get the hell outta here! This is a prison, don't forget that . . . That's what they want us to forget, so they make it nice and easy for us. We get three square meals a day, a nice swimming pool, school, a crafts shop, they even let us get away with a little drinking and a little screwing on the side! Just enough to make us forget that our real purpose is to get out!"

"Hey, what more do you want?" Sadsack asked.

"I want out!" Mike shouted and slammed his fist against the night stand. "I'm getting too used to this place . . . hell, I'm only a step away from the vegetables! The only difference is I can move around! Don't you see that?" he pleaded.

"Maybe we can plan something," Ronco agreed.

"Let's gang bang the Nurse," Buck offered.

"Let's lock up old man Maloney in the laundry room like we did last year!" Sadsack laughed.

"Panty raid!"

"Burn the place down!"

"Smoke some weed—"

"Kid stuff!" Mike interrupted. "I wanna do something really big! I want a breath of fresh air—"

"Like what?" Buck asked. We were all listening now; Mike's enthusiasm spread to us and we leaned forward to hear his idea.

"Why don't we talk the doc into letting us go into town," Mike grinned.

"Alll-raght!" Ronco exclaimed and slapped his hands.

"Fat chance," Sadsack groaned.

"We can try!" Mike insisted.

"He owes us one!" Ronco shouted. "Remember we made a deal with him to behave during the Christmas party when the little old ladies of the Committee came around with their webbed socks of candy and crap! We stayed cool! And we helped keep the little kids in line!"

"Right. We sure did—"

"We can borrow that big bus that's never used!"

"Samson can drive it!"

"We can invite all the girls!"

"Yaaaa-ho! Gang bang! Lord, here I come!"

"Ooooh my—"

"Hey, we could go to a Saturday movie," Sadsack suggested. We grew excited at the prospect of the outing.

"Let's go talk to the doc!" Mike shouted.

"It's worth a try!" Ronco cheered.

They went out singing:

> *It's been a blue, blue day!*
> *We feel like running awayyyy*
> *From this place!*

19

The spring light bathed us with its glorious warmth, welcoming us into the fold of the church. Easter Sunday and we stood nervously in line, waiting admittance, glancing at the first holy communion girls who stood by us, full of the fragrance of holiness and fresh soap and lace . . . their cheeks were blushed with red, their eyes closed, they prayed, small, tender lips pursed in prayer . . . And I, in that shining light of early morning, blinded by the dazzling sun, felt the earth begin to turn beneath me, saw the nervous faces of the communion boys swirl around me, looked up and saw the giant tower of the church turning around and around until I thought it would come crashing down on me. Innocence! I cried, what is our sin? Lord, how have we sinned? I cried aloud and faces turned to look at me. I searched the girls' faces for a clue . . . I looked for the sin they had confessed in the dark confessional, and when they turned and looked at me they blushed that I had dared to ask . . .

After the mass, after the solemn procession into the cold church, after fidgeting on the hard wooden pews and kneeling on weathered, splintered wood, after the sacrifice of self to God . . . and the emptiness and loneliness, I turned again, sought in the soft, pink faces my sin, dared to look at their fragile hands clasped together and held to lips which trembled with prayer . . . asked again where was my innocence, which of these girls of the windfall light had stolen it away with her quick glance, with a toss of her head, with a whisper. And the silence of the church assured me that I would find my answer in the first communion girls, because they had shared my time of innocence and my first confession. I felt like gathering them in my arms and wrenching the truth they held from their warm, peaceful bodies . . . instead we marched out, once again in the glorious light of spring, swimming out of the darkness of the church into the pain of the bright light, and the miracle of miracles that was to reveal itself to me that dreadful day . . . for before the cheer could go up from the proud, waiting parents the Lord blessed my girls again, teased them with his power, stripped the veil of innocence and revealed the soft, pink flesh of their eager tongues . . . Great, white petals of snow floated down from the clear sky. We turned and looked up and shivered at the sight. The people turned their faces upward and crossed their foreheads. The wet flowers were a mystery, a silent snowstorm sent by God . . . petals as huge as silver dollars, glistening for a brief moment in the shining light, revealing the intricate pattern of their crystal bodies, revealing the dread and mystery of God . . . blessing us, cursing us . . . And my girls, my girls! I screamed at their nakedness! They stripped back the lace veils which had covered their faces and reached up to gather the falling petals in their mouths! They stuck out their warm, pink tongues and received the flakes of snow as calmly and innocently as they had taken the host from the priest's hands! They did not question the mystery! They did not see the fear in it! They had remained innocent! I screamed and flung myself away from the crowd and raced for the river where I could hide myself . . . .

"What the hell you screaming about?" Sadsack cursed.

"You okay?" Mike asked.

"Bad dream," I heard Buck whisper.

"I'm okay," I nodded and opened my eyes and felt the instant light blind me, and saw the snowflakes of my dream floating by the window. "I'm okay—"

"Aow, jee-sus! Will you look at that! It snowed!" Sadsack complained and spit on the floor. "Friggin' snow!"

I closed my eyes and tried to recapture the fading images of my dream. The river . . . the river had received me, hidden me. I had waited all morning in the shadows of the giant trees, and at noon the people came down the winding path where I had met la Llorona . . . singing, carrying great baskets full of food, led by the girls in white . . . down the winding path to the edge of the river where they set up tables and set the food for all to eat . . . and the men talked and laughed and sneaked away to take drinks of whiskey and wine . . . and the women talked to the girls about their duties to God and to men . . . I watched, hidden in the shadows, afraid to approach even my mother who searched for me among the boys who threw rocks across the water to see who could make them skip the greatest distance . . . skimming across the water which was mine, my river . . . and later the holy communion girls sang and danced, played their own game, spread flowers from their Easter baskets on the grass by the bank and held their hands as they danced in a big circle and watched me out of the corners of their eyes . . .

Someone in the hall sang:

Peter Pecker had a dog
And what a dog was he!
He took it to his mistress
And it bit her on the cock–

Tail, gingerale, five cents a glass
If you don't like my story
You can kiss my royal asss–

Ask me no questions and I'll tell you no lies
If you ever get hit by a bucket of shit
Be sure to close your eyes–

Ice by the bucket
Ice by the cube . . .

And the song faded.

"Listen to those idiots!" Sadsack moaned, "What are they so happy about? Bet the trip's cancelled 'cause of the snow!"

"A little snow's not goin' to stop this cowboy!" Buck said cheerfully.

"Yeah, Sad, where's your spirit?" Mike added.

"I planned on the movie and now I bet it's cancelled," Sadsack repeated.

"No way!" Buck grinned. "I'm goin' if I have to push my chair all the way down town! Mike said he fixed me up with Rosita, and is she pur-ty! Hot dog! Pur-ty as a filly on a spring day, and hot to trot! Yahooooo! Hey, Tortuga, you goin'?"

"Sure," I nodded. At first I hadn't planned on going, but Ismelda had said, you can't sit here forever . . . You need to get out. You need to begin to see the world. How is it out there? I asked, and she answered, nothing's changed, nothing's changed . . . "Sure I'm going—"

Ronco came in, dressed in a double-breasted, pin-stripped suit about two sizes too big for him. He had tied the baggy pants around his ankles so they ballooned out like the old zoot-suit pants, and he had found a broad-brimmed hat and sunglasses. He was carrying a pile of clothes for the rest of us, old discarded clothes which the Nurse had dug up for our trip to town.   .

"Oraleeee! You look like a real killer!" Mike laughed.

Ronco grinned and the thin mustache he had penciled over his lips curled up at the edges.

"Just call me Bogart," he said hoarsely.

"Oooo-weeee!" Buck whistled, "You're goin' to have to beat the women off you with that outfit!"

"Dig that!" Mike exclaimed. "Great! Great! Did you get the suit from the Nurse? Any left?"

"Plenty," Ronco said and dumped the clothes on the floor. "I got something for everyone." Mike dug into the pile. He found a tan suit for himself and laughed. He found a levi jacket and tossed it at Buck and

Buck immediately put it on and grinned. "Just what I needed! Hot dog! Find me some boots Mike! Boots! Hot dog!"

Mike found an old woolen cap and stuck it on my head, and for Sadsack there was a flea-bitten fur coat and a fisherman's hat which even made Sadsack smile. We were excited as we put on the wild outfits.

Ronco took out his shaving mug, lathered the soap up good and foamy and helped us shave. We splashed his watered down after shave lotion on our red faces and slicked our hair down with his pomade. By the time somebody shouted the bus was coming we were ready, nervous and excited. A sense of freedom filled the air. The rest of the boys who were going shouted up and down the hall. When we saw each other we laughed, but we were happy. We followed Mike and Ronco into the recreation room, singing our ward song:

> *Oh we're the boys of the institute!*
> *One, two . . . one, two . . .*
> *We love to drink and we love to screw,*
> *And we like the girls that like it too,*
> *One, two! One, two!*

The girls were already waiting for us. Normally they ran around in hospital-issue denim pants and shirts like us, but today they were dressed up in skirts and nylons. They had all teased their hair in wild hair-dos and had painted themselves with bright lipstick and blue mascara lashes. They looked grown up and exciting and they smiled coyly at us.

Buck went crazy. He let out a wild yahoo, tossed his hat in the air and headed straight for Rosita. Mike found Sandra as everybody surged towards the door and the waiting bus. I looked for Ismelda and saw her standing by Samson, helping to load the girls in chairs. When she saw me she smiled.

"Ready for the trip to town?" she asked.

I nodded. "Are you going with us?" I asked.

"I can't . . . a new girl just came in and I volunteered to stay with her. It looks like it's going to be a lot of fun," she smiled. Then she leaned and whispered in my ear, "It'll be good for you, just don't go get drunk in town—"

I laughed. "I won't," I said, "but I wish you were going—"

"Ready! Ready for the wheelchairs!" the Nurse shouted.

Samson lifted me, chair and all, and tossed me into the back of the bus. He slammed the door shut and ran around the side to the driver's seat. Everyone shouted and laughed and scrambled for seats, and when the bus lurched forward a loud cheer went up. I pushed towards the rear window to wave goodbye to Ismelda. She stood by the hospital door, waving and hugging her light sweater around her shoulders. The sun glistening on the snow around her blinded my eyes as I stared at her. Dressed in her white nurses-aide dress she reminded me of the girls in my dream. I waved back, waved until the bus dipped downhill and she disappeared from sight.

"Free at last!" someone shouted above the din.

"Yahoooo!" Buck responded and pulled Rosita on to his lap. She smiled and put her arms around his neck. He went crazy.

Somebody lit cigarettes and passed them around, and those who wanted took tokes.

"Is somebody smoking?" the Nurse shouted from the front seat, and Mike innocently answered, "Noooo m'mam."

A couple of girls sang high school fight songs while most of the fellows moved around and tried to fix themselves up with dates for the movie. Tuerto and Mudo wrestled on the seats and chased each other up and down the aisle. Mike and Sandra disappeared in a passionate embrace. I could hear Ronco and Sadsack shouting and calling, but I couldn't see them. Danny watched passively. He huddled in a corner and covered himself with the long coat he had started wearing to cover his arm and hump.

After Ismelda had disappeared from view I relaxed, settled into my chair and turned to watch the antics of the crowd. The bright sun shining on the snow and the images of the dream which kept sweeping over me made me dizzy, and I thought I was going to be sick. So I sat back quietly and tried to focus on something that would hold me still and make the nausea subside. The loud shrieks and shouts in the bus and the landscape flashing by the window mixed into a single vibration which rumbled in my stomach and increased the sickness. I wondered if I should have taken the trip to town; I wondered if I was ready . . .

Then something else pulled me from my musing. I sensed someone's eyes on me. I looked at Danny, but he seemed lost in his own thoughts, quietly staring out the window at the cold, empty streets. I turned and met Cynthia's stare. I hadn't seen her since the day I arrived. She sat quietly across the aisle with two other hunch-back girls with twisted backs and wrinkled faces. They were the ones the kids called the night people because they kept away from the other kids during the day and wandered the halls by night. Once when I was sick, after I had seen the vegetables in Salomón's ward, I thought I had seen Cynthia one night. I had heard them whispering around my bed like I had heard them around the gurney the afternoon I arrived, whispering about my fate, the terrible ordeal I had been through, Salomón's judgement, their own curse which had ravaged their bodies so completely that they were doomed to the night because they knew they were repulsive to the other kids. Only Ismelda and Salomón loved them, they said. They knew everything that had happened to me.

At least I thought I had seen or heard her during the time of that deep despair, I couldn't remember. Now she was sitting across the aisle with her two friends, glancing at me from time to time, exchanging whispers and giggling. They were dressed in white, a first communion white of silk and lace, and I had to wonder if Cynthia, or someone like her had been there the day we all made our first communion, the day we lost our innocence . . . the day which kept returning to me when I felt feverish or great moments of joy. I smiled, and yes, I could see them dancing in that glade by the river where the sun glimmered in the just-new cottonwood leaves . . . Did they know I had met la Llorona that day? Had they seen my nakedness and heard my curse? Were they with Ida and June and Rita and Agnes when they called my name . . . called me back into their arms . . . .

Tor-tuuuuuuu-gaaaa . . . they called, and the cry echoed down the river valley.

"Tortuga! Hey! We're here. Look."

I opened my eyes as the bus slid to a stop in the ice and slush in front of the movie house. The marquee said the Frankenstein movie was playing. It must have been a Saturday, because a small group of high school kids stood in line at the ticket window. They turned to watch us.

A wild cheer went up as soon as Samson opened the door. "Let's go play the pinball machine!" Tuerto shouted, and he and Mudo bounded out the door towards the cafe across the street.

"Hey! A drugstore!" Sandra shrieked. "We'll be right back!" she told Mike. She grabbed her crutches and scrambled with the other girls for the drugstore next door.

"Come back! You hear me? Come back!" the Nurse shouted, but nobody paid attention. In the meantime Samson quietly unloaded us and set us down on a wide sheet of ice which covered the sidewalk in front of the theatre.

"Hey, how about a drink before the movie starts?" Mike asked Ronco. He pointed at the bar down the street.

"You bet!" Ronco nodded.

"Me too!" Buck shouted.

"No! No!" the Nurse shouted and grabbed Mike's chair, almost slipping on the ice as she did, "You do that and we're going straight back up the hill! It's already bad enough! Everyone's supposed to stay in one group!"

"Okay, okay, hold your horses," Mike grinned, "I was just kidding—"

"Call the others back," she said, not letting go of his chair. Mike put two fingers to his mouth and whistled.

"Jee-sus, what's happening?" the dimpled girl in the ticket booth asked. Her mouth and eyes were opened wide. Around us the high school kids jabbed each other and laughed. They were mostly football players because they all wore letter jackets. Their girlfriends also wore sweaters and jackets with letters.

"We just escaped from the crazy house," Buck answered and pasted his face against the glass pane. The girl shrieked and jumped off her seat.

"It's all right, it's all right, we're from the hospital," the Nurse explained. "We called in about bringing the, the kids—"

Mike whistled again and the girls came rushing out of the drugstore. "The old bag in there told us to get out!" Sandra cried and took Mike's arm.

"Why?"

"She said we were a bunch of freaks, and we just wanted to make trouble . . . All I wanted was to buy some lipstick—"

"Ah, screw her," Mike said, "let's see the movie."

"Yeah, screw her," one of the girls repeated and threw a finger at the drugstore. "Sticks and stones may hurt my bones, but names will never hurt me!"

Across the street Mudo and Tuerto came careening out of the cafe with the cook on their tails. "You little bastards!" he shouted and waved his broom.

"Okay, Nurse, we're ready," Mike said.

"Line up! Line up for tickets!" the Nurse shouted.

Mike groaned. "Nurse, we don't have to line up. You know how many there are, right? So just buy the friggin' tickets—" He led the way into the theatre lobby and we followed. The startled manager asked for tickets but we swarmed past him. Everyone rushed for the popcorn and candy counter.

"Hey, what's this?" one of the surprised jocks cried out. He was a big guy with short, crew cut hair. "Have the freaks escaped?" His friends laughed.

"Fuck off!" Mike snarled. He stopped his chair in front of the bully and was ready to go at it, but Ronco pulled him back. "Come on, Mike, let's not waste time on the apes, let's go see the movie!"

"Yeah, dah apes!" Mudo muttered as we swept past the jocks and their cheerleader girlfriends.

Laughing and armed with popcorn and candy and cokes we entered the dark theatre. Mike led us to the front row where there was room for our chairs. Those who could threw aside their crutches and others lifted themselves from their chairs to sit on the theatre seats. Then amid much confusion and whistling and calling we settled down as the camera light flashed through the musty, dark air. We cheered the cartoon and booed the Movie-Tone news which showed us giant bombers high above the clouds dropping bombs on a small village somewhere in a dark jungle. Burning children screamed in pain, a scream we could not hear above the roar of the planes and the exploding bombs. The small theatre seemed to shake and tremble with the explosions.

I closed my eyes and tried to recall the images of my dream instead, but I couldn't. The booming voice of the news commentator would not let me slip back into my private world. And the greasy, foreign odors that clung to the movie seats filled my nostrils with body smells of prior passion and frustration. How many, I wondered, had come here to see their fantasies played out on the screen? How many lonely lovers? How many crippled bodies? How many dreams woven into the cracks and fabric of the dingy walls? I smelled the sweat of old desires . . . I heard the groans of love about me as in the dark my crippled friends groped for each other . . .

Tortuga, someone whispered, may I come and sit with you and hold you to my bosom in the dark?

I looked across the darkening water of the river . . . the dancing girls lifted their skirts to their knees and called for me to join; the tambourines beat a sensual dance.

I am here, I answered, hiding in the shadows of the cottonwood trees, here at the grove where the cattails grow so thick beside the river . . .

"Heeeeey! Tortuga!"

"Look! There's Dr. Steel!"

Cheers shook the theatre. The movie had begun. On the screen a mad doctor mumbled to himself, hidden partially by the jars and beakers of his laboratory, he did resemble Steel, he did turn and speak to . . . He told us he wanted to create a new man, a superman, someone not heir to the insane passions which ruled mankind . . . Look! he shouted and his arms swept outward and revealed his laboratory, I have all the scientific tools at my disposal to rival God! I can create a better man! I can create a man who will be free of the wickedness which plagues mankind . . . And I can infuse him with the fire of science, yes, I can revive his dead cells with this! He shouted, pulled aside the cloth which covered his secret machine, a table with wires running to the apparatus, electrodes to be implanted in the brain, glass bottle and tubes for feeding . . . and suddenly he pulled the switch and the machine sputtered alive with electricity, hot, flashing electricity which sputtered from one pole to the other . . .

"That's Steel all right!" someone shouted.

"Playing God!"

"A little cut here, a little cut there!"

"Bull!" Sadsack scoffed and farted in the dark.

"Oh my!" Billy cried.

"Looks like surgery day—"

"Yeah, here come the patients! Right out of the vegetable ward!"

We looked as the doctor and his assistants haunted the cemeteries and collected the cadavers he needed for his experiment. Later, in his laboratory, in the secrecy of night, he scrubbed them down and dissected them carefully, like a used car lot mechanic looking for the best used parts.

We laughed uneasily. The creature which took form under the mad doctor's hands was one of us. We too were patched up with steel pins, braces, implanted nerves and muscles. We too knew how it felt to be created again, to breathe new life again. We watched intently as the dark clouds of winter swept around the laboratory and the wolves howled in the forest. The doctor didn't notice anything. His eyes burned with the mad obsession of creation, he stopped eating or sleeping, he was driven to finish his new man. And the poor grotesque monster grew as the doctor sewed and patched together the different parts of human bodies. We cringed in the dark; even Steel had never gone that far. This was life and death. This was a part of the nagging question we faced when we thought of the vegetables . . . poor creatures kept alive, mummified, denied death, cheating death, until the mad doctor came to haunt their ward with his machine, forcing them to come alive, forcing them to walk . . . oh God pity them if that should happen, what worse fate than to be dead and walking in the desert . . . alone, each one alone . . .

"Hey! Lookee!" somebody whispered.

I looked and saw the doctor rub his hands. His eyes were wild with fever. He was done. Now he was ready for the final step. Damn the people and their fear of life. Now he would show them that the secret of life was his, he shouted. He threw the switch of his machine, the generator whined and green flashes of fire hissed across the poles. The monster jerked with life. I winced with pity, remembering how painful the rebirth of my own nerves had been. The monster's face twisted with pain and the movie house vibrated with the terrible force of the generator as the pulses of fire went crashing into his brain.

"He's gonna do it—"

"Shhhh . . ."

The doctor laughed crazily and threw the switch again, and again I felt the fire flow through my nerves and spasm the muscles. The monster twitched again, his eyelids fluttered, he tugged at his straps.

"Get up!" Mike shouted.

"You can do it, Frankie!" Ronco added.

"Shut up in front!" someone shouted from the back.

"Damn kids!"

"It's the freaks from the hospital!"

"Quiet! Quiet please—" the manager ran up and down the aisle like a shadow.

On the screen the doctor walked away, broken hearted, his monster had not moved. In the dark Rosita giggled and told Buck she couldn't reach him through his bandages.

"I'll sure fix that!" Buck responded, and he stood up and began to unwind his bandages. Even in the dark we could see him tossing the bandages in the aisle.

"You crazy sonofabitch!" Mike shouted, "Take it off!"

"All the way!" Ronco clapped his hands.

Everyone began to clap and shout, "Take it off! Take it off!"

"Quuuaaaaa-yet!"

"Down in front!"

"What's going on down there!"

"Damn creeps!"

"Creeps yourselves! Can't you see Buck's doing it!" Ronco shouted back.

Alone on the screen, long after his master had gone, the monster's eyes fluttered open, he lifted his head and looked about the room, and he tore at his straps and freed himself. In the dark Buck finished tearing away the bandages, pounded his bare chest like Tarzan then jumped on Rosita. They disappeared behind a seat. Everybody cheered. Others followed Buck's example. Braces and corsets were removed and thrown in the aisle. Crutches and wheelchairs and coats and sweaters joined the clutter. Kids crawled on the floor, groping in the dark, forming a twisting, squirming pile which became an orgy. The girls moaned and the boys kissed them frantically. Groans filled the dark corner we had moved into. On the screen, too, our hero had met his love; he gazed at the blonde woman with love-glazed eyes.

A girl panted and moaned, "Oh my God, ooooh—"

Even Billy was drawn into the panting, sweating pile. I heard him say, "Oh my . . . I can't . . . no . . . Ohhhhh my—"

I looked around and saw that only Danny and Cynthia and I remained outside the pile of wet, groaning bodies. Desire filled my stomach and tingled in my thighs, but I couldn't move. I thought of Ismelda and wished she was here, wished I could hold her in my arms and dive into the pile with her, sucking, biting, ravaging her warm lips . . . then turned to the screen where our hero searched the misty marshes for his love. He, too, was driven by the human flesh he had inherited. He, too, braved the howling storm and the wrath of the aroused townspeople to reach his love. He, too, burned with the wet-acid of life and sought its release.

Suddenly, I, too, was filled with the need to love. My grotesque hero on the tattered screen reached out and touched his woman. For a moment she responded. Love filled the movie house. I smelled it, wet and clinging to the pants of the frantic boys, smeared on groping fingers, confused on smacking wet lips and nipples which grew erect with caresses never felt before. Everyone was giving, everyone was receiving.

The shadows moved from body to body, filling themselves with love. In the dark there were no twisted bodies, only the caresses of aching fingers which tore into the flesh to get to the soul.

That's what Salomón had said. That love was the only faith which gave meaning to our race across the beach. The path of the sun was the path of love. I needed to love!

That's it, I whispered to myself and laughed. I need to love! I need to reach out and embrace my life! Like one of Salomón's butterflies I squirmed and struggled to crack the darkness of my chrysalis! I laughed and reached out. I felt the strength in my arms and legs and at that moment I thought I could stand and walk. I laughed and cried, come help me break this shell! Come help me beat this fear. Desire washed over me like liquid fire; my loins ached with love and my heart pounded madly in my chest.

"Ismelda," I whispered, "I am full of love—" I felt her body in my arms.

"Tortuga," Cynthia whispered, "I need your love—"

She pressed close to me and put her arms around my neck. In the flashes of dim light her wrinkled face was soft with love. I reached out to hold her and felt the curse of her hump. For a moment my desire drained away. I remembered the night I came to the hospital and how Cynthia had met me in the dark, and for a moment her face was the face of the girl in the iron lung deep in Salomón's ward. I cringed with fear. I turned away and on the screen our hero, too, had met his love. He reached out to hold her, and suddenly a scream formed on her lips and terror filled her eyes.

"I know you love Ismelda," Cynthia said to me, "but love me for now . . . just for now . . ."

The woman screamed. It was a scream of fear and terror. We turned in time to see her strike at the monster. He cringed under her attack. I love you, he whispered hoarsely, surprised that she responded with blows.

"Get 'er, Frankie!" someone shouted, probably Mike.

"Yeah! Put it to her! Screw 'er!"

Popcorn rained on the screen and hisses filled the small theatre. We were angry because she repulsed our hero's love.

"Eat 'er up!"

"Give it to her!"

"Yeah!" I shouted and cursed the stupid woman, "Give it to her!"

"Kiss me," Cynthia begged, clinging to me, crawling up my lap to press her twisted face against mine. "I've never been kissed before—"

I looked into her eyes and swallowed the scream at my throat. I reached around her hump and drew her close to me. Somewhere beyond the clamor which filled the theatre I heard the rattle of the tambourines . . . and in the light which flashed across Cynthia's face and in her eyes which held a love for me I suddenly saw the first communion girls waving at me . . . .

Oh Cynthia, I cried, have you danced with the girls who held my innocence in their young hearts? Were your legs and arms once as supple as the limbs of my girls? Did you wave to me from across the river . . . that Sunday we took the host and felt the silence of God in our hearts . . . that bright spring day when they mixed the miracle of their god with the pagan rites of spring and dared to shout for all to hear, come dance with us! Oh pain of innocence! Oh pain of love . . . I am full of love . . .

"Yes," Cynthia whispered, "yes . . ."

I tightened my embrace and the dread, which was never mine to begin with, melted away. Cynthia's breath was warm and sweet on my face. Her skin was as soft as any woman's flesh. My need to give my love pounded in my heart and ran hot and wet in my loins. I laughed and saw her as my woman, grown ripe from that first spring day, blossomed into a luscious fruit on the path of the sun, offering me her pure and crippled love . . . I ran my broken hand along her stomach and caressed her small, swelling breasts. She moaned and closed her eyes, and I drew her close.

"My heart is full of love for you," she whispered.

"And I am full of love—" I answered. Her lips opened to receive mine, and I felt the flicker of her tongue push into my mouth as she opened me up to receive her love. I gasped then sucked as her saliva mixed with mine, warm and sweet and syrupy. Her small breasts, swollen with love, pressed against my chest and made the fire of the kiss race into my stomach and legs. My blood throbbed with love. Her fingers caressed my face and hair.

I reached eagerly into her, biting at the warm lips that dissolved in mine, tearing at the flesh which moaned so softly and made mine grow with power.

In the still cottonwood air the tambourines vibrate; their soft resonance is like the swirl of butterflies filling the green spring day.

I am full of love, I whispered, and widened my embrace, took Cynthia in, made her dissolve into my love. Somewhere Ismelda waved at me and smiled, and I turned and waved. I am full of love, I shouted, and she smiled and beat her tambourine tenderly, softly, bringing out its moaning song.

In the suck of our kisses I heard Salomón hum a song for his cripples, and I turned and waved to him and saw the butterflies of love start their journey across the desert.

Love sang and laughed in my throat. It tickled as we rubbed. Cynthia tightened her arms around my neck and pulled herself up on my lap, and I pulled her toward me, still clinging to the kiss, still sucking at the hot juices which mixed in our mouths, crushing each other in our mad embrace.

"Tortuga, my brother . . . my lover," she smiled, and the last brittle remnants of my shell fell crashing to the floor. Around me, in the dark groans and moans I heard other shells break and fall away. Love released us from our chains and filled us with its ache, a sweet pain whose only answer was the touch of a caress. I looked around and heard myself laughing in the dark. I laughed as hard as I could, and shouted, then turned to bury my wounded soul in sweet Cynthia's body. I kissed hard and sucked the blood from her warm lips. She bit back and made my lips tingle with love. She laughed and moaned and twisted like a woman at the peak of love, pulled me into her web of love, shared her warm thighs with me, caressed my awakened body and pulled it into hers.

On the screen the woman had screamed again. She beat back our hero and called for help. I cursed her and the hollywood hero who ran to help her, and I cursed the men who gathered with torches to destroy the doctor and his creation.

There is no fear in love, I felt like shouting, like Salomón would shout.

Look! I cried, don't you see! And I turned and kissed Cynthia, and Ismelda and Dr. Steel and KC and Danny, Tuerto, Mudo, Mike, Ronco, Sadsack, and yes, the poor creatures who rested in the iron lungs deep in Salomón's ward, I cradled them in my arms and cried and kissed their frozen lips and mixed my tears with theirs.

I reached into my dream, made it appear before me, made it appear on the screen for all to see, saw myself running across the river, my chest naked and glistening in the bright sun, shouting, waving at the communion girls who waited for me with open arms. I'm coming! I shouted, I'm coming!

I embraced them, finally, broke the web of separation, turned and embraced the monster on the screen, cursed the woman who feared him but embraced her also, kissed my grandfather's beard and his bald head, my mother, my father, everyone I could find I kissed in anger and in joy! My love and passion flooded the desert. I was drenched in sweat.

Cynthia trembled and pulled me down, but I couldn't hold her. Her weight pulled us sideways, my hand slipped from around her hump and the chair tipped over. Her braces scratched my legs as we went down. I reached out and tried to brace our fall as we tumbled to the floor. And as quickly as it began it was over. Cynthia balanced herself then scrambled up and righted the chair. She helped me sit.

"I won't tell Ismelda that you loved me," she whispered and slipped into the dark.

The catcalls and cheering turned in my direction.

"Hey! Is that Tortuga? Is Tortuga getting some?" Mike called.

"Yeah! Tortuga's making out!" someone answered.

"Híjola! Tortuga's getting some!"

"He's not a turtle anymore! He's a lizard!"

"Oh my, el Lagarto—"

Everybody laughed and cheered three times for el Lagarto. I laughed with them. My heart was pounding and my legs and arms were trembling, but I felt great. Yeah, I thought, el Lagarto on his way home.

Flashes of fire returned our attention to the screen. A mob of angry men armed with rifles and torches had hunted down the monster. They cursed at him and taunted him.

I raised my fist and cursed back. "You sonsofbitches! You can't kill our hero! He's going to screw your women and screw all of you!"

"Yaaaaaay!" the kids took on the cheer. "Leave our hero alone!" "You tell 'em Lagarto!"

We hissed the angry men and cheered our hero. Popcorn, candy wrappers, a pair of panties and dixie cups full of ice splattered against the screen.

"Down in front!" the people in the back shouted. "Shut up!"

"Fuck all of you!" Mike shouted. "Can't you see our hero's in trouble!" But it was too late. The monster had been driven back in confusion. All he wanted to do was to talk to them, because he, too, was a man, but they had turned on him. For a moment he turned and looked at us, but we couldn't help him. If we could have we would have warned him about the fear in people, but now it was too late. Hate curled on his lips and anger burned in his eyes. He had no choice but to protect himself.

"Get 'em, Frankie! Get 'em!" we cheered when we saw him raise the club.

"Don't let 'em push you around, Frankie!"

"Give it to them!"

"Down in front!" "Quaaaaaaaaa-yet!"

The mob pulled back, cursing the creation of the mad doctor, and setting fire to the castle. Inside the laboratory our hero turned on his creator. Full of anger and frustration he blamed the mad doctor for his torment. They clutched at each other and stumbled around the laboratory like two giant bears locked in a death dance. Outside the mob cheered as the flames licked at the castle walls. The roaring fire danced in their evil, frightened eyes.

I shuddered and turned away. Our hero and the doctor crashed against the same machine which earlier charged the monster with life. Now it sputtered with fire and hissed as it burned them alive. A loud explosion rocked the theatre as the castle collapsed in a shower of sparks.

In the bright light the mob cheered. We remained silent, tears wet our eyes. Someone sang a mournful,

Poor ole Frankie
He never got a kiss . . .
Poor ole Frankie
He don' know what he miss . . .

"That was a dumb ending," someone whispered in the dark, but we were too tired even to throw popcorn at the screen. We felt double-crossed by the ending.

Then Sadsack started screaming in the dark. I couldn't tell what was happening but Mike later told me that Sadsack had tried to make it with a girl who wore leg braces and had gotten his tool caught. He screamed bloody murder until Mike and Ronco pulled him free.

"You damn weirdo," I heard the girl curse, "no wonder they call you Sadsack! You can't do anything right!" Then she stalked away. Everybody was laughing and trying to find out what had happened.

"My tool! My tool!" I heard Sadsack groan, "Oh, it's ruined!"

"What's going on here? What's the matter?" the manager cried. A crowd had formed around Sadsack, wanting to know what happened.

"It's okay, everything's under control," Mike assured the manager. "Okay, gang, let's go home!"

The clothes from the pile had already been reclaimed, the wheel-chairs righted and crutches returned to their owners. We filed out, leaving the nervous manager scratching his head and shaking it from side to side. We were exhausted but happy.

On the way out Buck slapped my back and said, "Damn that Rosita's a beautiful woman . . . I'm goin' marry her someday. And that Sadsack's crazier than a bronc that ate loco weed! Whooo-wee, did you see what he tried to do?"

We laughed. "It was crazy," I said.

"Fantastic!" Buck said.

I had to agree. I looked for Cynthia, but I couldn't see her in the crowd and when we got outside into the blinding, glaring light we heard a loud commotion and I forgot about her.

"Something's up!" Buck shouted and pushed his chair forward. I followed. Right outside the theatre the jocks had surrounded Mike and Sandra. They were razzing them in a bad way.

"Hey, the movie freaks got loose!" the ring leader laughed.

"I didn't know there was a circus in town," his girlfriend added.

"Step right this way and see the one-legged woman—" I heard him shout. I broke through the crowd in time to see Mike swing and the big jock double over.

When his girlfriend leaned over to help him Sandra rammed her with her crutch and shouted, "Step this way and see the girl with a crutch up her ass!"

The girl screamed and jumped up. Sandra swung her crutch again and drove it into the girl's stomach. One of the high school boys grabbed Mike from behind and they spun on the sheet of ice. Then Ronco shouted his war cry and went crashing into them.

"Eeeeeeee-jola! Chingasos! Blows!" He crashed his chair into the kid that held Mike, swung him around and hit him as hard as he could in the face. I heard the jock's nose crunch and saw the blood spurt out. Mike and Ronco had powerful arms, and the jocks had underestimated that. That and the fact that on the ice the wheelchairs were steadier than sliding feet.

A third boy jumped in, but by that time Buck had whipped out his rope. The lariat zipped through the air and when Buck jerked the noose tightened around the boy's neck and flipped him off his feet.

We cheered. Cries of "Fight! Fight!" filled the cold air. The Nurse, who had spent the movie time drinking coffee across the street, rushed into the pile shouting, "Stop it! Stop it!" and when she hit the ice she slid into the free-for-all and went under. "Saaaaaam-son! Help me!" she cried out.

Ronco tore into the rest of the jocks. He'd hit one then push him towards Mike, and Mike would clobber the poor bastard and trip him into the pile. And everytime the jock that Buck had lassoed regained his footing Buck would shout, "Yahoo! Ride 'em cowboy!" jerk the rope and send the bully crashing into the ice again.

Those of us who couldn't get into the middle of the brawl let loose with snowballs. The girls had jumped in to help Sandra, too. They grabbed the cheerleaders by the hair and spun them around the ice. It was a bloody, screaming free-for-all. Even Samson dipped into the pile and pulled two jocks off Ronco. He held them up by their collars, grinned, then slammed their heads together and tossed them aside. We cheered and he took a short bow, repeated his act then courteously helped the poor Nurse to her feet.

"Everybody in the bus!" the Nurse shouted. We drew back and began to board reluctantly. The jocks had pulled back. They had been whipped, and now the manager ran around threatening everybody with the sheriff. The people who had gathered to watch the fight stood around laughing or looking dumbly with open mouths.

"Get in the bus! Get in the bus!" the Nurse shouted. Mudo and Tuerto climbed down from the top of the bus which they had used as a good position to clobber the jocks with snowballs and ice chunks.

"Dirty fighters," the jocks called out.

"We showed you!" Mike called back and raised a fist.

"Hot dog, we got those sombitches!"

"They can't mess with us and get away with it!" Ronco laughed.

Samson loaded the last chair and closed the door. The manager was having difficulty holding the jocks back. They realized they had been beaten and they were mad as the crazy hornets they had sewn on their jackets. They surrounded the bus and pounded furiously on it. Some of the kids pulled down their windows and spit on them.

155

"We'll get you the next time!" their leader swore.

"Yeah! Don't ever come back to town you damn freaks!" a girl added.

They scooped up snow, packed it into hard snowballs and bombarded the bus. But Samson had already closed the door and started the bus. As it jerked away from the theatre the snowballs splattered harmlessly against its side. We threw fingers and waved.

"You couldn't fight your way out of a paper bag!" Ronco taunted them as we drove away. He turned to us and added, "Damn I wish I had a drink—" He grinned. One eye was red and his upper lip was cut and bleeding.

"Pick on someone your own size next time!" Mike shouted.

"Mike! Boys!" the Nurse tried to calm us down, "Everybody sit down! I have to count to see if anybody got left!" Her hat rested awkwardly on the side of her head, her hair was disarranged and she shouted for order, but she was smiling. It was the first time I had ever seen her smile.

"Yah, yah, 'an don' go-go mess wid us!" Mudo stuttered and we howled with laughter.

"Sticks and stones may hurt my bones! But names will never hurt me!" Sandra yelled, but we were already out of reach of their snowballs and they couldn't hear us.

Samson turned the chugging bus up the hill into the bright afternoon sun. We settled down to lick our wounds and to recount the battle. The boys who had received cuts told how they got them and compared them, and they shyly let the girls fuss over them. Everybody was exhausted, but floating high with the excitement of the fight. The girls picked up the tune of our fight song and sang.

> *Oh we're the girls of the institute!*
> *We like to smoke and we like to chew*
> *And we love the boys that like to screw!*

Everybody joined them in a resounding, "One-two! One-two!"

We laughed and cheered and filled the bus with thunder. We talked about the movie and about the fight and how great the adventure had been, and then we settled back into our seats and chairs and relaxed as the slow chugging bus made its way up the hill. Bobby Dee, a small kid who could really play the harmonica warbled a tune, and a long-haired girl next to him sang softly, the words from Cawliga, the Indian who never got a kiss, the man who was like Frankenstein in the movie, the man who was like all of us . . .

156

Poooooooor ole Cawliga . . .
He never got a kissss . . .
Poooor ole Caaaaaaw-liga!
He don' know whaad he missed.

We listened quietly to the sad song. Even Samson, squinting into the light, hummed the tune. The Nurse straightened her cap and sighed relief. The words of the song drifted out the open windows to mix with the warm spring air which had come to melt the snow. Somewhere a meadowlark sang. The air was full of love and strange longings. I looked across the aisle at Cynthia and she smiled and blushed. She smoothed her skirt around her lap and sat quietly. I smiled and turned to look across the valley at Tortuga. There was a trace of spring green on his sides. Beneath him the river was a sheen of silver light in the setting sun. The glaring light flashed across my window, and I strained to look at the budding cottonwood trees which lined the river . . . smiled, looked and saw the circle of white beneath the trees, my first communion girls dancing in a ring . . . holding hands and dancing in a wide circle, a dance of spring . . . and I remembered it was almost Easter. They turned and looked at me as the bus climbed the hill, and I thought I recognized them, knew them all . . . Ida and June and Agnes and Rita . . . innocent faces taken from the angels of limbo, the babes of the Virgin in the picture at church . . . and dancing with them for the first time was Cynthia. The light filled the bus, filled it with spring's song, glowed white as it enveloped us, filtered through the bare spring trees and danced off the white dresses of the dancing girls . . . reflected from the windows of the bus and swirled like a kaleidoscope as the bus turned and turned, climbing the hill, becoming the end of a bright dream, the kind one has on summer days . . . and they had smiled and waved, out of that time so far away, so much a part of my memory, they had waved and welcomed me . . . they were waiting for me to return, crippled lizard that I was, I would find peace in their arms, I would shine like a new mystery in their hearts . . .

The bus floated in the strong, white light of spring. Overcome with joy and love I closed my eyes and listened to the song forming in my dreams . . . .

20

I returned to therapy every day. After a workout with KC, I sat in the whirlpool bath and felt the stiffness in the muscles drain away as Tortuga's waters massaged me with their magic. Since the incident at the pool Danny had stayed close to me. He was always near-by. When I looked at him and let him know I was aware of him he would look startled, as if he had been caught staring, then he would move away. Otherwise, he stuck close to me, watching me, closely following my progress.

Once he gathered enough nerve to draw close to me and whisper his anguish. "What do they look like?" he asked, and before I could answer he was gone. His entire side was withered now, and his arm bent him over until he shuffled like an old man weighted down by the hump of age settling on his back. The next time he drew close he almost cried as he hoarsely whispered, "W-Why are they being kept alive? Why?" I felt his pain and I was filled with pity for him.

I knew he was afraid, afraid he would wind up like one of the vegetables in Salomón's ward. His uncurable disease was drying him up and pulling him into their world. Sometimes he whispered that he heard them calling him, and he cursed them. They had become his only obsession, that's all he wanted to talk about, and so everybody had deserted him, even his two friends Mudo and Tuerto. They were still playing their pranks and practical jokes, but Danny had withdrawn from everybody. When he wasn't following me he wandered the halls alone, muttering to himself, rubbing his withered arm, and cautiously working his way to the door which led to the vegetable patch and the other wards. They told me he spent a lot of time looking at the door, as if he was building up the courage to enter the dark hall, and instead he always turned away in a fit of anguish.

He was suffering all right, and I felt sorry for him. Sometimes he would look at me and curse me, and it was because I had been to see them and he couldn't.

"You could've drowned in the pool!" he hissed at me, reminding me of my torment, trying to draw me out.

"It didn't matter then," I said.

"And now?"

"Now it matters," I shrugged. "I couldn't face death alone... I found that out. And now life is important to me, even Salomón's vegetables are important—" I paused. "In fact, they might be the reason I'm alive. Don't you see that?" I asked and reached out to touch him, but he drew back and snapped at me.

"Even after you saw them? You still think life is important after you saw them? Well what about them? What about them being there to rot the rest of their lives, not being able to move a finger! Not being able to feed themselves or wipe themselves! What about them?"

"I don't know," I shook my head.

"You don't know anything!" he shouted. "And you still believe what Salomón says about singing. You're crazy, you can't even sing!" he sneered. "How can you believe that creep after what he pulled on you, huh?"

"I trust him," I answered.

"Trust him? Oh God, you can trust him!"

"Talk to him," I said in desperation, "go talk to him."

"It won't do any good," he moaned, "it's no good... I'm being punished—you know what Salomón said about that..."

No, Tortuga, Salomón had said, the garden of cripples is not a place of punishment. Don't you see that punishment would give meaning to our existence. If we could say we're being punished then it would follow that God is punishing us, and we would be worse off than we were before... we would go on fabricating lie upon lie... It's very difficult to accept the fact that our existence has no meaning to the absent god. The only meaning it has is the meaning we give it... we can't blame the gods. That's too easy, but natural. Man has always taken his fear and pain and suffering and made strange gods from those shadows of his soul. Those gods are shadows, Tortuga, reflections of our weakness... I have read all the myths, and that's how it has been... shadow upon dark shadow of the cave dancing to the light of the flickering fire, dancing itself into a form in the mind of fearful man... and none of those gods could return and say I do not exist, because once they were given the substance of thought they generated their own power, they grew stronger, they no longer needed man... Oh, there have been a few heroes who have tried to steal the light of the cosmos, the eternal light which burns away all shadows, but they were few... Prometheus, hero of the Greeks, petty thief of fire and light... fails to gain his own freedom and thus fails us because in the end he turns and blames his punishment on that sham jury on Olympus and the fornicator Zeus! Oh God, if only he had not needed to give meaning to his punishment... what a great hero he would have been. He peered into the light of heaven, he touched it! And then he cries to the gods of Olympus and begs their forgiveness! Oh what a waste . . . what a tragedy to us . . .

Even Christ, in his triumphant hour upon the cross . . . at that moment when he can free himself from the darkness forever, when he can most be man and god at the same time . . . he fails us, he turns and blames his father who has forsaken him. So even the new myths are incomplete. Our heroes have not been able to suffer alone. In their last moment of anguish and pain they turn to the shadows dancing on the wall . . . turn to the past and the darkness . . . Even the modern Sisyphus cannot serve us. He is like us because he feels the interminable pain of that huge boulder he must push up the hill. He is a god crippled from that incessant labor. His spine is bent, his shoulder humped and cut to the bone, he knows pain and he knows the time of eternity which he will suffer . . . So in many ways he is like us, a poor vegetable pushing up against the boulder, reaching for the light, knowing he will never be free of that task . . . But he, too, fails the test. Because on his way down the hill he raises his fist and curses the gods who condemned him to eternal punishment! Don't you see, his punishment would be complete if he did not curse the gods . . . if he could walk alone! Only then could he be free! Only then could he turn and look around and see that old friends from Corinth wander the valleys of Hades . . . and yes, he even has the pleasure of an occasional country woman . . .

And is his torment as severe as that of my cripples? Monotonous, yes, and difficult. But think, on the way back down the hill he can feel the cool breeze on his sweaty body, and he can feel the fatigue of his labor drain away as he walks slowly down the hill . . . Ha! Sisyphus is a lucky king compared to us! Far in the distance someone plays a lyre, old melodies of home, and from time to time a friend comes by and they talk and drink wine and remember the days when Corinth was in its glory. Which one of us would not gladly exchange our place with him? No, Tortuga, we are beyond the last Greek hero . . . we are beyond all the heroes of the past . . . We have come to a new plane in the time of eternity . . . we have gone far beyond the punishment of the gods. We are beyond everything that we have ever known, and the past is useless to us. We must create out of our ashes. Our own hero must be born out of this wasteland, like the phoenix bird of the desert he must rise again from the ashes of our withered bodies . . . and he must not turn to the shadows of the past. He must walk in the path of the sun . . . and he shall sing the songs of the sun. It may be that we will find someone who crossed the desert in Filomón's cart, someone who suffered like us as he felt the fire in his body go dry and the juices die in his bones . . . someone who has felt the paralysis of life, and walked in the garden with his brothers and sisters, and who will sing of his adventures . . .

160

"Yes," I nodded and looked at Danny, "I know what Salomón said."

"But what does it mean?" he pleaded.

"I don't know—"

"But you should know!" he insisted and grew angry, "He made you walk in the garden! He made you see the vegetables! You should know why! No! You do know, but you're just not telling me . . . that's it! You and Salomón and all the rest know, but you're not telling me! I see it now!" He trembled with anger. He grabbed me by the shoulders and shouted into my face, "You want me to go see for myself! That's it! You want me to go into Salomón's ward and crawl in one of those machines and stay there forever! You want me to become one of those rotten vegetables! I see it now! I see the plan now! To get me in there!" He laughed crazily and swore at me. "Well you're not ever going to get me to go in there and become one of those vegetables! I'd rather die! You hear me you little bastard lizard! I'd rather die!"

He pushed me away and stalked out of the room, shouting, "No! Never! Never!"

21

That same afternoon I stood and walked the parallel bars for the first time. The word had spread that KC had given me permission to walk by myself, so quite a few kids came to watch. Everybody knew that walking the bars meant real freedom, especially if one didn't have to wait around for braces, and my legs didn't need braces. I would need crutches for awhile, but no braces.

The therapy room was crowded as KC pushed my chair to the end of the bars. "You're on your own, honey," she whispered. I looked down the long bars and at the full length mirror at the end. I nodded. I was ready.

Ismelda stood by me. "A lizard that can stand up becomes a man," she whispered. I smiled.

"You can do it, honey," KC said and helped me up from my chair. I gripped the bar with my right hand and pulled myself up. I felt the weight strain my trembling legs and locked my knees so I wouldn't fall. My legs quivered, but they held.

"Atta boy," Mike nodded from the corner.

"Do it!" Ronco smiled.

"Hot dog, that dude's ready for the round-up," Buck drawled. They crossed their fingers and watched me carefully.

I lifted my right leg and took the first step. My body moved stiffly over the fulcrum point, swayed momentarily, flushed hot with sweat, trembled like the earth trembled when Tortuga moved, then it settled down and I lifted my left leg. The kids cheered. Somewhere in the background Danny's dark eyes bore into me, then he cursed and hobbled away. At the door Dr. Steel paused to watch. He looked at me and smiled, then he nodded at the other doctors and they moved on to the surgery room.

"How's it feel, babe?" KC asked.

"Okay," I answered. She walked alongside me, watching carefully, ready to move if I toppled. Ismelda walked on the other side. The trembling was gone. With each step I took I felt stronger. I moved ahead, breathing hard and sweating. At the end of the bars I stopped to rest. I looked up and saw myself in the full length mirror. I didn't recognize myself. I was skinny and stiff and twisted with the weight of the cast I had carried for so long. My hair hung nearly to my shoulders. I wasn't the person I remembered from before the paralysis; I was a new man, a just-born man trying to coordinate my movements. Who was I, then, I asked and looked around the quiet room.

Are you okay?

Anything the matter?

What's happening? Whad he say?

It's okay, take a rest. You'll be fine . . .

Who am I? I asked. Who was born in that shell of plaster? Am I the same boy that went into the heart of the mountain and heard Salomón whisper the story of his butterflies? Was I the same man who walked through Salomón's ward and suffered the pain of its existence? How long had I been in the hospital? And what did it all mean? I looked at myself in the mirror and saw the layers of my past fall away, like the sheaths of an onion strip away to expose the little green heart at the core.

"Wanna try it again?" KC asked.

"Sure . . . fine," I answered. The faces in the room swam about me. They were here to celebrate one more step of my freedom. I smiled. I held back my tears. How could I ever take another step in my life without seeing them? Would I ever be free of them? Or was this my new weight? The memory of them would always come rushing down on me, whispering to me, forcing me to remember every incident, every detail, every crippled arm and leg, every twisted back, every scarred face, each breathing iron lung which guarded life in the dark wards . . .

Ismelda touched my hand. "You're all right, Tortuga . . ."

I turned away from the mirror and slowly walked back to my chair. Samson held it and I plopped into it. Behind me there were shouts and clapping, echoing as if from far away. Someone shouted the mountain was moving and there was a stampede of what sounded like goat hooves over the tiled floor to the windows. I heard the Nurse shout that it was medication time, and I felt KC's strong arms help me into the whirlpool bath. Mike and Ronco and the others gathered around me and shouted and slapped my back . . . then the water splashed like hot pee into the steel tub and soaked me with its magic. I closed my eyes and floated in it, allowing it to wash away my tiredness and the tears I was fighting to hold back. Somewhere I knew Dr. Steel was cutting into sensitive flesh, groping for a nerve, splicing tendons . . . and the flesh, drugged though it was, quivered from the pain . . .

Tortuga! Salomón smiled, look! See the strings of geese flying north! Can you hear their joyful cry in the night as they follow the river north! It's time to sing again, Tortuga, time to sing!

163

"Yes," I nodded, "yes—"

"What's that?" KC asked.

"I'm okay," I answered, "just a little tired . . ."

"The first walk is always the most tiring, honey, but it's gravy from here on."

I stood up and she threw a large towel over me and dried me down. I was sweating again by the time I finished dressing, but I felt good. And I felt sad, because I knew now I was leaving. It was only a matter of weeks, maybe days, and Steel would give me my walking papers.

"How do you feel?" Ismelda asked as she pushed my chair back to the ward. She had waited for me.

"I feel fine," I answered, "I feel like I could walk back to the ward."

"You probably could. I heard the doctor say you can have a pair of crutches tomorrow . . . after that it's just a matter of time—"

The recreation room was deserted so she pushed the chair to one of the large windows. She faced my chair so I could look at the mountain. She sat on the sill and for a long time we were silent, but I knew we were thinking the same thing. The test today told everyone I was ready to leave. Even before the walk on the bars Mike and Ismelda knew I was ready because I had been practicing standing around the bed, so I was strong enough. The walk on the bars had been a public show for KC and Steel, now they were satisfied, but it had been more than that for me, it had been a step which seemed to seal another part of my destiny. I was ready to leave. I was ready for the journey north.

"Damn, I can't remember how long I've been here," I said as I looked across the valley at the mountain. Spots of spring green appeared on its once barren sides.

"It doesn't matter," Ismelda smiled, "the important thing is that you're going home—"

She said it, we looked at each other and relaxed. I nodded and smiled at her. She held my hand and said, "You were great today . . . I was proud of you."

"I felt strong. I think with crutches I could walk all the way up the mountain—"

We looked at old Tortuga as he bathed in the afternoon light. "The ground is thawing up there," she said. "The thaw always creates a movement in the earth. Old Tortuga acts like he's coming out of a long winter sleep. He groans and moans . . . soon the wild flowers and the grass will be greening—"

"I didn't know anything could grow up there," I answered.

"Oh yes," she said softly and her bright eyes looked into mine, "just like algae and moss and little bugs grow and live on the backs of old sea turtles, bushes and wild grass and flowers live on Tortuga. It's very beautiful to walk on the mountain in the spring."

164

"You've been up there?"

"Yes. When I was little I took care of Josefa's goats, and the mountain was their favorite place. They could have had all the green grass they wanted along the river, but you know goats, they had to take the roughest path. So we climbed the mountain, they taught me how, and soon I loved it as much as they did. We knew all of Tortuga's secret springs . . . there were seven. And when the day grew warm we climbed to the top where we could rest in the shade of a giant juniper which grows there. From there I could look out across the desert in all directions. Like the mountain, the desert seems barren at first, but it isn't. When you look close you can see the life which lives in it: small, hardy plants which hang on for dear life, cactus which blooms in bright, lush colors, lizards and birds which look like the color of the landscape . . . in the desert you have to look closely to find life, but it's there. Just like it is on the mountain. All these places around here were once so holy. There are writings and signs carved into the huge boulders of the mountain—like there used to be drawings and names on your cast . . ."

She talked about the mountain as if it was a living being, a giant turtle she had climbed in the ocean of the desert, a creature alive with history and old memories, and as she talked she brought the time of the past into the time of the present, and the stories she told seemed equally to fit people as well as the birds and lizards and coyotes. She knew all the animals and plants of the desert and the mountain, she called them by name the way Salomón called each of his vegetables by name, and she told me of the places where she had slept and dreamed . . .

"Why did you leave?" I asked.

"I became a woman," she answered, "and I came to take care of a turtle-man."

"Now I want to climb the mountain with you, and see everything you've seen, and learn the names of the animals and the plants, and breathe the fresh air—"

"Oh, you will! We will! You're almost ready. In a few days your legs will be strong enough, and it will be warm. The desert and the mountain will flower again, the butterflies will be dancing everywhere! But first—"

"What?"

She held my hand tightly and looked at me. "First you must return home," she said and her voice trembled. "But there will be plenty of time for us when you return. Did I tell you Josefa smelled the wind this morning and pronounced that spring was definitely here! It's come early she said. And once the greening starts there's no stopping it! Look!" she pointed at the valley and the mountain. "See! The river is already moving with fresh spring water! And the snows of winter are feeding the desert life! See!"

I followed her gaze and through her eyes I saw the beauty she described, the beauty I had not seen until that moment. The drabness of winter melted in the warm, spring light, and I saw the electric acid of life run through the short green fuses of the desert plants and crack through the dark buds to brush with strokes of lime the blooming land. Along the river farmers plowed the yawning earth. Strings of geese, strung out like the rosary of the resurrection, cried in recognition as they spotted the hump of the mountain, a landmark on their way north. Beneath them the river thrashed and shed its dry, winter skin. Tortuga's hot pee poured from the hidden springs and mixed with the snow-water which came rushing from the northern mountains.

"Yes!" I cried, "I see it! I can see it!" I turned to hold Ismelda, but she was gone. The brush of her kiss lingered on my lips, but she was gone. Her warm tears wet my cheeks. She had shared her beauty with me, but now she had to be alone, as I had to be alone to understand what the coming of spring meant to all of us. I touched my lips with my tongue and tasted her sadness. Around me the strands of golden light fused me to the mountain and wove Ismelda's love into my soul.

22

"Where's Sadsack?" I asked. I hadn't seen him for a few days. I had been so busy practicing on the parallel bars I really hadn't noticed his absence.

"Got sent out for special surgery," Mike said.

"Lost the one good leg he had left," Ronco added.

"Got gangrene from a naughty girl's braces, so they had to cut it off!"

"Let that be a lesson to you, Tortuga." They laughed and raced out for mail call.

I didn't know what they meant, but Sadsack was gone. His bed was neatly made and his corner empty and quiet. There was no groaning and cursing in the morning. Sometime during the night a pack of shadows had stolen into the room, and, like scavenger rats, they had scurried off with his comic books. The room was picked clean.

"But he can't just disappear?"

"They had to put a splint on his tool," Buck exclaimed. "He's either up front in isolation or they sent him to another hospital."

Poor Sadsack, I thought, a few days and he would have been moaning and complaining about my leaving. I sat by the window and looked at the mountain. The spring wind blew the winter haze out of the valley early in the morning so everything was bright and clear. I was thinking of home when Mike shouted, "Hey! Got something for you!"

He and Ronco had returned with a large package and a gang of inquisitive kids following them. "It's for Tortuga!" a boy shouted and pointed at the package.

"Biggest one I've ever seen!" his friend whistled.

"It's for you, Tortuga," Mike said.

"Damn, looks like a rope and saddle!" Buck exclaimed and sat up in bed.

"Wha-Whad i-i-is it?" Mudo stuttered. He and Tuerto had joined the crowd which filled the room. Even Danny had come to see what was in the package.

"Let's have a guessing contest," Tuerto grinned, "and whoever guesses right gets Tortuga's bed when he's gone!"

"Yeeeeah!" the little kids shouted.

"Shut up!" Mike yelled. "We're not going to have any crazy contest and nobody's getting Tortuga's bed unless I say so! Let's just let him open the thing!" He put the package on my lap and handed me the letter that came with it. It was from my mother.

"Bet it's a suit for going home," somebody whispered.

"Maybe something to eat—"

I opened the letter first and read it aloud. Because we received so few letters we always read what we got aloud. Everyone listened intently, pretending it was their letter from home.

> My dearest son,
>
> We can't tell you how happy we are. We got the letter from the doctor telling us you're coming home—At last all of my prayers are answered. It has seemed like an eternity to me, but now I am happy. The doctor says you are walking. A miracle. The day I received the letter I went to the church and lit candles, and I prayed all afternoon. Now I will never know that place where you suffered so much—there was no money to go. And the battle here has continued. It is like a war. Nothing is settled. The workers are without work. But we have faith and we keep fighting and praying. Oh, it has been so long you will not remember anything. Do you remember Crispín? The old man who lived across the alley? He is dead. May God rest his soul. He died and with him so many dreams died. But he died fighting for justice. That is why I am writing. He left you his guitar, the one he would play in the evenings. We were all at his bedside and he said he wanted it sent to you. He did not tell us why, but he said to send it immediately. He said not to wait till you got home. To send it right away. He said you would know why. So now you have this beautiful blue guitar. Keep it safe and return with it. May the blessed Virgin Mary and all the saints watch over you. I pray to God you return quickly. With all my love.
>
> Your Mother.

"A guitar," Mike whispered as I put the letter aside and tore the brown paper wrapping from the package.

"Who was Crispín?" Ronco asked.

"An old man," I said. I felt a loss, but I could not feel sadness. Instead my thoughts were suddenly alive with Salomón's instructions. Even now I could see him lying in his bed, smiling as I opened the package which would reveal the blue guitar. He knew! He had known all along that Crispín would send me the guitar! That's why he kept saying I would learn to sing. But how did Crispín know? Did all of these people know something about my destiny which was revealed to me only in flashes of insight, like now, when everything suddenly seemed to fall into place and make sense.

"Open it," Mike nudged me.

I tossed away the wrappings and dug through the wadded newspaper. A flash of blue appeared, and as I lifted the paper I struck a string and a note warbled in the package.

"It is a guitar!" someone said breathlessly.

I reached in and held it up. It glistened blue in the sunlight. It glowed with the light of the sun.

"Damn! It's beautiful," Mike said softly.

"I've never seen anything like it," Buck whistled.

Silence, then exclamations of awe, greeted the guitar.

"God, you're lucky. Nobody has a guitar like that. Not even Franco!"

"Play it, play it!"

"Yeah. Play a song!"

Then the revelation I had turned to frustration and anger. How in the hell could I play a guitar with only one good hand! I could barely move my left hand! And a person needed two hands to play a guitar! Had Salomón conspired with Crispín and Filomón? Did they all know each other? No, they couldn't! It was Salomón's doing! He had put the thoughts in my head to make me believe I would be a singer! Well I didn't want to be a singer! I only wanted to get the hell out of the hospital!

"Play it! Play it!" the kids shouted, "Play a song!"

"Hey! Quiet down you little bastards!" Mike yelled and shut them down. "Can't you see he just got it! He needs to learn how to play it."

"Yeah, he needs practice," Ronco nodded.

"He needs more than practice," Danny sneered at the door. "How in the hell is he going to play it with only one hand, huh? If you believe that then you're crazy!" He glared at me, as if he had triumphed over me because he knew my left hand hung uselessly by my side, the fingers stiff from the injury which had shattered the bones and nerves. Then he turned and walked away. I wanted to curse him also, because the anger was building inside, and I wanted to curse Salomón too, but the memory of the old man and what he had done for me kept me still.

"Ah, Danny's sour grapes," Ronco said. "There's lots of guys that can play guitars and fiddles with one hand—"

"Sure," Mike agreed, "he just needs time to practice. Come on," he said to the kids, "let's clear out of here. Tortuga needs to be alone for awhile." The kids nodded and filed out of the room, talking about the beautiful blue guitar.

I did need to be alone. I sat staring at the blue guitar, feeling the polished wood which had once been cradled by the old, blind man, touching the strings which seemed alive with a sad song. But I couldn't answer the questions which kept tugging at me, irritating me with their insistence. I barely remembered the old man, I hardly knew him. So why had he entrusted the blue guitar to me? The answer to the riddle lay with Salomón; it was he who started the chain of events rolling, he and his story about me becoming a singer. That was nonsense! I couldn't learn to play the uitar in a million years . . . more important, I didn't want to learn. I on, wanted to get out of the hospital and go back home and try to lead a normal life. That would be hard enough for a cripple I had already learned. I didn't want to be saddled with the guitar and what it meant. When I was stronger I only wanted to return for Ismelda, settle along the river, farm, raise goats, try to forget the suffering and the pain I had felt and seen in Salomón's wards . . . That's all I wanted. Now here was the guitar sitting on my lap, as alive with power as one of Salomón's stories and filling me with questions again . . . feeding my imagination with the possibility of Salomón's wild dreams for me, daring me to strum its strings and sing . . . I cursed and gritted my teeth. Damn Salomón! Damn them all! I'd give the guitar to Salomón and show them! Let it rot with him and the vegetables in their dark ward. I wasn't responsible for what had happened to anyone! I didn't want the responsibility! They could have it and do anything they wanted with it! I only wanted peace and quiet . . . With this resolution in mind I slung the guitar over my shoulder, picked up my crutches and headed for Salomón's room.

It was dinner time so the hall was empty. I could hear the clinking of dishes and the sound of laughter from the dining room. I hadn't been to see Salomón in a long time, and I hadn't thought about the vegetables, so I had to pause and work up my courage to enter the dark hall which led to their ward. The hall was very still and dim. My footsteps echoed in the dark. Somewhere behind me I felt Danny following me. I turned and saw his shadow melt into the darkness. I shrugged. He would only come as far as the door that led into the garden, but he wouldn't enter. He was afraid. And once at the door I had to wonder if I could control my own fear. I hesitated, then pushed open the creaking door. The whooshing sound of the iron lungs greeted me. As usual, the vegetable patch was dark. The large, sad eyes of the vegetables turned to follow me as I walked down the enormous room. The door to Salomón's room was ajar, and when I pushed it open it creaked as if with pain. The room was dark and still; dust covered everything, and the once green and clinging vines lay withered on the floor. For a moment I was frightened; there was no sound of life. The room was stale and musty as a crypt.

170

"Salomón," I whispered and walked in. I was relieved to see the dim light by Salomón's bed. At first I thought he was reading, but as I approached the bed I saw a strange light which emanated from the figure of a person who sat at Salomón's bedside. The figure was dressed in white. I thought it was one of the old nurses who roamed about the ward tending to the vegetables. Perhaps she had come to read to Salomón and had fallen asleep. I turned to Salomón and whispered his name again. I drew close to the bed and saw that his eyes were closed. HIs complexion was pale, the ashen color of cold wax. I couldn't hear him breathe. For a moment the fear that he was dead gripped me, and I hated myself for having come with so much anger. I touched his forehead and prayed that he was alive. The room was cold and silent and I shivered.

"Salomón . . . it's me."

Then barely in a whisper I heard Salomón's voice flutter alive, like one of his unfolding spring butterflies . . .

Ah, Tortuga, I'm so glad to see you. I see you've come walking like a man . . . I'm happy for you my friend, my comrade. And what is that slung around your shoulder? Could it be the blue guitar? Has it come . . . has it come at last? That means Crispín is dead . . . passed into another form of this vast drama we are weaving . . . But he left you the guitar. He sang his time on earth and now it's your turn. Oh, how can we be sad when a man passes away but leaves us so much of his life . . . leaves another to take up his place. Now it's your turn to sing, Tortuga. My heart is full of joy that this has come to pass!

Relieved that he had spoken, my anger flared anew. "I don't know what you mean by all this nonsense!" I shouted. "I don't want to be this singer you keep talking about! I didn't ask to be brought to this damned prison and I didn't ask for Crispín to send me the guitar! Don't you see I'm tired of all the suffering and pain I've seen! I only want to get out of here . . ." I sobbed. The impotency I felt made me shudder. Blind rage suddenly overwhelmed me and without thinking I unslung the blue guitar and sent it crashing against the wall.

"There are your damn songs!" I shouted. "You sing them! Or find somebody else to sing them! I'm tired of playing your games! I want my own freedom!" I slumped into a chair by the bed and sobbed. The echo of the crash reverbrated around me; the sad, harsh notes of the violated guitar echoed in the ward. I knew the vegetables were listening, holding their breath and listening. I didn't care. I was tired, tired of everything that I had seen. I only wanted to forget the pain of my past, and yet I knew I couldn't. And I knew that no one else could do what I had to do. The questions would always be there to haunt us. New cripples would find their way into the desolation of the vegetable patch, and they would keep

171

raising the question over and over . . . until someone answered it, or until we knew in our hearts that it was not by design that we suffered. I was just one of those persons at a particular place in time who had asked himself the question . . . there had been others before me; there would be others after me. Destiny had suddenly converged on me and illumined my path. My rage and my anger would pass, Salomón knew that, and then I would take up the load again.

Tortuga, I know it's a long journey . . . and we don't know why we're chosen to walk the path of the sun . . . but we do know that it's our destiny to walk in the light and to leave the dark shadows. It's a road of suffering and pain, but we can bear it now . . . we're not alone anymore . . . there's no whimpering and crying anymore. You've felt the roots of sadness, my friend, you've seen the mountain's heart . . . you walked through the halls of the orphans and the cripples of this life . . . and you held us in your arms and offered us love . . . Oh, we sang with joy when you offered us your love! Our pain and suffering had meaning in your heart! We're not concerned with why we're here anymore . . . All that's behind us. Now is the time for singing and rejoicing! Now is the time to dip into the electric acid of life and burn our souls with its joy! Don't you see, my friend, you're the one hope that the darkness will never cover us completely! Even battered, crippled men will follow the path of the sun . . . bathe in its light . . . sing its songs . . . Oh, Tortuga, don't be angry with me to-day . . . not today . . .

Suffering without redemption, I thought, oh what a hellish place we've been cast into . . . and yet his voice could still echo with joy . . . Why? What inner strength had he found that eluded me? I looked at his thin, withered body. Of all of us he had suffered the most. Time had suspended him in this cruel plane, and instead of begging and whimpering he had cast off his past, he had dared to become a new man . . . and he had reached out and helped the other cripples around him. Perhaps he didn't know it, but he had gone beyond those heroes he talked about, even in this ward of hell he had dared to question the gods and the ways of men . . .

I cursed myself for complaining. I, who was ready to leave the hospital, I had so little to give in return. I had suffered, but for such a short while, and he, he had suffered the weight of eternity . . .

His eyes were closed; he hardly seemed to breathe. Quietly, so as not to awaken him, I picked up the blue guitar and caressed it tenderly. I ran my fingers along the string and they vibrated with golden strands of sound. All right, I said to Salomón, I'll sing you a song . . . there is much to sing about. I want to sing about going home, and about returning for Ismelda and her love, and I want to sing about climbing the mountain, and about walking through the dark halls of the cripples . . . oh, there are so many things that lie so heavy on my soul that must be sung. So I strummed a chord and sang my song:

> I'm going home . . .
> To keep the promise of the spring
> To see the friends I left behind . . .
>
> I've wandered far . . .
> Far beyond my land of birth
> Into deserts full of pain
> Into a darkness without end . . .
>
> I've got to sing!
> A song of love I left behind
> Of the journey of the sun
> And the love and death it brings
>
> I've got to sing!
> Of the desert that I crossed
> Of the pain that I have felt
> And the love that made me well . . .
>
> I'm not afraid!
> To shout my song across the land!
> To the orphans of our love!
> To the cripples that lie bare
> On the desert of this life!
>
> I'll sing this song!
> Of the rising of the sun
> And the journey I must run
> And the love that I will bring . . .

The words kept tumbling out, jumbled, full of pain, stumbling to convey what I felt, filling me with relief while I sang and releasing my soul from its shell. I didn't know how to sing, but I would do it, I would do it for Salomón and Mike and Jerry and all the poor vegetables who lay listening to my song. I was glad Crispín had sent me the guitar, with time I would learn to handle its responsibility. That's all I needed, time and practice, like Ronco said. But I swore that I would learn to draw the soul out of the blue guitar and learn to sing.

I looked up. A smile played on Salomón's lips. The room was very still. The figure at the bedside was gone and the room had grown dark. I got up quietly and looked at Salomón for a long time, then I leaned over and kissed him. His lips were cold; his breath was still. I wanted to say goodbye to him, but I couldn't. The words choked in my throat. I knew that I would never see him again, but that didn't matter, because I would be taking him with me . . . I would be taking all of them with me, in my heart, in memories that were to awaken in the future and call me to sing. That's the part of the song which wasn't complete yet, because I knew I would be awakening on many a night, and the rustle of the wind or the fragrance in the breeze would remind me of this love I had shared with them and I would be condemned to go to the guitar and continue the song, continue finding the verses until the entire story was told. Someplace the song would say that we never said goodbye because as long as we dreamed and remembered nothing was lost . . . they would all be crossing the desert with me, helping me find my way back home.

I turned quietly and walked away. I stopped at the door which led to the dark rooms, the ward where I had gotten sick at the sight of so much suffering. Now I opened the door and stepped in. The endless rows of iron lungs and respirators were silent. I walked softly down the aisle, looking at the bits of curled life which rested in each machine. I knew they had heard my song. That was why it was so peaceful here in the dusk, they knew I was not afraid now. I held the tears back, I was not supposed to cry for them, I was supposed to sing and laugh with them, but I couldn't help thinking about Salomón lying so quiet and peaceful in his dark room.

23

When I returned to the ward the grapevine was alive with the rumor that Dr. Steel was going to release me.

"Dr. Steel wants to see you," somebody whispered.

"You're going home, Tortuga, going home!"

"You're a free man!"

I nodded, and I smiled, but the news of my release and its sudden elation was mixed with the sad feeling I had felt as I sang my song for Salomón . . . I knew then the song wasn't complete, that there were more sad verses to be sung.

I found Steel reading charts in the nurses' station. As usual, he was working late. He looked up over the rim of the glasses he used for reading.

"You want to see me," I said.

"How do the crutches feel?" he asked.

"Fine, but I think I could get along without them." I settled into a chair. I felt tired and weak, and in the pit of my stomach I felt sick. The weight of the afternoon settled heavily on my shoulders.

"Tired?" Steel asked. I nodded. "Keep the crutches awhile," he said. "You know most of the kids throw them away as soon as they get out of here. That desert is strewn with cast-off crutches and braces—can't say I blame them. Hey, is that the guitar I've heard so much about?"

I knew the kids had already told him about it. I unslung it and handed it to him. He took it and looked at it, turning it tenderly.

"It's a beautiful thing," he nodded and handed it back to me. "It must have meant a lot to the man who gave it to you." He took his pipe from the desk and filled it. He only played with it and sucked on it when he was nervous. "The x-rays I took yesterday are fine," he said. "I had your release papers typed today, so you can go anytime you want. Tomorrow, day after . . . the driver goes down town in the morning to pick up the mail and he can drop you off at the bus depot—" his voice trailed. "The nurse will help you get ready, pack anything you have to—" He stood up. He was no longer the young doctor I had met the day I arrived; he looked old and tired. He worked twenty-four hours a day, slept in a small room by the surgery rooms, was always on call, had to train the new doctors and put up with the administrator and the Committee . . . and he had to cut us up, glue us together with steel pins and braces. He saw us learn to feed ourselves and walk and then leave, and he remained. I wondered what penance he was doing, but I didn't ask. He had chosen to do what he had to do. There was no use thinking about it any other way.

"This is the only thing I'll be taking with me," I said and patted the guitar.

"It's a precious gift to be traveling with," he nodded. He picked up the charts to complete his late round, then he put them back on the desk.

"Are you going to see Salomón?" I asked.

He shook his head. "I'm tired," he said, "I think I need a rest—" I watched him walk up the hall. It was better this way, I thought. Steel knew what happened in the ward as well as anyone, and it was better this way.

I went back to the room and when I entered someone flipped on the lights and a loud cheer went up. Everybody knew I had gotten my walking papers.

"Damn Tortuga!" Mike grabbed me and hugged me, "You're a free man! A free man!"

"Congratulations," Ronco smiled.

"Hey! We oughta have a party for him!" Buck cried out, twirled his rope and sent it snaking out to loop his chair.

"Damn right!" Mike agreed.

"I'll fix some drinks!" Ronco clapped his hands, "some of my specials—"

"Oh damn, not the orange juice and shaving lotion again," Buck groaned, "you know that stuff gives me the runs."

"Let's do something different, I mean really great for Torruga!" Mike said and put his arm around my shoulder. I think he suspected that I had been to see Salomón.

"Oh boy, Mike's thinking!" Ronco laughed.

"What?"

"How about a swimming party," Mike whispered, "after lights go out."

"Hey, all right!" Ronco nodded. "We can pick the lock to the pool easily—"

"And we can invite some of the girls!" Buck cried. "I can hardly wait to see my mamacita in a bikini!" He smacked his lips.

"She won't need one," Mike said.

"Hey, whad you mean?"

"Why man, if we're going to swim in the dark we don't need bathing suits!"

"That's right!" Ronco shouted hoarsely. "Great idea! Everybody goes nudey! Ajúa!" He grabbed Mikes chair and spun it around.

> *Root-too-toot!*
> *Root too-toot!*
> *We're the boys of the institute!*
> *We love to swim, in our raw skin*
> *And we love the girls that . . .*

". . . That aren't too thin!" Buck finished the improvisation.

"Right!" Mike slapped him. "Give me one that I can get ahold of! A mamasota that's got a lot of security to her!"

"Hey, wait a minute," Buck balked. "I'm not going to have my Rosita runnin' around naked in front of a bunch of horney bastards! No way! Besides, I love that girl—" He got serious. "I respect her, and I'm goin' to marry her someday—"

"Buck, it's dark in the pool! Nobody's going to run around rapeing girls for-crying-out-loud!"

"Yeah, no messin' around, except what you want to do," Ronco nudged him in the ribs.

"Yeah, it's just what you want to do," Mike said.

"Yeah?" Buck thought aloud.

"Yeah."

A slow grin spread across Buck's face. Then he smiled. He grabbed his hat and threw it in the air. "Yahoooo! Let's go! I'm ready podnars!"

"Great! Great!" Mike nodded and they got to discussing the plan of action. I turned to Danny who had been standing quietly by the door. "Why don't you come with us, Danny, it'll be good for you."

Danny shook his head. He stared at me and tried to make me back down, but I didn't. "I got other things to do," he whispered and jerked out of the room, muttering to himself.

"Poor bastard," Ronco shook his head, "he's going crazy. Just goes around talking to himself all the time . . . claims he hears God's radio waves telling him what to do . . ."

"It's that damn arm," Buck said. "How would you like to sleep with that thing lying next to you, rotting all the time . . ."

"He's too wrapped up in himself," Mike shrugged, "he's got to quit feeling sorry for himself and come out and join the world, but he's given up."

"Well, back to the party," Ronco said.

"Right. Ronco and me will go tell the girls to get ready, you guys cover the ward here, and remember, it's only for the big boys. The squirts have to stay in the ward tonight."

"Yeah, we don't want to contribute to the delinquency of minors," Ronco said and they went out laughing.

A wave of excitement swept through the ward. By supper time everybody knew about the secret swimming party, and the small kids giggled and whispered that we were going to swim naked. We swam with the girls everyday at the pool, played water basketball and horsed around with them, but one of the therapists was always with us, and we didn't swim naked in the day; tonight it was going to be different.

Nobody ate dinner. We sat around the huge dining room and played with our food and glanced at the girls and they whispered to each other and looked at us. After supper we waited for the lights to go out and talked about the swimming party. Most of the fellows had girlfriends in the girls' ward, and somehow the swimming party was a natural end to the romances which had blossomed at the movie. Spring was tugging at all of us, and the excitement made us restless. The girls had agreed to swim naked, and that made us hot and expectant.

I wondered if Ismelda had heard about the party. Of course she wouldn't be there, and if it wasn't that the party was for me I think I would have skipped it. I had too much on my mind to really enjoy it. I was thinking about the trip home, I could leave the following morning if I wanted, and I was thinking about Salomón. Deep in his ward he lay sleeping, dreaming, smiling at our crazy antics, always happy for us, always telling us to do more, to embrace life, to get tangled in it and never mind the pain . . . I was tempted to go back to his room, before the party, just to talk to him and check on him, but before I had made up my mind the lights were switched off and the ward grew dark. Shortly thereafter Ronco appeared at the door and whispered, "We're ready."

"Oh my," Billy whispered. I heard him gasp. He was afraid. We had talked that afternoon, and he had told me that he wanted to go awfully bad to the swimming party because there was a girl he liked in the girls' ward, but he was afraid to get naked in front of anyone. We talked for awhile and he finally decided that he had to do it, that he had to lose his fear. He looked at me in the dark and I nodded and he shook his head. He was ready.

"Did everybody stuff pillows in their beds?" Ronco asked. We had covered the pillows with blankets so it looked as if a body was asleep in each bed.

"We're ready," Buck replied.

"Let's go," Ronco motioned and we moved out into the dark hall. Other shadows joined us.

"What about the small kids?" I asked.

"They've been threatened to stay in their rooms and keep quiet," Ronco whispered. "Tomorrow we'll have special games for them in the recreation room, so they're happy. Little bastards—"

We moved down the hall quietly. Once the lights were out the night nurses never ventured out of the nurses' station, so it was easy to get past them. Two of them were smoking, drinking coffee and nibbling at snacks as we slipped by and headed for the pool. We were extra careful at the windows because the spring moon was bright, but the hospital was quiet and we got to the pool without an incident. Mike had picked the lock; he held the door open while we slipped in. During the day the pool was noisy and turbulent with swimmers, but tonight it was peaceful and quiet. The moonlight sparkled on the clear, chlorine blue. I looked at the water and remembered the night Danny had dumped me in, and I wished Danny had come with us. Like Mike said, he needed to get outside himself and join us in doing things. The disease was driving him crazy, but try as we might we couldn't draw him out. I shrugged, slipped off my pants and shirt and entered the water noiselessly and joined the others. We swam quietly around the pool and waited for the girls.

"Here they come!" Mike called, and the whisper spread like a shudder over the water. We turned and saw the door open and the girls slipped in. Then Mike closed the door and in the light of the moonlight the girls disrobed and slid into the water to join us.

At first we were only shadows in the green, spring water, then as our eyes grew accustomed to the dark we became beautiful golden fish and graceful turtles sliding through the quiet water. There was no shouting and noisy splashing, only the silent group of male fish swimming slowly around the shy mermaids who had entered the water, calling to them with our bodies, courting them with the prowess of the spring dance. They swam in the inner circle, dipping in and out of the water, coyly calling us. Their glistening, shimmering bodies rode the crest of waves. We laughed, waved at them, listened to their silent song and gurgled with a joy we couldn't express as we bathed in the moonlit water. Hot and excited we swam the wider outer circle, closing in on the mermaids who swam counter to us and smiled for us to join them. The air was pregnant with a dripping electricity which could not be contained. Like lovers showing off for their beloved, we dove in and out of the clear water, rippling with flesh and fin the water of the mermaids, becoming merman for them, we smiled across the clear water and dove to greet them.

Oh, Salomón would have cried with joy to see so much beauty! I saw in it a verse to be added to my song. The tension of the spring which had pierced the earth to thaw the land now coursed through our bodies and quivered in our limbs. We were no longer the deformed, twisted bodies which on land limped and dragged the heavy weight of steel; we had become graceful golden mermen and mermaids, part fish and part men and women, swimming to the dance of spring, comingling our terrible energies in the water. Wild cries clawed at our throats until the tension and silence were almost unbearable. The circle tightened as we closed in on the mermaids, swimming like golden fish at spawn, wetting the water with our hot pee and slippery juices, drawn by the fragrance and the song of the mermaids, we dove and splashed towards their beckoning smiles and their virgin, naked bodies.

I paused and looked to keep from drowning in the beauty which unfolded before my eyes. I saw that in the water we were like birds in the air, full of power, graceful, elegant in our movements. We unfolded like sea flowers in our liquid element, gracefully reaching out to touch fingertips in the strands of golden water. We fanned out like sea moss, undulating back and forth until hands clasped, and the mermen pulled the mermaids to their sides and they swam as one, disappearing into the depths of the water, rising to breathe the warm, spring air, diving again to complete the courtship dance, tinting the water with virgin blood, making it swirl and bubble with the thrashing of their love . . . then all was silent again, and the water was quiet. Couples rose to rest in the sea castles by the shore . . .

The dance dissolved as quietly as it had begun. The melody rested on the water, spent of its energy. Overhead the spring moon shone through the skylight. Across the pool Cynthia smiled at me. She had been my partner in the dance . . . now she was content to sit by the side of the pool and dry her body in the moonlight, content to dream her dreams in the pale light. Like tired seals we had climbed out of the water and flopped down to rest. We were exhausted from the swim. Around the pool the lovers sat resting, touching hands, quivering from excitement, bathing in the silent intimacy they had shared.

I sat alone and looked at the glistening bodies of my brothers and my sisters. I was full of joy, as full of joy as I had been with love at the movie. I had shared these moments of ecstasy, felt the present slip into the past until I saw the communion girls swimming in the pool with me, welcoming me and calling to me like Cynthia had called. Somehow I was swept up in the energy of destiny which would force me to join into the fate of those who shared my journey . . . perhaps that's what Salomón knew and why he had predicted the blue guitar would come to me. Curse of chance or force of fate, I was entwined in it, seeing at times through the illusion of time and soul with perfect clarity, lost and cursing the dark way most often, wanting Salomón and his vegetables to enjoy moments like this and yet knowing that deep inside they were always with us. So this was only a part of the song . . . it was not yet complete.

I stood and draped a robe around my wet body, folded my clothes under my arm and slipped out the door. I walked slowly back to the ward,

I was very tired, but when I got to the room I couldn't sleep. I turned on the radio and wished Ronco was back so I could share one of his cigarettes, maybe that would calm my thoughts. The day had been too full, too loaded with those realizations which kept fitting together like notes into a melody. Each peak and valley of the day had been full of emotion, more than I could take in one day because each one kept sweeping over me and pulling my thoughts back and forth . . . but through them I was beginning to see what I had to do. I knew Salomón was right.

I sat by the window and looked across the valley at the mountain. It was clothed in the blue velvet of the spring night, but like me Tortuga, too, was restless. I felt him tugging at his moorings, nervous to toss aside his shackles and swim into the sparkling night sky. It was a strange spring madness, full of the sounds of home which were calling me, full of Ismelda's love which slept in the night, thick with the tragic love songs which flowed from Buck's radio.

It was the radio that should have warned me. For an instant it blared loudly, the sound came crashing into the room like death's call. And in the valley the lights of the town flickered brightly, and then as quickly as the energy had come it found its equilibrium and settled to its former level. It was as if a star had died in the galaxy and charged the earth with its dying gasp . . . or as if a new sun had been born and lighted anew the golden strands of light that anchored our earth to space. I had been dozing and the brief flicker of light nudged me awake, I shook my head and wondered what it was, then the unsettling darkness drew me down again and I slept. If I had looked carefully I would have seen Tortuga angrily rear his head and curse the night.

I tossed restlessly in the troubled waters of sleep, pulled back and forth by the energy which filled the night sky and made it glow, bothered by the dry gusts of wind which shook and rattled the hospital. Sometime during the night I heard Mike and Ronco drag in and fall asleep . . . the sounds of music drifted through the night. I dreamed a mermaid came to sing to a crippled turtle-man, and he strummed the strings of a dark, blue guitar, strings woven from her long, black hair. She sang a song, and when the song was done they swam north on the rising crest of the river.

24

I will remember it the way Ismelda told it to me. She sat by me and held my hand for a long time, and I knew she was afraid that she would cry when she told me they were all dead, that someone had pulled the switch that night and sent the entire ward into darkness . . . They had no chance, locked up in their iron lungs, without the force of the air to lift their lungs they suffocated quickly . . . All of them.

I will always remember the way the sun rose over Tortuga's hump, bringing with it the wail of the sirens and the terrible screams of terror which filled the halls. At first I thought it was a part of the terrible nightmare that haunted me that night, but no, the sun was up and shining, covering everything with its light . . . it would admit only the truth, and the truth was that Dr. Steel had sealed off the ward and we weren't to leave our rooms, not even above Mike's protest and mine. So all morning long while the police cars and the ambulances moved up the hill we could only watch from the window . . . and we knew immediately what had happened. Someone had pulled the switch in the vegetable patch . . . everyone was dead . . . all of them.

I will remember the screams of terror which filled the ward, the shouts of the nurses and the doctors, the small kids crying . . . and then the silence which fell over the ward as we sat by the windows and looked out as they carried the small plastic bags out of the ward and loaded them on the ambulances. Once only did someone say — somebody pulled the switch — and then no more was said. Once only did Mike and I say, we should be there— and when Steel shook his head we returned quietly to our room. There was no need to be there. Their end had come.

Then there was the silence which followed. We did not look at each other, we did not speak . . . words were useless, and we had been through it before. Now there was only the shock, the terrible fatigue which lay in our stomachs and throats and made us numb, now there were only the questions which we had asked so many times before tumbling through our tormented minds. Then Ismelda came. She sat by me and after awhile she told me she had been to Salomón's room. He had not been afraid.

There was a smile on his angelic lips. Filomón had come for him, and tenderly they had lifted him into the wagon which had originally brought him here. So he has good care for the new journey, she said. I opened the window in his room, she told me, then I opened all the windows to let in the sun and the spring breeze. I looked into her eyes and saw myself reflected in them, saw her opening the windows, felt the grief in her heart. It was over very quickly, she said, like most tragedies . . . now all that remains is for us to live with it. How will you be, Tortuga. I told her that I had seen Salomón that evening and played my song for them . . . and then in my troubled dreams I had seen her, and finally I told her that I would have to leave in the morning. I wanted to get out as soon as possible. I did not want to be consumed by the grief, it was not what Salomón would want. He would want me to start my own journey home. I know, Ismelda said. She kissed me lightly on the cheek and then she disappeared.

In the afternoon I wandered aimlessly around the ward. The kids gathered in small groups and talked about what had happened, but I stayed away from them. I wanted to be by myself. I wanted to feel everything in the hospital exactly as it was that day, so I would never forget it. And I wanted to be alone to sort out my feelings. I didn't know yet what I would do when I saw Danny, but I knew before the day was up that I would have to see him. I didn't want to ask him why he had done it . . . I think I already knew. In a way, we all knew . . . somehow we had been with him when he threw the switch. But I had to see him, and my concern was not one of anger or justification, it was that I wanted to know if he was fully aware of what he had done. And I wanted to be by him because I felt he needed me.

I looked for him in the ward, but I couldn't find him. When I asked Mike he said, "Danny's in the emergency room. Last night, or early this morning sometime, he took a surgical saw and cut off his arm . . . He was in surgery all morning. He lost a lot of blood, but I think he's going to make it— Didn't you know?"

No, I said, but it all made sense. All the questioning and all the wondering and the pain had suddenly made some sense to Danny, and that's why he had done it. So I couldn't even be angry anymore. Cursing him would just be one more excuse for us. Still, I had to see him, now more than ever, because I knew I would be gone in the morning. So I made my way to the recovery rooms which were part of the surgery unit.

When I found Danny's room the nurse who sat by the bed looked up at me and put aside her magazine. "Did you want to see him?" she asked. I nodded. She stood up and walked to the door. "You can only stay a few minutes," she said, then added, "he's under sedation . . . he hasn't talked." Then she went out.

I went to the bed and looked at Danny. His eyes were closed. His face was cracked with pain and age; even his hair had grown gray in spots. The bandage at the shoulder where he had severed his withered arm was spotted with blood. I felt pity for him . . . any anger I may have felt drained away and I was left feeling weak and tired. I felt sorrow, for him, for all of us. We had all grown old and tired during our long stay at the hospital.

The steel and the plastic which kept us patched together could not erase the effects of the pain we had felt, that showed in our eyes and faces. Even now while Danny slept, searing pain burned through his veins and throbbed in his heart. They had hooked him up to the machines. A plastic tube dropped from the glass jar which sparkled with light and entered his arm. The yellow liquid drained slowly into his blood . . . the new bread of heaven, forced in by the very people who had created the hell which brought us here. Drainage tubes carried away the poison the body would use on itself if allowed, and next to the bed sat a stainless steel machine, glistening with bright, polished chrome and colored lights which flashed on and off, secret messages to the panel at the nurses' station. The machines were new, every day they brought in a new one, everyday the workmen opened the walls to run more wires, wires which could monitor the vital signs of the dying body. And the new respirators, more efficient than the old dark and awkward iron lungs, now lay next to the bed, pumping air, recording, monitoring, forcing the breath of life into Danny's tired body . . .

I wondered if he would rip them away when his sedation lifted . . . I wondered if he really wanted death, or was it only the death of his arm he had sought? Had he tried to tear the darkness he thought was evil from his body? I sighed because I knew we had failed him . . . .

"Danny," I whispered and touched his forehead. He was hot with fever. He groaned and his eyelids fluttered open.

"Ah, Tortuga," he whispered, "you've come at last . . . I knew you would come— I've been so afraid, Tortuga, so afraid . . . A terrible darkness seems to suffocate me . . . but now that you've come, I feel everything's going to be all right . . . Oh, such sad things have happened to us . . ."

I nodded and rubbed his forehead. "Yes," I said, "sad things . . . but it's all right now . . ."

I rubbed his forehead and he closed his eyes and seemed to rest easier. Somewhere I heard the sound of Filomón's carriage crossing the desert, laden with the dry roots which he would lay to rest in new desert sand. Old desert plants are tough, Salomón had said, they'll take root most anywhere. You can tear their limbs, burn them, uproot them and keep them from water for years, but then you throw them in new earth, give them a little sun and before you know it they're sending down that green fuse, seeking water in the sand, sprouting green . . . yes, green,

green buds to greet the sun . . . and in the path of the sun we're all constantly growing into different shapes and forms . . .

The nurse returned and said my time was up. I nodded and looked at Danny.

"Is he going to be all right?" I asked.

"That depends on him," she answered, "you know that—"

Yes, I knew, I nodded and went out, but I couldn't return to my room. I wandered around the hospital for awhile, seeing it for the last time, looking clearly into every part so I could take it with me when I left in the morning. The pool and the therapy rooms were empty and silent; even the recreation room was deserted. I found my quiet spot by the window and sat to look at Tortuga. The mountain basked in the setting sun. High on its rocky sides little sprigs of green were pushing out of the dark crevices of earth and rock. The long winter sleep was over; it was time to seek the sun. The mantle of lime green fitted the old mountain well. I had to smile. So the old remnants and seeds and dry roots which had lived in the dark bowels of the hospital for so long had moved to Tortuga's shell where the sun was brighter. That's what Salomón had said, that bits of moss and algae and small animals sought out the turtle shells to live in peace and without fear. Later, the hot summer winds would come and burn everything away, but the roots would curl into the mountain and live on, and their seeds would be scattered like butterflies in the wind, and after the dreaming in cocoons there would be whispers of the love they had shared . . . so the cycles kept sweeping over us like the sweet syrup of time, and each passing washed our eyes open to a new form of life . . . .

I paused in my thoughts and turned, thinking I had heard Salomón's voice, but no, I was alone. It was just that my thoughts were making connections with everything, and without knowing I was humming a song. It was a song about the mountain and about Salomón, Ismelda, Mike, Ronco, Sadsack, Jerry, Danny, the doctor and the nurses and everyone who had come into my life at the hospital. I sang to them as I watched the sun set on Tortuga and saw the rich, green mantle turn to royal magenta. I sang and filled myself with hope, a hope against the dark fear which returned to haunt us and force us into dark shells, a hope which rejoiced in what Salomón had said . . .

It was in the quiet of evening, when the doves flew against the setting sun and their mates cried along the river, that we gathered to begin our procession.

Throw away your crutches! Ismelda shouted, and we threw away our crutches and braces and wheelchairs and gathered around her and Josefa. They dressed us in thin, flowing robes, robes so airy they made us float, and Josefa lit firebrands for us, torches which we held up in the gathering dusk.

For a moment Tortuga glowed a soft, salmon pink as the sun kissed the wild horizon of the west, then an Indian war cry split the air as the fiery rider on the unbridled red horse checked his steed long enough for Jerry to dismount and join us, then the jubilant cry thundered again and the flaming horse disappeared into a shroud of clouds to the west. We cheered and welcomed Jerry and embraced him, and he smiled then stood back, silent and inscrutable as always. He had brought a drum and he played for us an evening chant. Someone shouted for me to play the blue guitar and I unslung it and joined Jerry in his praise of the sun and the mountain.

Is everyone here? Mike asked. He had gone to the front of the line because Ismelda said he could lead the march. I looked around and saw that everyone was with us, even Sadsack was in line. He had groaned and complained once, but when he saw it wasn't a time for complaining he smiled and joined in the singing. And Danny was with us, quiet and withdrawn but strangely beautiful in his robe of dream-web. Ronco was there, and Billy and Franco, we were all there, climbing and winding down the trail to the river, crossing the bridge over the evening waters and finding Ismelda's path up the mountainside . . . behind us the doctors and nurses from the hospital and the people from the town watched in awe as we made our way up the mountain.

Night fell and the torches lit our way. We danced to the drum beat and the soft notes of the blue guitar as we climbed, and along the way we paused to dance around and sing to the plants and flowers which dotted the side of the path.

This is Salomón's army, Ismelda said, sentries of the spring night who guard our way . . . she called them each by name, and Salomón smiled.

When we reached the top we found a wide meadow and in the middle of the meadow a giant juniper tree. We joined hands and Ismelda led us like a winding vine around the tree, dancing a May dance in the spring night. Our souls were as free as the stars which sparkled above us; we ran and played like Josefa's goats . . . Tortuga smiled on our happiness; we wove our strands of light and love into his heart, and he stirred with old longings. He moved to dance with us, awkward at first, his leathery legs so long anchored to the earth were stiff with cold. But like us, he cast away his bonds in the magic of the spring night. He ripped them free and the earth shook with tremors as he moved. Far beneath us the townspeople screamed in terror that the earth was ending. The thin core of lava which led to the earth's heart snapped free, like the thin wire which had kept the vegetables alive had snapped, and the fiery blood spurted and went cascading into the valley below. Tortuga's underground rivers tore loose from their secret channels and swept into the hissing streams of lava, and the blood-water went tumbling and churning into the town below, sweeping away everything in its path and covering everything. The earth trembled as the huge mountain tore loose from its mooring . . . all around us the screams of drowning people and the atomic horror of the holocaust split the heavens with a thunder of destruction, and for a moment we too cringed and held each other because we saw the end had come. A loud lamentation filled the darkness. Ghosts arose and walked, and many tried to climb the mountain to be saved but they were dashed against its sides. They cried for forgiveness! They cried for love! But it was too late . . . their words were false. Look! Ismelda pointed, and we turned and saw that the mountain was rising safely into the starry sky, while behind us the earth thundered and exploded as the forces of the fire and water dashed over the land to make it new again. Mike cheered, and we all cheered, because we were rising like a glowing sun into the indigo of night, rising to take our place in the spermy string of lights which crowned the sky. We sang and danced on the back of the turtle that once free of the earth could swim so gracefully in the ocean of the night. So the earth was the beach that we had crossed . . . and what we should have known is that we had to join hands and cross it together, because it was only for an instant that the sun bathed and fed us with its love . . . then the night came and around us the roaring suns of prior ages welcomed us into our new destiny . . . .

25

The following morning I awoke early. For a long time I sat thinking about the dream, then I got up quickly, because I knew that as beautiful as it was I couldn't remain in it . . . I had to move out into the world. I walked to the showers. The hall and the bathroom were strangely quiet and empty at the early hour. The sun was just coming over Tortuga; it bathed the bathroom in streaks of golden light. I got in the shower and spent a long time under the refreshing water, washing away the lethargy of sleep and the exhaustion of the tragedy, trying to remember the time I had spent in the hospital so that as it flashed through my mind I could wash away the pain and agony in Tortuga's waters . . . so that he would flush them down to the river, back into the earth, to the mouths of the waiting, parched roots who struggled to flood the desert with life . . . but I couldn't give my thoughts wholly to the water . . . I had to walk on earth . . . in the path of the sun . . . there would never come a time when I did not turn to hear a sound, to look at a fleeting shadow, to catch a moment of love before it disappeared into the vast expanse of the wasteland . . . there would never come a time when I would turn and not see the shrunken bodies and the sad faces of the vegetables, and hear Salomón saying something to me, sad though it might be . . .

No, I could not wash away the time of sadness. It was etched into my face. I dried myself in front of the mirror and I did not recognize the person I saw. My eyes seemed empty and vacant, as if they were looking ahead to a point in the future, as if they did not want to see the emptiness of the rooms where we had lived so close to life, and had lost it after so long a struggle . . .

I combed back my long, black hair and shrugged. I knew what I had to do and that was the only thing that mattered. So I dressed in the blue denim shirt and levis the hospital issued, then I put on the brown corduroy jacket Ismelda had given me. It smelled clean and new. I ran my fingers along the sleeve and felt the texture of the material. For now, that was all I could do, understand that I could feel again and that in a little while I was going to walk out of the hospital. I looked one last time in the mirror and I couldn't keep from smiling. So, Ismelda would say, the lizard has put on the clothes of a man, strange lizard. Then I turned and walked back to the room.

Mike was awake and sitting in his chair. "You ready?" he asked and rubbed his sleepy eyes.

"I'm ready," I answered. "I wanted to start early, so I would have time to go by Ismelda's —"

He nodded. "Hey, you look good," he smiled and reached up and straightened the collar of my jacket. For a moment he looked into my eyes and I knew he was happy for me. Then he turned and went to the window and looked out. "It's a beautiful day to be moving north . . . following the river, just like the geese. They've been flying over all week . . . sometimes I think I can hear their lonely cries in the dark, and I imagine they're flying over at night . . . going home. You know, last night I had a dream . . . I can still remember it clearly. I dreamed we all got together and climbed the mountain—"

He was talking and rambling because it was difficult to say goodbye. We had shared too much, and there were no words to explain the depth of that sharing. For a moment I thought I heard him say, "I'm sorry about Salomón, and—" then he waved his arm as if erasing the thought. "There's nothing to say. It's done. I guess I was thinking about the little kids—it's harder on them. How do we explain it to them?" He turned and looked at me. "I feel sorry for you, too, Tortuga."

'I shrugged. "I'll be all right, Mike—"

"I know you will," he nodded, "it's just that you have a way of getting wrapped up in these things . . . I don't know if you'll ever be free from them—"

I understood what he meant. I wanted to tell him that none of us would ever be free, but Buck yawned and sat up in bed.

"Hey, Tortuga! You ready? You leaving? Damn, I had a good dream last night, dreamt we had all left this goddamned place!"

"Who's leaving what goddamned place?" Ronco called from the door. He pushed his chair in, took a look at me and clapped his hands. "Hijola! Look at Tortuga! Just look at that man! Why he looks like a goddamned regular! Have you had your bm today?" he asked and we laughed. "It's true," he smiled, "you know that bitch of a Nurse isn't going to let you out if you haven't had your bm!"

"Maybe that's why the rest of us haven't gotten out," Mike said, "because we're too goddamned constipated!"

"We're a danger to the world if we ever get out!" Buck added.

We laughed, easily, to break the tension. We all knew that going home seemed so small a triumph against the backdrop of the tragedy in the garden, but we also knew we had to keep going, that time for mourning was always short for those of us who had lived so close to death. So we laughed, shuffled our feet, cleared our throats and waited for the actual moment which would separate us.

"You got a good day for going," Ronco said, "and man, I had a good dream last night . . . felt like a fairy flying on top of old Tortuga . . ."

"Good dreams, good luck," Mike said.

"Hey, did you give him the present?" Buck asked.

"Oh yeah, almost forgot," Mike nodded and dug into his pocket. "It's a kinda going away present," he said and handed me a guitar pick.

"We got it blue to match your guitar!" Buck smiled.

"Now you'll have to learn to play the damned thing," Mike added.

"That's going to be worth seeing," Buck laughed, "old Tortuga strummin' the guitar with one hand."

We laughed again and filled the silence, laughed at the sadness of a one-handed guitar man.

"Well, I guess you're ready," Ronco said and cleared his throat. "Hey, I got a little present for you, too—" He took a couple of dollar bills from his shirt pocket and forced them into my hand. "My old man sends me money from time to time, and I've been saving some for when I get out . . . anyway, you might need some . . ."

"No, thanks, I don't think I'll need it; I've got everything I need—"

"Take it," he insisted, "maybe you'll wanna get something along the way, when the bus stops." He grinned and I nodded. It was his present to me and I couldn't turn it down.

"Okay, thanks," I said and stuffed the bills in my pocket.

"Got everything?" Buck asked.

"Got your ticket?" Mike added.

"It's waiting for me up front . . . and the Nurse said the driver would take me into town . . ."

"Hey, you goin' by and see Ismelda?" Buck asked. I nodded. "Hot dog!" he exclaimed, "He's goin' see his girl!"

"Well, you better get going," Ronco said, "the driver goes into town in half an hour—"

"Yeah, get going . . . you've hung around here long enough," Mike said. He reached out and shook my hand then he pulled me down and hugged me then pushed me away. "Take care of yourself . . . we don't want you back in this place—" He turned his chair and went to the window. I shook hands with Ronco and Buck and told them goodbye.

"Yeah, take care of yourself—and listen, if I ever come rodeoing up north I'll look you up! We'll get drunk together, find us some wild women and have a rip-roaring time!"

"Sure—"

"So long," Ronco said, "take care of yourself . . . you're looking great."

"Thanks," I nodded then walked to the door. At the door I turned and looked back and I told them thanks for everything then I walked up the hall to the nurses' station.

Old man Maloney was starting his early rounds. He paused for a moment and nodded, which was as much of a goodbye as he could give me, and I nodded back. At the nurses' station the Nurse was loading the morning medication cart. She looked at me and asked me how I felt and if I had eaten breakfast. I hadn't eaten, I couldn't, but I nodded.

"Do you have everything you need?" she asked and looked at the guitar, and before I could answer she said, "You didn't come with much, did you?" She handed me a slip of paper and told me to take it to the front desk where I was to pick up my bus ticket. She also told me the doctor would probably want to see me. I hadn't expected her to, but she did say "Good luck," then returned to her cart.

I walked down the hall towards the front offices. Samson was bringing in a new kid, a boy about my age who had his back in traction. He stopped the gurney and waved and I waved back. I walked across the empty recreation room. My footsteps echoed in the enormous, empty room. The sunlight streamed in, warming the room. Outside, in the patio, the gardener was spading the dark earth, turning it over for its breath of air. I thought about Salomón and how well he had taken care of his garden, and I looked across the valley at the greening of the mountain, and the light which radiated from it blinded me. It was strong spring light, good light for the awakening plants, good light to travel in . . .

A few reporters were already in the reception room when I entered. They were waiting for the arrival of the governor and the Committee. Mike had said that today was the day of the hearing. What had happened here had created ripples all the way to the capitol, and now the governor and his aides were forced by the news media and public opinion to find out what had happened. I wondered if they would really ask themselves the questions which had tormented us for so long in the ward, the question that drove Danny to his insane answer . . . or would they merely go through the motions, find someone to blame, then wash themselves of the matter and return to their private lives. We who had been involved in Danny's doing could never erase it from our memory . . . we were a part of it. Each one of us had been with him in his terrible agony, and we had been there when he pulled the switch. We could never retreat from that; we could never forget it. And the governor, I thought as I looked up at the portraits of the somber governors which lined the walls, will he be able to come to the right decision? Will he care? I looked at the portrait which had been added since I first came to the hospital. It was an intelligent face, but a cold face. I wondered if he could have walked in the dark wards of the hospital and come to the right decision; I prayed for him, then I walked to the reception desk where a thin, partridge breasted woman handed me my bus ticket and told me the doctor wanted to see me.

The reporters looked my way as I walked to Steel's door, but they said nothing. I knocked and went in.

"Hey, Tortuga," Dr. Steel smiled from behind a stack of papers, "I see you're ready." He looked tired. I knew he hadn't slept. "Let's give you a final check—" He made me unbutton my shirt for a final, cursory examination. As always, his exam was thorough but his movements were off.

"What's going to happen?" I asked.

"Well, the governor called for an investigation, he's on his way here now; the Committee is talking about firing all the staff; and the reporters, well you saw them, they've gathered around like vultures since the— since it happened. They're all looking for a scapegoat, someone to crucify—"

"Is that going to be you?"

"Probably," he nodded and tossed his stethoscope on the desk. "Button your shirt; you're ready." He walked to the window and looked out. "I'm glad you're going," he said, then he added, "you know what to do."

"Yes."

"I wouldn't mind what's going to happen now, if, if only we learned something from it. But as is the case with so many tragedies, we'll be aware of it for only awhile, only while the headlines are screaming at us, then everybody lies back, pretends it didn't happen . . . forgets . . . If something good would come of this, if only a wider and deeper understanding of this so inconsequential but precious life we share—" He stopped short and looked at me. "We both know what happened—"

I nodded. Then for awhile we were silent. "Maybe that's enough," he finally said. "Maybe all this won't mean something until later . . . a long time from now—" He looked out the window and was lost in his thoughts. When he turned I was waiting for him and he smiled. "Go on, get out of here, Tortuga . . . And take care of yourself, okay?"

"I will. Thanks for everything—" He waved and slumped into his chair. I turned and walked out into the noisy reception room. It was packed with people, most of them reporters hanging around the door. One of them pushed up in front of me and shouted in my face, "Hey, kid! Is he in there? Is the doc in there?"

I went around him and pushed my way through the noisy crowd to the door. I had just reached it when someone shouted, "The governor! The governor's here!" Outside three black limousines had just driven up. Flashbulbs exploded as the reporters fought for position. The governor and his aides, all dressed in dark suits, disembarked and pushed through the crowd. The reporters barked questions, but the group swept past them and towards Dr. Steel's office. I turned and found the driver and told him I was ready.

192

"Hey, don't you wanna stay and see the excitement?" he asked.

"No," I shook my head. I remembered him from the day I arrived.

"Have it your way," he smiled and popped the gum he chewed, "but we ain't ever had this much excitement here . . . not even when that little Indian boy got lost and froze up in the mountain—Hey, don't I know you?" he asked as we stepped out and walked towards the car. "You're the one they call Tortuga, ain't you? Well I'll be damned. Going home, huh?"

I nodded and we got in the car. "You're early for the bus, you know that don't you. We could go back in there and watch the fireworks for awhile. What say? Boy, it's not everyday we get the governor down here. Man, are feathers going to fly!"

"I have to see somebody in town," I said.

"Oh, if that's the case, fine. Let's go! Speed-o at your command." He started the car and we drove down the hill. He left it in low gear so he could lay back and smoke. "How long you been here?" he asked and offered me a cigarette.

"A long time," I said. I took a deep breath of the cool air that came in through the open window, and I looked at the mountain and the valley. The weight of the hospital began to lift. I was suddenly free, and it felt good. I wondered what I would tell Ismelda.

"Don't smoke, huh," he said and tossed the package on the dash. "That's okay . . . I just like to offer. A lot of the kids like to smoke . . . nothing else to do. You deserve it after doing time back there. How about a drink? Wanna drink?"

"No, thanks—"

"Anybody that gets outta that place oughta have a drink and a good piece of ass, that's the way I think. Anyway, who you gonna see in town?"

"A friend," I answered. The sun was very warm. It felt good on my arms and legs. Across the valley it warmed old Tortuga's hump. It was a good day to be on the path of the sun.

"—Filomón said to keep an eye out for you," Speed-o was saying, "he said to tell you everything went okay on that last trip he took. I don't know what that means, do you?"

"Yes," I nodded. I knew. He went on talking about the thing that had happened at the hospital, but I wasn't listening. I was looking down at the bottom of the hill where the road turned into the town. Off to the right the glistening river gurgled south. Near it lay a small cluster of adobe houses which I recognized from Ismelda's description. She and Josefa lived in one of the homes; I was sure I could find it. When we were close enough I asked the driver to stop. He pulled off the side of the road.

"Here?" he asked. "There's nothing here, except some old houses—"

I jumped out, closed the door then leaned on the window. "How much time do I have before the bus comes?" I asked him.

"Oh, a couple of hours, but are you sure you wanna get off here?"

"I'm sure," I nodded. "The bus will come along this road on its way up north, won't it?" I asked. He nodded. "Will it pick me up here?"

"If you got your ticket, sure. Just flag it down. It picks up people along here all the time."

"Thanks," I said and stepped back.

"Have it your way, daddy-o," he shrugged. "I guess I'll go back up the hill and see what's happening. Good luck!" he called and spun the car around and headed back up the hill. I watched it for awhile. The sun on my back was warm. It was thawing the earth, sucking up the ice and creating mirages of heat and moisture. The morning shimmered, and the dull building of the hospital became lost in the waves of the tremendous energy which seemed to be turning the earth round and round.

I turned and walked down the dirt path between the houses. Behind the houses, in the small fields, men moved back and forth with their plows, using the old single plow with horses they turned the earth and prepared it for planting. Beyond them I could hear the soft hum of the river as it ran full with the spring run-off. The men called to each other as they plowed and cleaned the irrigation ditches which would bring the precious water to their fields. It was a festive time, the coming of spring. Women visited. Their homes were open to receive the fresh, spring air. At one of the houses a woman paused in her work to look up at me. She had emptied the cotton of her mattress on a large canvas and was beating it to air it. I remembered my mother . . . Two small boys racing a hoop with a wire ran past me, calling to another friend to join them as they ran. I felt their joy and excitement. Even in the middle of the wide desert there had been some life festering under the pain and the paralysis, waiting for the spring to renew itself. Filomón had been right . . . Salomón . . . all of them.

The bleating of goats made me turn. In a small corral by the side of a house Josefa tended her goats. We saw each other at the same time and she waved and started to shout, but something made her stop. The smile faded from her face as she looked up at the hospital on the hill, then turned to look at me again. Instead she motioned towards the small house. I went to the door and knocked and Ismelda came running out.

"Tortuga, oh Tortuga!" she cried and threw her arms around my neck. "You look so beautiful . . . and you're going home, oh, I'm so happy for you—"

She took my hand and we walked towards the river. We walked hand in hand along the sandy bank and then we stopped and stared at the brown, churning water for a long time, but we said nothing. We walked some more, until we were out of sight of the houses, and there we sat down on the warm sand. The green river grass grew around us. Across the river the mountain rose and glistened in the bright, warm sun.

"I had a dream last night," I said as I looked at Tortuga.

Ismelda looked into my eyes and nodded. "It was a beautiful dream to share," she smiled.

"Maybe someday we can make that dream come true—" I said, and I told her I loved her and that someday I was coming back for her . . . someday when I was stronger and I could understand the magic and the joy which flowed through me and tortured me so much . . . someday when all that we had seen and shared would have a meaning. I held her in my arms and kissed her warm, dark hair, her eyelids, her throat, her face and cheeks which were wet with tears, and she held my face in her gentle hands and told me she loved me and that she would be waiting for me forever. I felt her hummingbird kiss, the flicker of her moist, warm tongue reaching into my soul with its sweet pollen and nectar. We turned in each others arms, like two naked lizards rolling in the warm sand, surrounded by the purple plumes of the salt cedars and cushioned by the green grasses of the river . . . We turned in our embrace, throbbing with love, naked and innocent as the sun which warmed us, as alive as the pounding of our hearts which hummed to the tune of the cresting waters. We rose into the golden strands of light like two mating butterflies, rainbow colored and whispering secrets . . . Time stood still as we felt the turning of the earth and the sun . . . and we dissolved into each other. I dreamed my first communion girls in her eyes, and they smiled and waved at me from across the river, and they called my name and forgave my sins . . . I reached out and felt her touch . . . and for a moment nothing existed except the sphere of time which we had turned into our own world.

Across the river Tortuga smiled at his cousins playing in the sand. The air was full of laughter. We whispered, full of joy, words with so much meaning that they would stand forever against the erosion of time and pain . . . and then Josefa called, the bus was coming and for now I could not stay. I still had to find my way home. We both knew that. Our time would be complete when I had found my way out of the desert, and could return. I rose and helped her to her feet. We walked slowly to the edge of the road and I waved the dusty Greyhound bus to a stop.

"I'll be waiting for you," Ismelda promised.

"I'll come back," I said, "in the meantime, keep coming into my dreams—"

"I will," she said and squeezed my hand. "I'll always be with you . . ."

She kissed me lightly and I turned and boarded the bus. For a moment I stared at the bus driver. He resembled Filomón. "Going north," he winked and took my ticket. On the seat just behind him sat a dwarf, an impish young man who smiled and reminded me of Clepo. "Probably going home," he said. He nodded at my crutches. They had picked up other stragglers from the hospital before it seemed.

"Need any help?" the driver asked.

"Thanks," I said, "I can make it."

"It's going to be a long trip," he smiled, "find a comfortable seat."

"Plenty of room! Plenty of room!" the dwarf sang.

The bus was empty, and glowing with white light which sparkled through the windows. I walked up the aisle and found a seat where I could wave to Ismelda. I threw my crutches under the seat and placed the blue guitar next to me. Then I pressed my face against the window and Ismelda laughed. She threw me a kiss with the tips of her fingers, then the bus jerked forward and I had to crane to see her standing by the side of the road, dressed in white and waving goodbye and wishing me good luck. She was like someone from a dream, a dream of childhood when one is innocent, standing in the bright light of spring, surrounded by the first green grass and sprigs of spring.

I waved until the bus crossed the bridge and she disappeared from sight. I turned and waved goodbye to Tortuga, and I promised to see him again when I returned for Ismelda. Then we entered the desert and I settled back in my seat and closed my eyes. A thousand thoughts and whispers fluttered through my mind. Someday I would make sense out of them, but now I only wanted to rest. I felt very tired.

Around us the desert opened its arms to receive us. It gaily wore its spring-green coat. Off to the side, hidden in the thin line of budding trees, the river flowed south; it flowed from the north, from the green mountains that were home. That's all I wanted to think about, home. I wondered who would be waiting for me, and what would they say when they saw me. What kind of a life would I make for myself . . . Life? At that moment I thought I had learned something about life by struggling so much for it and then seeing it lost when its fragile ribbon was cut, but I never really knew how boundless and limitless its magic and memories and hope could be until I heard Salomón whisper,

Ah, Tortuga, didn't I tell you you'd be going home when spring rolled around . . . And here you are, crossing the desert again, leaving behind the magic mountain . . . but oh how much we shared under its protection! Good times, sad times . . . but today we won't dwell on the sadness of the past! No! This is a new journey! This is the journey of your return home, and what's a journey without a song! Sing us a song, Tortuga! Make a song of rejoicing from all that you have seen and felt! Sing a song of love, Tortuga! Oh yes, sing of love!

196

Startled, I opened my eyes. I expected to see Salomón sitting next to me, but no, I was alone. The bus glowed with the bright light of the sun. Around us shimmered the desert mirages. Up front the driver hummed a song and the young boy at his side tapped to the rhythm. Butterflies played in the sun, visiting the first hardy flowers of the desert. I closed my eyes and smiled. It was a good time to be going home. I reached for the blue guitar and cradled it in my arms. My fingers felt the strings and strummed a melody, and I heard the words of my song fill the bus and flow out the open window and across the awakening desert.